WIND AND BONES

by

Kristin Marra

2010

WIND AND BONES
© 2010 BY KRISTIN MARRA. ALL RIGHTS RESERVED.

ISBN 10: 1-60282-150-X
ISBN 13: 978-1-60282-150-7

THIS TRADE PAPERBACK ORIGINAL IS PUBLISHED BY
BOLD STROKES BOOKS, INC.
P.O. BOX 249
VALLEY FALLS, NY 12185

FIRST EDITION: MAY 2010

CREDITS
EDITORS: CINDY CRESAP AND STACIA SEAMAN
PRODUCTION DESIGN: STACIA SEAMAN
COVER DESIGN BY SHERI (GRAPHICARTIST2020@HOTMAIL.COM)

Acknowledgments

Infinite thanks to the following souls:

Rad for gambling on a new writer. Cindy Cresap for phenomenal insights and editing. Sheri, whose cover makes me smile every time I look at it. And my intrepid beta reader Gill, who goaded me into submitting this book.

My first readers Lisa Brodoff and Lynn Grotsky are the best writer's cheerleaders on the planet, and they're all mine. Rah.

Jeanne Winer set her own novel aside to encourage me and delivered a seminal lecture on plot to an audience of one.

My sister Shelley, my personal Montana sheriff expert. My brother Joe always said the Hi-Line is worth writing about. My sister Rose still holds down the fort in northern Montana.

All the Greenbergs, Winers, and Kaftans, the best in-laws any lesbian could dream of. They gleefully support every word I write. How did I get so lucky?

Dr. Green picked me up, dusted me off, and convinced me I was capable of writing a book and having a good life.

And, finally, thanks to the amazing people of Montana's Hi-Line. To be of you is an honor. This book is in homage to your strength, resilience, humor and all that damn beer you've bought me over the years.

Dedication

To my extraordinary partner and mainstay, Judith. My love,
you still wow me every day.

To my world-class daughter, who is waiting to star in the film
version. Hold that thought, Buzz.

CHAPTER ONE

The truth is, if my father hadn't dropped dead with a long list of unfinished business, I wouldn't have a story to tell. I was sitting in my local Vietnamese restaurant, eating a bowl of pho, when the call came.

"Hi, Jillian-baby, it's Billy."

"Hey, Billy-boy, you coming out for another Mariners game?" I was watching kids in a playground across the street and getting ready to slurp another pile of pho noodles.

"No, sweetheart, I'm calling about your father. I hate to have to tell you, Jilly, but he…well, he…passed away just a few hours ago."

"What?…How?…Why?" I was a journalist even in crisis.

Then everything inside me quit moving. Those kids playing across the street were stop-action recorded in my brain forever because my eyes glued to them.

"His heart…it just…stopped. We were at the café as usual, a bunch of us guys, you know, sitting around. Your dad, he stood up, said 'I don't feel so good,' and fell over dead. I swear, he was fine just seconds before, discussing the problems on the Martin farm."

"But he was only seventy-two. He never mentioned his heart…"

"I know, sweetie, but he kept secrets. We all know that."

"Yeah…Okay, I'll be there soon." I glanced around, had no idea what to do next except pack a bag of black clothes and get to Montana. "There's a flight to Great Falls every night around eight. Lands around eleven. I can get into Prairie View around two a.m."

"No need to push it now. I got a room for you at the Heritage Hotel in Great Falls. I'll drive down in the morning and get you. You can use your dad's car while you're here in Prairie View. And, Jill…"

"Yeah?"

"Plan to stay a while. There are some…things you'll have to deal with beyond just burying your dad. Pack for a few weeks at least."

"Do I really need to? I don't think I can stay…"

"Sorry, sweetheart, but there are some serious land problems that need decisions. It's going to be up to you to represent him for the next several weeks. His attorney will fill you in a few days after the funeral. Give you some time, you know."

"'Kay, Billy. Listen, I'll take that room in Great Falls, but I think I'll rent a car. I don't wanna drive Daddy's."

"Are you sure? It's no problem, me coming to get you."

"Thanks, but that will work best for me, I think. Oh, and will you call Connie for me, tell her what's happened?"

"Already done."

"Thanks. See you tomorrow, then." And that was it. The call.

❖

I was befuddled, numb, and unable to put two coherent thoughts together. It was different than when Grandma died five years earlier. Grandma's death hurt bad, left a chasm in my life. And I grieved from the second I knew she'd died and still did. But my father's death hollowed me out. I was cast adrift, unfeeling and empty. I was forty-one years old, an orphan. On my own. I had expected him to last at least twenty more years, making loads of money, popping Viagra, and watching over me.

Besides all that, I was going to have to spend too much time in Prairie View, facing my father's legacy, my ambivalence toward my hometown, and my heart-scarring history with Annie.

CHAPTER TWO

We all pretend I was born on April 22, and we all pretend I was born in Prairie View, Montana. Both pieces of fiction come from the birth certificate my father had fixed up at the courthouse. He owned half the politicians in the building, so it couldn't have been too hard.

Everyone knew my mother dropped me off at my grandma's door when I was a few months old, claiming I was Dean's daughter. Where she had me or on what day, we never established. My grandma didn't think to question her. That's because of the kind of man my daddy was and, according to Grandma, I was just another product of my dad's acquisitive nature. She was often too forgiving of her thoughtless philanderer son.

As far as I know, that's the last time I ever saw my mother. She did leave a note, though.

Dean,
This is your baby.
Her name is Jillian.
I gave her a life and a name.
You do the rest.
You are a son of a bich.
Eva

Yeah, that's how she wrote it. A damning indictment, and she couldn't even spell it right. I found the note when I was nine, rooting around in my dad's jewelry box when no one was home, except Connie, our housekeeper. The note was buried beneath all the forgotten, formerly precious stuff that collects under the ring tray in every jewelry box. Even at that age, I could pinpoint the misspelling. It embarrassed me. I also felt bad about the "bich" invective against my poor grandmother, who had wrapped her love around me the second she held me. I still wonder what inexplicable sentiment kept that note in Daddy's jewelry box. His incomprehensible death made that question unsolvable.

I do know what Mama might have looked like because my father was unvarying in his choice of women. "Dollies," my grandma called them. And they were all of a type: big tits (these women never had breasts) thrusting out of western-cut shirts. Ass-gripping, high-waisted, boot-cut pants, topped off by large, silver-buckled belts with names tooled on the backs…JoAnne, Dawnie, Betty. Short, they all had to be short, under 5'4". And, you got it, they all resembled Dolly Parton. It was a look my father couldn't resist. When one of them things would bounce into a room, Daddy was lost to me, but only for a few days. After the perfume wore off his shirt, he was pretty much done with her and back to bathing me with his lavish attention.

Sometimes, I liked to think my mother was following my career. That she had both my Pulitzer Prize announcements framed on her living room wall. That she'd read my work over and over again wondering how much of my journalistic success came from her. Mostly, though, I was pretty sure that the only avid reading my mother did was her *TV Guide*, peering through a cigarette haze, wondering who was going to win *American Idol*.

I'm certain that I'm a memory she would like to forget. But I'm old enough to know she hasn't forgotten having me; she's just tucked me way back in her brain, somewhere in that back forty we all have for stashing painful memories. My back forty is full of them. Why should my mother's be any different?

To say I wasn't mothered would be an enormous lie. Grandma did it all. She was the quintessential small-town mother, involved in the school, church, and garden club. She made my Halloween costumes, overdecorated my birthday cakes, and cheered me through victories and heartbreaks. Oh, I was mothered, all right. I just called my mother "Grandma." No big deal, except when Theo Lamaster teased me about having a dead mother or when kids asked why my mom was so old, their noses wrinkling when they said the word "old."

Do I look like what I think my mom looked like? I'm relieved to report, no.

"Jillian, you're an O'Hara through and through."

"I know, Grandma."

"My lands, you look just like your grandpa. God rest his soul."

"I know, Grandma."

"You're the same string bean height as your daddy was at your age. And look at your hair. You look like a little Norwegian girl, even though you're Irish through and through…at least on your daddy's side, and that's all that counts around here."

"I know, Grandma." This would be when I should have asked about my mother's ethnic background, but we always pretended she didn't exist. In fact, I doubt my grandmother ever asked anyone about my mother.

"So like your daddy. And I bet your hair will darken when you get older, into that lovely brown honey color your dad has and Grandpa had, too, until it thinned away, poor man. The boys are going to go wild for you."

"I don't know about that, Grandma."

It was true, I didn't know about that. I would try to wrap my mind around boys going wild for me. All I could conjure in my imagination was them going wild about picking me for their side when we chose up for baseball. I was as good as any of them and better than some.

I did play dolls with the boys, though. We'd take my dolls up the hill behind my house, build mini combat bunkers, place the dolls in strategic battle positions and blow them to bits with the most powerful firecrackers we could buy. A few cheap Barbies rendered hours of vicious glee. Those are among my most satisfying playtime memories.

In sixth grade, Grandma caught me kissing Kathy Dolman in our garage. I was in pubescent bliss from that kiss. Grandma saw it in my eyes, I'm sure. And bless her soul, all she said was, "Time for dinner, Jilly." She never again talked about boys going wild for me. She would smile and give low-key encouragement when I'd have a date with a boy during high school. But she somehow knew I was different, even if she couldn't say the words. I'm sure she was relieved that I didn't follow up on the Kathy Dolman behavior in public. She trusted me not to embarrass the family, but she never interrupted my closed bedroom door sessions with my high school sweetheart, Annie.

I'm sure Grandma didn't want to know for sure about my lesbianism because then she'd have to put ugly words to my behavior. Those were the only words to describe me back then. People had no context for me; neither did I, for that matter. But I knew enough to keep my mouth shut, maintain a boyfriend for a few months here and there, and plan my escape from the town that was becoming more like a prison every year.

❖

"Jilly, baby, what do you want to be when you grow up?"

"An author, Daddy. A famous author like Charles Dickens or Madeleine L'Engle."

"But, honey, not many authors get famous. And they don't make much money."

"Don't we have enough money already?"

"I suppose we do, baby, but more is always better." Always snickering after that statement. "I think you could be a writer. Just marry a rich man." Another snicker. "It's just as easy to marry a rich man as a poor one."

Marriage? Believe me, I tried to see myself walking down the aisle of our Catholic church, gripping my father's arm, wearing that white dress. I'd try to envision myself with a bucket of kids, wiping their boogers, driving them to basketball practice, spanking their behinds just to show them who's boss. I tried, but couldn't gel the image in my brain. It was elusive, just like imagining a man across my table eating dinner and gazing into my eyes, or driving me in the car with his arm wrapped around me It was like imagining being Queen of England; I sort of knew what the parts were but couldn't fit them together in my brain. Actually, the queen thing was easier to work with.

CHAPTER THREE

I couldn't drive my dad's car around Prairie View. I'm a hometown girl made good. How would my journalist persona be served by cruising around town in a fat new Oldsmobile, CB antennae on top? Truth be told, I couldn't pull up to the church for the funeral in something that wasn't me. I was that insecure.

I had lived in a small town long enough to know that what people perceive you to be, you become. They wouldn't have it any other way. That's why I had to leave Prairie View, Montana. It's all so damn complicated. I had escaped living there, but my small-town identity still lived in me, always waiting to pull the rug from under my giant ego.

In Great Falls, I rented a sweet Nissan Murano, burgundy with gold trim. Butch with class, great sound, forty-seven miles on the odometer. And I headed north to the Hi-Line of Montana. A place of hundreds of thousands of acres, so desolate, so nowhere, known only to those who live there. Even Montanans from other parts of the state lived in ignorance of the vast north that pushed down on them from the top of the map.

My ritual for driving to Prairie View included one regular stop. There was this rest area about thirty-five miles south of town that I couldn't pass up. It was the place where I readied myself for the onslaught of bittersweet memories and associations that awaited me in Prairie View.

RATTLESNAKES SIGHTED. STAY ON THE WALKWAYS.

That was the sign that greeted any weary traveler pulling in to freshen up. My guess was travelers were wide awake by the time they scampered to the toilet and back again. And my sympathy went to anyone who, nervous eyes darting across the ground, stopped to give their little poochie a break in the grassy dog relief area.

I parked in front of my favorite sign in the world, rolled down all the windows, switched off the ignition, and sucked the first full breath I'd taken in twenty-four hours. A firm breeze rolled off the Rocky Mountains. The Hi-Line was rarely without a breeze from the Rockies, carrying soothing scents of sage, tilled soil, and hay. A breeze on the Hi-Line would be called a wind anywhere else.

The car metal warmed my back where I leaned against it, and I waited for my signal of home. There it came, the expectant bubbled call of the meadowlark and then, a little farther away, softer, the exuberant reply from its mate. I scanned the sage, squinting out sunlight to catch sight of the birds. There they were, skittering and bobbing above and through the wild hay and giant sage bushes. I caught a clear view of their yellow spring plumage just before the breeze whipped my hair into my eyes.

While trudging up the rise behind to the rest rooms, and making my way to the picnic tables, I kept half an eye on the ground, vigilant for rattlers.

"Yeah, Grandma, I'm watching out for snakes," I muttered to my grandma's ghost who still had her hold on me. It didn't matter where I was going when I was a kid, or what was planned. The last thing I would always hear as I left the house was Grandma shouting, "…and watch out for snakes!" The Hi-Line way of saying, "I love you."

My gaze drifted north across the limitless prairie as I sat on top of the picnic table. I stared at the Sweetgrass Hills, three dead volcanoes springing out of the flatness, lined up along the south side of the Canadian border. They had always been exhilarating to me, but today the anomalies drew a fatigued sigh from my chest. Daddy had a gawd-awful amount of land up north by the border, and I knew I'd be doing a snoot-full of driving around there before this epic was over. White exhaust smoke from an Air Force jet drew a messy figure eight over the far eastern Sweetgrass Hill.

A pair of red-tailed hawks caught my eye, and I lay back on the tabletop while I watched them do their twirly mating ritual high up on the airstream. I dozed off.

I must have been dreaming about Annie when a big old blowfly hit my temple and jolted me awake. My first waking thought was of Annie. When do I call Annie? Should I call Annie? "Shit. When will this end?" That was my usual Annie mantra.

Then I caught the scent of new wheat, closed my eyes again, and my mind floated to warm spring nights. Annie and I sitting in my Chevy, sipping Little Olys bought for us by someone's legal-aged brother. Annie would begin our make-out sessions by reaching across the bench seat and brushing a lock of my, by that age, amber hair. I'd look at her and watch the moonlight play with her extensive blond curls. She smelled of Sand and Sable perfume.

She always had so much sadness in her eyes before she kissed me. I'm sure my eyes were never melancholy with her, just lustful and needy.

"God, Jill. I love you. I can't explain why, but I need to do this." And she'd place a tender kiss on my lips, lick them, and I was hers. Every time.

At first, we never went beyond intense making out and a little breast touching, outside the shirts, but that didn't keep us from pushing ourselves onto each other, eliciting an orgasm right through our jeans.

The fall of senior year, however, our sexual explorations expanded. The first time we made full love was in my bed. My dad had taken Grandma to Hawaii as a special treat and left me on the honor system, though Grandma gave me the warning eye when they left the house. She didn't trust me for a second, but it wasn't bad enough to pass up a dream trip to Hawaii.

Consumed by the clumsy lust endowed to seventeen-year-olds, Annie and I spent two days in bed. We gave each other countless orgasms as we learned to finesse our sexual technique. Our bodies were carnal laboratories where we freely experimented with the elements of pleasure. We danced at the edge of a sexual precipice, pushing one another into a free fall over and over.

Every part of my body yearned for her touch, and she gave herself to me without reserve until Sunday afternoon. Then something shifted.

"Um, Annie…can I ask question?" I was lying with my head

between her breasts, occasionally licking the nipple that stood erect near my mouth.

"S…sure," she hissed at the stroke of my tongue.

"I lost my virginity this weekend. And I'm glad it was with you. I couldn't tell, did you lose yours? I mean…it doesn't matter or anything. I was just wondering." Her body beneath me stilled and the atmosphere in the bed went from loving and tender to motionless and cold.

"Don't ever ask me that again." And within twenty minutes, she'd showered, dressed, and left with an impersonal kiss on my lips. When you're seventeen, "processing what just happened" isn't in your vocabulary, much less in your skill set.

We continued to be lovers during senior year, hiding in my car's backseat, stealing time in my bed, because the pull between us was irresistible. However, as graduation neared, she rarely called me. She took her time returning my phone calls, and by May, it was probably clear to any outside eye that she had lost interest in me. I still believed in us, thinking that our planned escape to college in Missoula would give us the time and space to build our future together.

The morning of graduation, she called me. Thrilled at her uncharacteristic behavior of actually calling me, I didn't notice her distant tone.

"I don't want you to hate me," was her conversation opener, "but I have something important to tell you. I'm kinda…um, well, I'm pregnant."

I couldn't move, couldn't breathe, and certainly couldn't respond. Blood pounded in my ears; I was shaking my head. "Say that again?"

"I'm going to have a baby in December. Don't ask who the father is. That's not important. But we can't see each other again. Sorry. It's just too complicated and I can't talk about it. I'm sorry. When you get to college, I'm sure you'll find a nice guy. That will help you get over all this."

"A guy?"

"I'm sorry, Jill, but I gotta go. We'll talk sometime."

One month after graduating from high school, she married Wayne Robison, an obscure guy in our class whom she never mentioned before. We never did have that talk. I went to college and she had her first baby.

Occasionally, late at night, Annie would call me "just to have a chat." I'd lie on my bed and feel the warmth of her voice and presence. For maybe an hour, her attention would be directed at me. She'd relate cute stories about her little boys, gossip about our high school buddies, and, every so often, complain humorously about Wayne. But after about six years, the calls petered out. Christmas and birthday cards continued far longer with vaguely loving reminders of what we had shared. "I always think of you, Jill." Or "I'll never forget our friendship." Or "You're never far from my thoughts."

When I would visit my father in Prairie View, Annie and I would meet for lunch at a restaurant in a neighboring town. Or maybe she'd come to my father's house for a beer. But we'd never show ourselves together in a public place in Prairie View. It embarrassed me to think I accepted my relegation to the shameful secret box in Annie's closet, but I did. She was a married woman, after all, I reasoned. She couldn't afford to be seen hanging around an out lesbian.

And I would clutch each crumb tossed, seeing them as possibilities for us to have a future when the time was right. All such communication had ceased five years before my father's death, but I still left a peephole in my heart in case Annie ever wanted to take a look.

"Fuck." There I was, forty-one years old, lying on that picnic bench anguishing over things that happened twenty-three years earlier. After all those years, I was still entangled. So many mornings I would wake up with a bittersweet ache in my belly because of having an Annie dream. The dreams always had the same theme: Annie and I desperate to make love, but the dreamland circumstances would force us to make a date for later. When later would come around, I'd be held up, blockaded by some dream disaster, kept from my rendezvous with Annie.

I would always wake feeling sexy, bittersweet, and bereft. If someone happened to be sleeping next to me, I'd slip her leg between mine and urge her into bringing my release. I felt slightly guilty about that, but my partners were pleased with themselves. I never even considered popping their post-orgasmic bubbles with the overrated truth. Too much trouble, since all women's days in my bed were numbered anyway.

Peeling myself off the top of that picnic table, I resigned myself to the next few weeks. "Might as well get on with this." When I reached my gorgeous car, I got in and finger-combed my hair. I needed to give my appearance the once-over in preparation for my entrance into Prairie View. I sent blessings to my stylist, Charles of Seattle. Just four days before, he'd trimmed my hair to shoulder length, highlighted some burnished red into it, tweezed the eyebrows to perfection, took my $250, and sent me on my way.

"Perfect timing, Charles. You prettied me up for Daddy's funeral. Who would have thought?"

As I pulled out of the rest area, I realized I had never seen a single rattlesnake there, despite the warning. That improved my mood for a moment until I became aware of the surrounding plains and remembered their colorful, unfortunate, history. History reflected in faded, bullet-holed road signs declaring defunct promises of sanctuary ahead. "Etta's Best Home Cooking: Fresh Pie." "Stay-a-Spell Motel: Clean Rooms. Free TV." "Car Overheating? Bill's Engine Repair." None of those businesses had been open for decades, but their signs graced the landscape like neglected tombstones.

CHAPTER FOUR

Twenty minutes later, I took to the off-ramp from Interstate 90 onto Highway 2, which ran right through downtown Prairie View, population 4,222, or so the thirty-year-old faded sign declared. The town had died back to about 3,000 over the past two decades, but nobody seemed to notice, except me. Just like nobody seemed to notice that two grade schools, two drugstores, and several clothing stores were boarded up. Bars were doing great, though.

I cringed at the rural dinginess shrouding my childhood landmarks. Muting the CD player to gather myself, I was aware of the railroad tracks to my left that used to be a mighty arterial for the Great Northern Railroad Line. Now it was a through track for freight trains that barreled east and west, ignoring the little town that waited like a puppy trying to get attention.

On the other side of the tracks, across a large weed-strewn field, was my old high school. I could just make out the bronze statue of a wolf, the high school mascot, howling at the occasional cloud that would bother to drift overhead. That poor statue, always looking like a fat husky, was the butt of many pranks over the years. Nobody liked the darn thing when it was placed there as a crowning achievement of the community. Thirty years later, it still sat there dumpy and ridiculous. I suspect it had become part of the landscape, just like the bald hill looming behind the school, and nobody even noticed it anymore.

To my right ran a string of businesses in familiar worn buildings. At the truck stop, the locals were filling their fuel-inefficient cars, each car having at least one disturbing bumper sticker condemning gun control, environmentalists, or abortion. All the men wore either ball caps or cowboy hats and walked like their bones ached. Many of the women were puffy and pasty from spending the last seven months indoors. They all glanced at my car, out of the small-town habit of needing to know who was breaching their city limits. I didn't like this behavior when I was young; I didn't like it now. But I caught myself checking out whoever drove down my street in Seattle whenever I was outside.

There was the Dew Drop Inn, now a smoky casino, where I had my first job when I was fourteen. Daddy got it for me, said I needed to learn responsibility. But they let me go a few months later, after I ran my dad's truck into the owner's car, smashing the taillight. I didn't know I was supposed to report it. I had a learner's permit but hadn't learned anything.

Each building I passed, whether used or abandoned, held some history for me. Every once in a while, in the empty parking lots, a little dust devil would coil up then peter out.

Just as I was about to turn onto Main Street, I heard the *whoop whoop* of a sheriff's cruiser behind me. Having lived in Seattle for the previous twenty years, I drove closer to the shoulder so the cop could pass me and get on his important way. But the cruiser had its lights flashing and wouldn't move around me. I was getting irritated. Then I heard a graveled voice from the police speaker order, "Pull over, please."

"What? Shit. Ah shit! He's stopping me? Me? What did I do? Does he fuckin' know who I am?"

Then I faced the cold fact that he might not know who I am. I didn't live there anymore, hadn't in decades. It's true: you never got to be famous in your hometown. They knew too much.

I inched the Murano into the abandoned parking lot of what used to be Holmes Ford Dealership and recognized that my father's dominance in this tidbit of a town was over. The leadership torch had passed to people I went to high school with. A surreal and disturbing thought. I also realized that nobody around here gave a rat's ass about my two Pulitzers and all the aggressive skill it took to get them. The cop was parked behind me and not getting out of his car.

"Stay in your car, please." That speaker needed some work because it was distorting his voice, making it difficult to understand.

I slumped behind the steering wheel, rolled my forehead right and left on the warm leather wheel cover, and reviewed all the reasons he could have stopped me. "Hell, I was going a little fast, but everyone goes fast on that stretch of road. Maybe my taillight is out. Did I stray across the center line? No, must be the taillight."

Heartened by the taillight theory, I straightened and checked the rearview mirror. Officer Annoying still hadn't turned off his flashing rack of lights, making me embarrassed, agitated, and, truth be told, a little scared.

I noticed I was jiggling my left leg, a lifelong nervous habit, and it was making the car wobble. I thrummed my fingertips on top of the steering wheel and glued my eyes to the rearview. My face heated from a mixed bag of anger, mortification, and scorching sun on the windshield. Just when I realized he must be running a check on my license plate, I saw his car door open.

"Oh sweet…Mary…mother of God…who is that?"

And she emerged. Yeah, she. The cop was a girl…no, not a girl…a woman…a vision. And tall, taller than me, six feet at least. Officer's ball cap, long black braid, and reflecting sunglasses. And she wore a uniform, the two-toned chocolate and gray uniform of a county sheriff. I admit, I whimpered when I got a full view of those miraculous legs with the gray uniform stripes down the side.

"Definitely not a local girl. Be nice, Jilly." Then I remembered she was a damn cop bent on hassling the grieving me, and I forgot the babe angle. I was pissed off. Babe or not, she was making a bad twenty-four hours worse. "Nothin' I can't handle."

I used my side mirror to watch her approach, but could only see her from the waist down. I stared at her nearing black gun belt, complete with handgun and the brass belt buckle covering a flat belly. The ironed creases in her pants hung from her waist straight and smooth, accentuating the surrounding assets.

She was using two strong fingers to make a circular motion, so I opened the car door and started to climb out. Her left hand blocked the door from opening farther and her right hand rested on her gun.

"Remain in your car, please, ma'am, and roll down your window." Monotone. Controlled. Damn bossy. Well, I've weaseled my way around law enforcement officials in dozens of countries, so I figured this small-town frustrated detective wouldn't be able to stand up to my experienced machinations.

I decided to try the puzzled and conciliatory method first. In other words, kiss ass. "Oh, I'm so sorry, Officer. Was there something I could help you with?" They loved being called "Officer."

"Driver's license, proof of insurance, and car registration, please." She sounded bored, but her jaw was twitching under those exceptional cheekbones. The damn sunglasses hid her eyes.

I ruffled around in the glove compartment for all the car rental papers and fumbled through my purse to extract my driver's license. I remarked to myself that whenever I needed to produce my license under pressure, it became stuck in my wallet, making me look guilty because my hands trembled. There was a little bead of sweat trickling down the middle of my forehead.

"Excuse me, Officer, but could you please explain why I'm being stopped? I'm not sure what—"

"Please, ma'am, I would like to see your driver's license, proof of insurance, and car registration first."

I hate being interrupted when I'm speaking, and I really hate taking orders. Another bead of sweat. I decided to use the reasoned but still friendly method.

"Officer, uhhh…" I squinted at her badge. "Terabian, is it? Officer Terabian, I haven't done anything, as far as I know, to warrant being pulled over. I grew up in this town. I know the rules around here. I know—"

"Ma'am, this is my last polite request. Either produce the items I requested or we can visit the station together." Same bossy monotone. I handed her the license and papers.

"Okay, okay, but I have to tell you, I feel unfairly targeted here." I was slipping into the irritated but cooperative method.

"Keep your hands on the steering wheel, ma'am. Please stay in your car. I will be back in a few minutes."

"Why? What the hell? Where are you going?"

"Be patient. I'll be right back." That time there wasn't any "please."

Good thing she walked away because now I was into the pissed-off bitch phase and there was no methodology to that one. "Shit!" I was unraveling. I couldn't seem to find my diplomatic self. Then I remembered my dad had just died. "Oh God, Daddy." He wasn't around to save me.

Right there, sweating, detained by the police, the weight of my loss hit me in the gut. I was abandoned. Doubling over my aching belly, resting my head on the back of my hands, I pushed out body-tossing sobs.

Then I remembered I had to pull it together. Too many people would drive by and see this drama. I couldn't let that happen, not in this town. I did my shoulder relaxation technique from yoga, wiped away tears and snot, took some shaky breaths, and sat up, composed… sort of.

"That bitch is running a check on me. Wait 'til I go see her boss. She will rue…the…day."

Sheriff Terabian unfolded from her cruiser and returned to my car, carrying my papers and her ticket pad in her left hand. There was an intricate woven leather braid on that wrist. "Hmmm…definitely not from around here."

"I'm sorry, ma'am, but I'm going to have to write you two tickets. The first is for going forty miles per hour in a thirty mile per hour zone. The second is for not coming to a complete stop coming off the interstate. You will find the address for the county treasurer on the back of the tickets. You may mail your check there."

"And, Sheriff, can you tell me how much my increased insurance rates will cost?"

"Ma'am, that's not for me to consider. I expect that next time you will be better educated about the rules of the road."

"Well, Sheriff, I'd like to know where all the understanding cops went. You know, the ones who stop you, give a warning, then gossip about who's in jail and who got married? You know, those ones who care when someone's parent dies? How 'bout those ones?"

"Ma'am, I can't be concerned with your personal tragedies. My job is to keep the people of Prairie View safe. You were driving unsafely." She tore off both tickets and handed them to me. "You can contest these tickets with the justice of the peace, Ms. O'Hara. He's located in the courthouse—"

"I know where he's located, Officer, and, trust me, I will contest your targeting me on one of the worst days of my life."

"That's your right, ma'am. I'm sorry for your loss." And she strode away. Didn't even look back.

CHAPTER FIVE

Bolstered by my anger at the sheriff, I headed to the funeral home to make arrangements. I thought the anger would keep me from falling apart while I discussed Daddy's funeral.

The Prairie View Funeral Home was located just a few blocks from where the stupid cop stopped me. As I stepped into the office, the sheriff passed by in her cruiser, neither glancing my way nor slowing for the stop sign at the corner. "Hypocritical bitch," I said as I noticed Arnold Potter watching me from his desk.

"Jill O'Hara, I'm glad you're here," Arnold said, rising from his huge, but cracked, leather desk chair. "I'm sorry about your dad. He was an amazing guy, helped so many folks. Do you want me to handle the funeral?" He was fingering a Bic pen, the kind you buy in packs of ten.

Leave it to Arnold Potter to try to stake his business claim before the conversation got any friendlier. He was a good mortician but a tightwad and rich. Business was superb when you ran the only funeral home for an entire county, half populated by senior citizens. He never tipped waitresses.

"Yeah, that'd be fine, Arnold. Um, where's Daddy's body?"

"Didn't Billy or Connie tell you? I have your dad here. Would you like to view him?"

"I haven't talked to them yet, so...okay, I think I can look at him. I suppose I need to say good-bye."

"Give me a minute, Jill, and I'll get him ready for you. I don't have him in a coffin yet. He's still on his gurney."

"Don't worry about that, Arnold, just let me see him...whatever's convenient. I don't want to stay long. I'll just take a look at him and then make the funeral arrangements."

Arnold left the office, leaving me to stew in my anxiety. *This is real, Jilly, the real thing.* I'd seen dead bodies in my journalistic forays to famine and war zones, but they were never anybody I knew, much less loved. I could always separate from them, like they were mannequins modeling the tragedy I was investigating. This was my father.

"Okay, Jill, he's ready for you."

"Yeah, but am I ready for him?"

"Want me to go in the chapel with you, dear?"

"No…thanks. I think I need to do this alone." And it was in that fraught moment that I regretted not having a girlfriend to hang on to. Then I berated myself for thinking about my love life. I wiped my palms on my jeans several times.

The chapel reeked of furniture polish and snuffed candles. Across the room was a gurney with a form wrapped in a tight white sheet. Arnold had parked it at an unceremonious angle, right in front of the altar, like it was a UPS delivery. There was my father's hair, silver and thin, but who was attached to it?

Each step jarred me as I neared the form. Then I was looking down at a stranger wearing my father's hair.

"Oh, Daddy, what happened?"

And that's all it took. The second sob fest of the day bound my chest and escaped as a wail. I eased onto the nearest pew, put my head in my hands, and wailed again. The air forced from deep inside, and I knew cavernous grief. Wrapping my arms around my belly, I rocked, moaning.

After several minutes of this intensity, I noticed mucus was running down my chin, mingling with tears. There were boxes of Kleenex at both ends of every pew; I grabbed one and started wiping my face, still sobbing. I knew Arnold could hear everything, but figured it was a daily occurrence for him. I gave him credit for knowing to leave me alone when my grief was that acute.

I have no idea how long I sat by Daddy's body, rocking and wiping, but after a while, the raw emotion subsided and turned into a dark space in my gut. Blessed numbness set in. I touched the spotless shroud wrapped around my father and whispered, "Good-bye, Daddy." I brushed the frigid hard cheek with the backs of my fingers and kissed his solid forehead. Then I went back to the office to begin arranging the funeral.

In my haze of grief, I chose flowers, music, singers, memoriam flyers, recipients of memorial donations, an ash urn, and whatever else Arnold needed to get the funeral prepared.

I agreed to write the obituary that evening and e-mail it to Arnold. He reminded me the obit would be published in three different newspapers, so I'd want it to be accurate and decently written. I found it curious that he'd forgotten the one thing I was an expert at was writing for newspapers. But journalism was never this personal or this mundane. I'd developed a new respect for obit writers, people I used to disdain.

"So the Altar Society Ladies will plan the funeral reception in the church hall. Oh, and, Jill, one last thing, a little off the subject. But your dad and I had an agreement. He…helped me once…saved my business."

"Arnold, people tell me that all the time, but—"

"No, no, he really did. I owe him…you. This funeral is on me, except the flowers, of course." I had ordered three huge funeral wreaths at about $200 each. Arnold's largesse only went so far, but I wasn't going to argue. I was too depleted and it didn't matter to me anyway. I was done facing the world for that day.

"Of course. Okay, um, thanks. Is it really that important to you?" My dad had scads of money; I didn't need the favor.

"Yeah, it is."

At that point, all I wanted to do was stumble out of there and go lie down somewhere in a fetal position. I told Arnold I'd stop by a few days after the funeral and choose the headstone. I wanted to get one to complement Grandma's.

As I drove up the hill to Daddy's house, I noticed that cursed police cruiser parked on the street. The sheriff was yakking on a cell phone, but she looked my way as I passed.

CHAPTER SIX

After Grandma died, my father sold the old house on Second Street and built a huge monstrosity on the hill overlooking the shallow valley that held Prairie View. It sat up there like a toad surveying the pond, waiting to whip out its tongue and catch some unsuspecting insect.

My dad was like that toad of a house. Always lying in wait, ready to "bail out" any poor person whose farm, business, or family member was in trouble. Dean O'Hara, my daddy, would produce his magic checkbook and buy the troubled farm, business, or person. And they would be indebted to him. It made him powerful, somewhat of a despot, and grudgingly respected. That damn funeral was going to be huge.

I pulled into the circular driveway and parked outside the three-car garage. When I opened the back of the Murano, I found my black suit had fallen sometime during the drive and was lying in a heap. My suitcase had slid into it and bunched it up.

"Shit, what the hell else?" I hate ironing clothes.

Daddy hid the house key in the nose of the hideous wooden bear made by one of those chainsaw artists he was fond of. My father's taste in art was both western and dubious. His house was full of bronze animal sculpture and, the height of bad taste, taxidermy. Grandma wouldn't have dead animals in her house, so after she died, Dad went on a taxidermy spree.

When I opened the door of the house, I was greeted by a bared-teeth badger sitting by the boot jack. Its glass eyes were slightly off-kilter, giving it a simpleton look. I was going to cover every one of those monstrosities while I was there. They made me feel like I was flea infested. The house smelled of aftershave, pipe tobacco, coffee, and that certain spicy-sweet smell that comes with the testosterone-producing sex.

I threw my bag and crumpled suit on the foyer chair. The house was clean, meaning Connie, housekeeper and family friend, had been here. I checked the table where Dad's mail was always placed and found a note from Connie.

My Sweet Jilly,

I'm so sorry about your dad.
I can't believe it's real.
I've informed Father Wallace in case you need him.
Please call me if you need anything.
There is a casserole in the fridge. 1 hour at 350°.
I'll be in tomorrow to check on you.
I mean it, call me.

Connie

Food. I had forgotten all about it and realized I hadn't eaten in twenty-four hours, except airplane peanuts. Connie, as usual, knew what needed to be done. She had been with our family since she was in her twenties, raising two boys who went on to do great things in law and construction. I didn't know for sure but, I suppose, my dad had something to do with setting them up. I wondered how they paid him back. People were always paying him back. I wondered, with such successful sons, why Connie continued to take care of Daddy.

I preheated the oven, opened a bottle of pricy Cabernet, popped the casserole in, and sat at the kitchen table. I sipped the wine and appreciated that Dad did have a sense of fine wine. I watched the sun droop toward the west and listened to the kitchen clock *tick...tock...*a cherrywood number with squirrels and pheasants carved in it. What was I going to do with all this overbaked décor? For that matter, what was I going to do with the entire house?

The phone jerked me out of my perplexing thoughts. The caller ID read B. Stover.

"Thank God, you're around," I said into the receiver. "I was worried you'd be away on one of your 'excursions.'"

"No, baby girl, I'm right here. Do you need me?"

"Oh, Billy-boy, you don't know the half of it. Have you eaten? Connie left a baked ziti casserole, and I've just opened a bottle of kick-ass cabernet."

"I'm there. I'll be over in about fifteen minutes. See you then, my Jilly-jill."

Billy Stover, friend, battle comrade, and keeper of secrets. We'd known each other since I was eighteen. Dad continued to believe I should have a work ethic, so I started a job at the Hi-Line Club as a waitress. Billy was ten years older than me and the swamper for the restaurant and bar. After closing, he cleaned up. While I was working, he would come down from his apartment upstairs, sit at the help's table, and order his on-the-house dinner. When not busy, I'd get into stimulating conversations with him about books, movies, and pot. We both loved to dip into the weed back then when our brains could afford the loss of synapses.

The following summer, when I returned from my first year of college, Billy and I started hanging out together outside of work. We'd get stoned and revel in our heady discussions. One night Billy made a confession that changed the way I viewed him and the culture of northern Montana.

"Billy, why, with your excellent brain, do you just swamp out the Club?"

"Okay, dearie, it's truth-telling time...and I expect your discretion." I nodded, thinking he was going to tell me he couldn't read or something.

"Jill, you know that extra room upstairs, next to my apartment, the one that always stays locked?" Now I was getting uneasy. Locked rooms held hideous secrets in all the movies. "Well, three nights a week, I run some games in there."

"Games?" I had no idea what he was talking about.

"You noticed that sometimes I come down to the kitchen and put together a relish tray? Well, it's for the games. Poker. Big, I mean *big* stakes. I serve the drinks, food, remove the rowdy, the drunk, the flat broke, and get a hefty percentage for all my work. Swamping the Club is my on-the-table front, while running the games is my under-the-table livelihood."

"There's gambling up there?" I'm sure my jaw was unhinged.

Back then poker games were illegal; they still are. Billy, I learned, had a little gambling empire going on right under everybody's nose. More shocking for me, it was a local open secret. If you had the money, you got to play in Billy's room. The owner of the Hi-Line Club got his percentage, gave Billy the apartment and a daily meal, and high rollers from all over the area would show up to play. Billy limited it to three tables and would often have people waiting in the bar downstairs for an open seat at a poker table upstairs.

It was the summer when I learned how much I didn't know. It was the end of my childhood. I found that I wasn't the only one with a secret. The whole town was full of secrets, and Billy knew most of them. Drunks talked to Billy; down-and-outs talked to Billy; lonely, rich farmers talked to Billy; hell, I even talked to Billy.

"I think I like girls way better than I like boys." I was nineteen, we'd just finished a joint, and I was going back to college in a few weeks. "Do you get my drift?"

"Oh, honey, haven't you ever wondered why I haven't hit on such a lovely specimen as you? You clearly aren't into men, and…maybe I like boys way better than I like girls."

I started rolling another joint.

That revelation realigned everything I had assumed about gay men always appearing nelly. Billy's body was beefy, in the muscular sense. He was one of those guys who walked funny because his muscles were pushing his arms from his torso. The legs of all his pants were skin tight because of his abnormal quad development. He lifted weights for a few hours a day. He was a consummate butch, at least to those folks he wanted to fool.

"But you laid that married woman from Cutbank only last week!"

"Just because I like an occasional bounce with a woman doesn't mean I don't have a preference. I sleep with lots more men than women."

He went on to explain how he'd always preferred men, but he also loved money. So he was using his "job" in Prairie View to set himself up to move to a gay-friendly place when he was in his fifties. Find a cute young boyfriend and settle down. I was impressed with his long-range planning.

"I'm doing very well in the investment world, thank you very much." I heard how swishy he talked when one knew the rest of the story. "I don't want a boyfriend until I'm older and desire companionship. As it is now, I trip off to Great Falls or Missoula once a month or so and find all the sex I need. And, yeah, I figured you for a lez a long time ago and was wondering when you'd tell me."

"Damn, am I that obvious?"

"Only to those in the know, dearie. And your…friendship with Annie Robison when you were in high school was difficult to miss." I cringed and sucked on the joint.

For the next few weeks, I learned more from Billy about my family and my town than I had learned in nineteen years. My understanding of the world sharpened from the secrets Billy revealed.

My family, I had assumed, made its initial fortune in real estate. Not true. My dad's grandfather was a bootlegger during Prohibition and ran booze all over the Hi-Line, making more money than he could spend. After the Repeal Act passed, all that money went into mostly legitimate businesses, except for off-color investments in gambling. The most visible business was beer and soft drink distribution. More money was made and, by the time Dad was born, my family's influence was statewide and even into southern Alberta. When my daddy took over, he was bankrolling every backroom gambling operation in the states of Montana and Idaho. Then casino gambling became legal, and Daddy had a cut in every casino, legally. His buying out a dying farm or bankrupt business was just a hobby for him. And Billy's business? Of course, he was financed by my father, too.

My emotions upon learning all this ran from feeling stupid, to angry, to powerful. But the long-term effect was that I fell in love with secrets, with the rest of the story. And my interest in investigative journalism was born.

I joined the School of Journalism at the University of Montana, and trudged to a master's in journalism. I moved to Seattle and wrote for a couple of the free rags popular in the city during the late 1980s. I was able to choose my stories and write long, indignant exposés about everything from police cover-ups to fraudulent university research labs.

In the 1990s, my work caught the attention of a national syndicate that contracted me to investigate early deaths of cancer patients using experimental protocols. My first Pulitzer. A few years and a dozen stories covering war and pestilence later, the same syndicate asked me to investigate some cozy dealings between sports franchises, software billionaires, and politicians, all at taxpayer expense. After receiving numerous threatening phone calls and letters, I completed that work and gleaned my second Pulitzer. The threats stopped.

And my father, what did he have to say about my success?

"You're a wonderful writer, honey, but you're making some important enemies in territories I don't travel. I'm worried. Couldn't you switch to fiction?"

"I don't know how to write fiction. I've never even written a short story and, besides, I find fiction to be too…confining, rule-bound. I like to go into the streets and get dirty when I research. I like learning the back story, the one people should know. Fiction comes from the imagination, and that's way less interesting for me than true stories."

"But what about your love for Charles Dickens? Doesn't he inspire you to write fiction?"

"Daddy, dearest, have you ever read Charles Dickens?"

"Well…not that I remember."

"When I think I can write fiction like Charles Dickens, then I'll write fiction. Until then, I'm just a nosy reporter."

Chapter Seven

F ive minutes before the oven timer pinged, Dad's doorbell played a few bars of the *Bonanza* theme. It was a no fail eye-roller. My dad was a walking western cliché and he was proud of it. Embarrassed when I was young, as the years went by, I found my father's efforts at being a stereotype charming. Except the taxidermy.

"Oh, it smells like one of Connie's gloriously garlic-laden casseroles in here. That badger's atrocious; can I have it?" Then Billy wrapped his arms around me and let me bury my face into his cologned neck. He stood, both feet planted, rocking me and rubbing my back. "Oh, poor, poor girl. I'm here to hold you up when you need me."

I didn't really cry so much as moan into his neck, and I felt like a little kid. I could do this with Billy. When his nephew died in Iraq, I held Billy for hours. He loved his sister's boy almost like he was the kid's father. We still toasted that boy and shed a few tears every time we were together. The whole tragedy would always break my heart.

"Yeah, the badger's yours." I sniffled into his collar. Then I looked at him, scrunching my eyebrows together. "What in the hell do you plan to do with that thing?"He grinned on one side of his mouth. "Never mind. I think I'd rather not know."

"Oh, Jilly-bean, just think of the possibilities."

"I have no idea. But let's eat and get a little smeared on Dad's good wine. He'd want it that way." I wasn't in the mood for one of Billy's twisted ideas.

The casserole was devoured, the wine polished off, and a new bottle opened to breathe. Billy and I lay at opposite ends of my father's enormous couch, discussing funeral arrangements, town politics, and how the two were so inextricably entwined.

"You know, dearie, the whole town in going to be there, including people who hold grudges against your dad."

"Of course, they'll be there to gloat and to verify whether they are off the I-owe-Dean-O'Hara hook. Should they be off the hook? I have no idea what kinds of agreements Dad made with people. I know there are plenty of them. Arnold Potter settled one with me today."

"Oh, yes, the Arnold story. Isn't he a piece of work? I suppose he's handling the funeral gratis. Trust me, he owes your dad lots more than the price of one of his cheap-ass funerals. I suppose you know that your dad actually owns the funeral home? Correction, you own the funeral home."

"Oh God, this is going to get so messy." I sat up and poured a glass of glorious Petrus. I reasoned Daddy would want me to.

"You don't even know the half of it, girlie, but I'm here to help. In the last few years, your dad shared a few things with me. You know, late at night guy talk, sitting over a glass or two, smoking his superb cigars. By the way, do you want his cigars?" Billy was staring at Dad's cigar box on the table.

"You can remove every tobacco product from this house, and take all the dead animals while you're at it."

"I'll stick with the tobacco and the badger. Gotta leave something for Connie. Now, we have to discuss the Martin farm before you go downtown tomorrow and say something not cool."

"Can't Dad's attorney in town fill me in on all that? I just want to drink great wine and not think for a while. I'll go downtown and see his lawyer in a few days."

"Um, actually, your dad created a new law firm in Great Falls."

"Created a law firm? What are you talking about? Damn!" I had sloshed a few tablespoons of the wine on my shirt. "That bottle cost over two hundred dollars. Shit." I marched into the kitchen to get a wet cloth and dabbed at the red splotch while I went back to the couch.

"Careful with this liquid gold, Jillie." Billy had refilled his glass almost to the brim. Sometimes he could be a lowlife. "Back to the issue at hand. Your dad's estate attorney is in Great Falls."

"No offense, but what was my dad doing telling you about his estate planning? I'm a little confused here."

Billy sat up and faced me on the couch with one knee resting on the couch back. "Here's what Dean, your dad, said to me. 'Billy, you're the only friend of Jill's I can trust. I don't know her friends in Seattle, and I'm not sure which ones she's slept with. You can't trust women you've slept with and dumped.'"

Billy was doing a pretty good imitation of my dad, I had to admit.

"I think your old dad sort of enjoyed the fact that his little girl was cutting a swath through the women in Seattle. Anyhow, since he knew you and I had never known each other carnally—"

"How did he know that? And how did he know about my sexual habits?" I was getting nervous. There were some things parents shouldn't know about their children.

"Well, I assured him that you and I never have, and never will, indulge in a biblical study of each other. He trusted me to be a stalwart friend to you. Which I will be if I can have his humidor." A total boor.

"The humidor's yours. Now what about the Martin farm? You said Dad was discussing it when he...fell over." I couldn't say the word "died." My lips just couldn't shape it.

Billy went into one of his windy explanations that included lots of digressions into snatches of yummy local gossip, the kind that thrilled the locals but bored the bee-jeebers out of anyone else. Okay, I was enthralled.

To sum up Billy's thirty-minute monologue, Daddy had been gradually including Billy into his business dealings. He and Billy were driving all over the Hi-Line, visiting my father's real estate acquisitions, setting up new ones, and coming up with new locations for casinos in seven different towns in eastern Montana.

The Martin farm was my dad's purchase that was causing a legal battle between the owner's sons and my father. They wanted that farm back and expected my dad to return it, one way or another.

That it was suspected the Martins were up to something shady on that farm wasn't surprising. Old man Martin's sons, Josh and Eric, had been messed-up troublemakers since the days they came into town for high school.

It was common that farm kids would go to rural schools, one-roomers, and move into town for high school. Sometimes they lived with a family, but other times they would have their own apartments.

Usually this was harmless enough because they were good kids and their parents had folks who would check up on them. It was different with the Martins.

The Martin boys were blond and muscled the way hardworking farm men became after spending their childhood bucking bales and picking rocks. The Martins became known for recklessly driving testosterone cars, dispensing drugs, and beating up anyone who pissed them off. Eric, the younger, had obvious mental issues, while his big brother, Josh, was just plain mean. Handsome but vicious described the Martin boys.

To make things more bizarre, the whole town was talking about Sheriff Terabian having a little affair with Josh.

"You mean that bitch is boffing Josh Martin? I hope he lives up to his family creed and pummels her once in a while." I cringed when Billy lifted a disapproving eyebrow. "Okay, that was out of line. Men hitting women sucks. She just pissed me off today, that's all."

"Honey, Sheriff Terabian is a great sheriff for this pathetic little burg. She has experience up the wazoo and has been the catalyst for a serious reduction in border crime. She does have bad taste in men, though, if the rumors are true."

"I never thought I'd see Josh Martin cozy up to the law. Of course, she's something I'd probably cozy up to if she wasn't such an ice pack. Funny, I really thought she's a dyke, but I've been fooled before."

"Haven't we all, baby girl." Billy gave his half glass of wine a melancholy look and slammed back every last drop in one gulp. I winced when I realized he didn't even taste it. My daddy's Petrus. "Do you want me to stay with you tonight? I hate for you to be alone in all this."

"I'm not alone, baby boy, as long as you, and all this taxidermy, are in the world. And thanks, but you go home and get some rest. I'll call you tomorrow. By the way, expect to be my escort at the funeral, will you?"

"I'll be here for you as long as you need me, hon. I'm canceling the games for that night. Some frantic oil man is going to miss losing money at my tables, and I don't feel sorry for him. We'll talk tomorrow."

Billy left, badger under one buff arm, an unlit cigar in his mouth, and an extra in the badger's. He looked pleased with himself.

"If only he were a girl…" I muttered as I watched him pull out of the driveway. Within a few seconds of Billy pulling out of the extensive driveway, a large dark motorcycle rolled into the circle of light cast by the security light. The bike continued down the hill behind Billy, the engine low and the rider covered in oiled black leather. I waited for the rider to disappear into the night, then closed the front door and turned off the brass lantern-shaped porch light.

I finished the wine by myself.

CHAPTER EIGHT

I was dreaming the theme to *The Magnificent Seven* as I woke up and realized it wasn't a dream but the phone ringtone my father had selected. The clock read 8:00 a.m. "That's seven in the morning in Seattle," I groaned. The caller ID read Prairie View Funeral Home. A wave of panic rolled over me when I remembered I had forgotten to write the obituary.

"Hi, Arnold, I'm sorry I didn't get the obit to you yet. I'll have it for you in the next few hours." I'm an expert at writing for the deadline after an overly indulgent night.

"That's great. I also wanted to let you know that I've sent your dad's body to Great Falls for cremation. It will be completed by late this afternoon. Jill, I left his scapular on, you know, his Catholic necklace? Is that okay with you?"

The details of managing a death were starting to overwhelm me. "I think that was the right thing. He never took it off…at least, as far as I know. Is there anything else? I want to get started on the obit."

"Not yet. Just know I'm here if you need anything, dear."

A crash downstairs startled me, but I remembered Connie would probably be in the house by now. "I think Connie's here, Arnold. I'll have her help me with the obit. Thanks for everything."

My head ached from the previous evening's wine, and I dreaded facing Connie in all this postmortem drama. Connie had been our housekeeper since I was in kindergarten. She was the closest thing to a family member I had left since my family had no aunts, uncles, or cousins. I hail from a dwindled line of scurrilous ancestors, and it looked like the line would die out with me.

My room had its own bathroom, so I got into the shower to clean up my act before the inevitable emotional scene with Connie. I started composing the obituary in my mind as I let the hot water beat my face.

I threw on my old college bathrobe that Connie had hung in the closet. "Heh, still fits. You're hangin' in there, old girl." I smiled to myself but then glanced in the hall mirror and saw my grandmother's features in my reflection. Chastised, I headed downstairs to the sound of the radio in the kitchen.

"Hey, Connie. Any coffee made?"

Connie's tough little body straightened as she turned to face me. She left the soapy casserole dish in the sink, threw the dishtowel over her shoulder, and ran to me. She grabbed me into a painful bear hug and cried muffled sobs into my bathrobe. We stood together, holding on, blubbering into each other for several minutes. As if a timer dinged in our heads, we stopped at the same time, pulled back, and gazed at our teary faces, a little embarrassed. Hi-Line folks were not much for showing emotions.

"I miss him already, Jill. I keep expecting him to walk in and tease me about my bad coffee that he drank every morning for thirty-six years. Who will I take care of now?"

I didn't know how to answer that. "Did he tell you his heart was bad? Could you tell there was a problem?"

"Yeah, I knew. I found his pills, lots of them, when I cleaned his bathroom. That was three years ago. He'd been seeing some doctor in Great Falls. When I asked him about it, he shrugged. Lord almighty, he made it clear that it wasn't my business and that I couldn't tell you. He didn't want to worry you, he said."

"And knowing him, even if I did know, nothing would have turned out any different, so please don't blame yourself."

"I can't help but think…if I'd insisted he see another doctor…"

"Don't do that, Connie. The last thing you need to do is blame yourself."

Connie swiped at her tears and shook her head. "I swear it's something about that Martin farm that has…had…him on edge. Usually he took all his business deals in stride, barely nodding at them as they passed through his bank account. But there was something going on with this one that bothered him. He wasn't his usual sunny self. And here's something else that worried me, he hasn't…hadn't…stayed out all night in months."

"What? Nobody? Not even once?" Even when he aged, my dad enjoyed women, as long as they had the tits he so appreciated.

"That lady sheriff came over one night last fall, all serious looking and such, just as I was leaving the house. I stayed a little longer, made them some coffee, and cut up some of my rhubarb pie, you know, the kind with just a few strawberries that he loves. Then I left. After that night, he was worried and wouldn't answer me when I asked about it. You know how he is…was."

"Connie, quit worrying about your language. I'm sure we'll all get him in the past tense soon enough. And, yeah, he kept things to himself."

"Sorry, honey. Anyhow, another thing, after that sheriff's visit, your dad had maps of the Martin farm strewn across his work table for weeks. I'd pile them neatly when I cleaned, but they'd always be open and spread around the table the next day. After a while, I just left them alone."

"Well, I'm sure I'll find out what that's all about, Connie. And you'll be one of the first to know." I wasn't thrilled at the possibility I'd have to visit the sheriff. There was nothing that annoyed me more than a closet case, and I was sure the sheriff was a closet case.

"Connie, I'm going to get my laptop and write the obituary. I'll let you see it first to make sure I've got all the information right, okay?" Connie nodded, wiping at more tears. I marveled at a housekeeper who would know her boss so well she could be involved in writing his obituary.

❖

I struggled over the obit while sitting at Dad's big oak desk in his office. Every once in a while, I'd peer around, expecting him to come in and tell me to get away from his private stuff. I swear, if you believed in ghosts, you could believe Daddy was with me in that room. I knew that seemed ghoulish, but it wasn't; instead, it was comforting. Like his body was gone, but he wasn't gone. It was the first glimmer of peace I'd felt since I had gotten that phone call two days before.

His leather couch was back against the wall with a matching

easy chair next to it at an angle. The bookshelves were jammed with valuable first edition hardback westerns, especially Zane Grey, Louis L'Amour, and Tony Hillerman. On the wall behind the desk chair, he had a satellite map of Montana with a penciled circle around the land just southeast of the central Sweetgrass Hill.

There was an original Charlie Russell on the wall opposite the desk and above the couch. Its lush colors portrayed a contented cowboy cooking over a small fire, his dog asleep next to him. The stars looked companionable and warm. That was an expensive piece I knew he hadn't bothered to insure. I'm not a western art fan, but I decided I would keep that piece because Daddy loved it so much.

Above the long window that looked over the prairie behind the house, was a seven point elk's head. Atop the bookshelves was a jackalope, the peculiar creature of taxidermic humor, a rabbit with antlers.

In between the desk and couch was the work table covered with farmland maps. The utilitarian table was mission style with four matching chairs. I kept looking up from my laptop, wondering about those maps. My desire to learn what Daddy was pondering before he died distracted my efforts at the obituary. But I was able to slog through it in ninety minutes, and while Connie checked it over for accuracy, I started scanning the maps. I wanted to think about something other than Daddy's life history. Getting obits right is hard, I decided. It was depressing to learn that a life as colorful and prominent as my father's could be boiled down into a short newspaper article.

Dean Fitzpatrick O'Hara
July 29, 1937–April 16, 2009

The Prairie View community was saddened to learn of the passing of one of our most prominent citizens, Dean O'Hara. Mr. O'Hara has been a businessman and philanthropist in our area since he took over his father's beverage distribution business, Hi-Line Distributing, in 1970. The O'Hara family has resided in our area since the early 1900s.

Dean O'Hara was born in Great Falls on July 29, 1937 to his mother, Margaret (Peggy) Shea O'Hara, and his father, Patrick Connor O'Hara. He grew up in Prairie View, graduating in 1955 from Prairie View High School where he was active in sports, chorus, Catholic Youth Organization and Key Club. After high school, Mr. O'Hara enlisted in the U.S. Army and served for two years, which included ten months in Korea. He was exceptionally proud of his service to his country and became an active lifelong member of the Veterans of Foreign Wars, Post 6105, in Prairie View.

In 1958, Mr. O'Hara enrolled in Montana State University at Bozeman where he majored in Business and Economics. During that time, he participated in numerous organizations and was a member of the Sigma Nu fraternity. Upon graduation from college in 1962, he returned to Prairie View to work in his father's business. When Patrick O'Hara retired in 1970, Dean took over the business and proceeded to expand it into the large company that exists today. His company has over 500 employees statewide and makes substantial contributions to the Prairie View economy and community organizations.

A lover of sports, Mr. O'Hara was an avid supporter of all local teams and often contributed uniforms and traveling expenses for our young people. He was also a devoted member of St. Brigit Catholic Church and Knights of Columbus. Over the years he served on the city council and school board and was president of Kiwanis for 12 years. He was one of the founding members of the Milk River Country Club and was single-handedly responsible for acquiring funding for its architecturally renowned clubhouse. Through his efforts, the clubhouse and golf links attract golfers from all over the northwestern United States. Mr. O'Hara was also a generous sponsor of many projects at the Taft County Medical Center and Hi-Line Nursing Home.

Mr. O'Hara was known for his caring for others and love of a good joke. He supported the arts and developed a renowned collection of Western art. He was beloved by his friends and employees. He is survived by his daughter Jillian O'Hara, a resident of Seattle, Washington.

He will be greatly missed.

A rosary will be held Friday night, 6:30 at the Prairie

View Funeral Home to be followed by an open house reception at the O'Hara residence at 206 Hillside Drive. Everyone is welcome. On Saturday the funeral will take place at St. Brigit Church at 10:30 followed by interment at the Prairie View Cemetery. After the interment, there will be a reception at the St. Margaret parish hall, sponsored by the Altar Society Ladies.

Mr. O'Hara's daughter asks that memorial donations be given to the Hi-Line Nursing Home for construction of its new kitchen.

As much as I loved my father, I admit it was difficult to write this without inserting all the snarky comments that came to my head. But I was sure the folks in Prairie View had their own to add, so I left the fun up to them.

CHAPTER NINE

It was those damned maps that kept me in Prairie View. I was geeky about maps, couldn't resist studying them when they were placed in front of me. Agricultural maps, city, road, and world maps, maps that illustrate major exports, any old map. They all had an allure that an information lover like me couldn't resist. It was a belief that understanding a map was going to help me order and control my world, make me smarter, and aid my survival. And there was some truth to that.

"Jill. Jillian? Jilly!"

"Hmm? Oh, Connie, sorry…these maps…they're, well… interesting."

"That's fine, and I'll leave you to them if you'd just show me how to e-mail this to Arnold, so he can print the funeral programs. He just called. Didn't you hear the phone? He needs to get the obit in the paper, too."

"Oh, right. I'll do that now." While I was attaching the obit to an e-mail, I asked, "So, why does Daddy have that circle in the area between the Sweetgrass Hills? Over there on the wall map?" I pointed to the large map.

"Isn't that near the Martin farm?"

"Oh yeah, the Martin farm. Wow, they're so close to the border."

I started remembering my youthful exploits at the Canadian border. "You know, Connie, we used to take farm roads and cross right into Canada, just to get beer. Never once were we picked up by the cops. I bet that doesn't happen anymore."

"Oh, don't be so sure. It's common knowledge that there aren't enough Border Patrol cops to cover the Hi-Line. Lord, they probably think a bunch of hicks like us aren't worth patrolling. But we all know better, huh?"

"Well, actually, I've been gone awhile, Connie. I'd like to think Homeland Security would be all over it by now."

"Oh, hell, Jill, the government has its head up its ass, as usual, no matter what they tell the public. I know Mike Hassett still moves lots of drugs back and forth. Has for years. We all know about it, but the Feds do nothing."

Mike Hassett was one of my brief high school boyfriends who had gone bad. He was bright but couldn't control his urge to make money the easy way. After a two-year stint in the prison at Deer Lodge, Mike made some connections that supplied him with just enough drugs to keep him comfortable and under the federal radar. Despite his despicable career, he was a nice guy. I always liked sitting down to a beer with Mike.

To outsiders it appeared that everyone on the Hi-Line lived a little on the other side of the law, but that's not really how it was The rules did get pushed a bit more, but that's the nature of the area. It was remote, unrelenting, and unforgiving. It took a particular kind of person to settle there, raise a family, and stay on for several generations. The kind of person who could do whatever is necessary to adapt. It was a place where badgers and rattlesnakes flourished. What did that say about the people?

I was getting hungry and realized I hadn't eaten a thing. Connie was really off her cooking game, and I didn't have the heart to say anything. "You know, I think I'm going down to the Grill for lunch. I suppose everyone will be wanting to comfort the grieving daughter."

"Oh, darn it, Jill, I forgot to cook you any lunch. I'm so sorry. Can I heat up a can of soup? Make a grilled cheese?" I shook my head. "Then would you like me to go with you?"

"Totally unnecessary, but thanks. I can handle the vultures… ehhh…the comfort givers myself. In fact, I need to get used to it, huh?"

To tell the truth, I wanted to wander into Annie's little boutique and coffee shop. Just to check in, of course. My palms were damp from my considering it. I knew all along that my plans to play it cool with her were pathetic attempts at keeping my heart safe. I was a little miffed at myself for thinking about her when my father had so recently left for the other life.

"Annie doesn't get to the store until around noon." Connie had a little grin, mixed with sorrowful eyes. "I'm sure she wants to see you. She could be a support for you, along with me and Billy. Besides, she'll be hurt if you don't stop in."

"One of the reasons I left this town, Connie, is so people like you wouldn't know so much about people like me." I bent and gave her a quick kiss on the forehead and a tight hug. I had a feeling we'd be hugging each other a lot from now on. It was a pleasant prospect.

Chapter Ten

I hadn't seen Annie in three years. The last time was down at the Oilman's Bar, one of the seedier bars in town. Actually, all bars in Prairie View would be considered seedy by Seattle standards. There were three types of bars in Prairie View: seedy, seedier, and seediest.

She was sitting at the seedier bar with Wayne, her husband, sipping a girly-looking drink. I came in with Billy to shoot some pool and have a beer. Annie and I caught each other's eye in the mirror behind the bar. My heart jammed; it looked like hers sank, considering the frown she donned. She rose to the occasion, however, and gave me a tepid hug. She didn't extend herself much to glance her cheek off mine. I took the hint and kept it to a hug you'd give a heterosexual acquaintance. Hands on each other's shoulders, cheeks tapping together, barely a peek into the eyes, hips a couple feet apart, of course.

Wayne invited me to join them, while Billy went to play pool and flirt with a farmhand. We talked about family news, town politics, and sports. As usual, Wayne was warmer to me than Annie. While it was good to be in her presence, comforting somehow, it was clear she wasn't interested in being anything more than a distant old friend. Ex-lover was not to be in our job descriptions for each other. I left the bar that night aching again for her. Her laugh. Her hair. Her eyes.

And that's why I made sure I didn't see much of her over all those years. Because every time I did, I would get reactivated like an LSD flashback, and my heart wouldn't have room for anyone else. Love unrequited, a toxic condition.

Now my dad was dead and I wanted to see Annie. I think I had some ulterior hope that her sympathy for me would encourage her to comfort my pain. However, all I had to do was remember that bar scene three years earlier and I knew better.

So I was floored when, knees shaking, I entered her store, and she shouted, "Jilly!" She swooped around a display case and clutched me into an almost loving hug. Well, hips still weren't touching, but it was a hell of a lot more expressive than that last time. I held on to her for several seconds and milked the bereft daughter role.

She pulled back and looked into my eyes. "I'm so happy you came in. I've been thinking of you all morning. I'm so sorry about your dad. I found out yesterday and feel terrible about it." At the lost look on my face she moaned "Awww" and hugged me again, a little tighter and a little longer. "Tell me how I can help, sweetie," she said into my hair.

"Oh, Annie, I…" I was a little kid all of a sudden. My voice quavered and embarrassing tears started spilling down my cheeks. My emotions were so intense that, even now, it's difficult to describe them. My father dead, my semi-estranged lifelong love comforting me. Having her arms around me, soothing me, was both exhilarating and strange. I buried my head in her shoulder.

After a few minutes of enjoying her closeness and floral smell, I pulled back to look at her. She held my eyes for a few seconds, then looked away toward the door of the back room. "Wayne, look who's here. It's Jill O'Hara."

Wayne emerged from the swinging doors separating the back room from the front. "Hey, Jill, good to see you. Sorry about Dean." And he came over to give me a warm manly hug. He smelled like cigarettes, Old Spice, and beer.

"Thanks, Wayne. Look, you guys, I just wanted to stop in and say hi. The funeral is Saturday. Maybe we can go out sometime later next week. You know, catch up and all." I wondered where that courage came from.

Annie looked pleased and thoughtful. "We'd love to, but aren't you on nights all next week, Wayne?" Wayne nodded. "Then you'll have to entertain just me. But, Jill, isn't there anything we can do to help for the funeral?" Annie was actually reaching out, so I decided to take her up on it.

"Well, look, Billy is going with me to the funeral. That's just two of us for the whole front pew of the church. Connie, her husband, and sons have the second pew. Would you two mind sitting with Billy and me in the front?"

They took a moment to look at each other, a slight nod from Wayne, and then Annie said, "We'd be honored. Your father was an amazing guy. He was always kind when you and I were in high school and, afterward, spoke to me whenever we'd run into each other downtown." The mention of high school put an uneasy look on her face.

"Thanks, you guys. It means a lot to me to have your support." We stood looking at each other, shy and speechless. I hated pregnant interpersonal moments, except when I was interviewing someone. "I have to get something to eat, so I'll see you Saturday, okay? The funeral will be at ten thirty."

"We'll definitely see you then, Jill," said Wayne. "Do you want us to wait so that we can all go in together?" Wayne was more empathetic than I gave him credit for. Another check in the plus column for Wayne.

"That would be great. See you then." And I scurried out of the store, uneasy at how well it had gone. Then I got uneasy about my unease. In other words, as usual, seeing Annie left me screwed up.

CHAPTER ELEVEN

I spent the next few days preparing for the funeral on Saturday. There was a rosary Friday night at the mortuary, with a reception at Dad's house following. The funeral the next day would include Mass, interment (why couldn't they just say burial?) at the graveyard, and another reception at the church hall. I had to help Connie get the house ready for the post-rosary reception, including hiring a last-minute caterer and buying a load of alcoholic and non-alcoholic beverages. The fancy Murano came in handy.

One chore I had to fulfill was to go to the graveyard and decide where Daddy's grave should go. To the right of Grandma or to the left? My father had purchased four plots years ago. Why four? One was supposed to be for my hellish grandfather, but he had adamantly expressed his wishes to have his ashes spread in Ireland. I think most folks, including my father and grandmother, were relieved to have Grandpa Paddy's remains as far from Prairie View as possible.

So Grandma had two plots to her left and one to her right. I wanted to see which plot had the best view, so my father's ghost would enjoy the dazzling sunrises and sunsets the Hi-Line is famous for. It's a common practice there to bury even cremated bodies in the ground, complete with headstones. It's one of the advantages of living in a state where vast land tracts can afford spacious resting areas for the dead. My father's urn would be planted next to his mother's.

The graveyard gate was open, so I inched my car along the well-maintained gravel lanes that separated blocks of graves. I fought back tears and my breathing hitched as I studied all the familiar names etched on the headstones. I learned something about small towns that was rarely mentioned. I could walk through the cemetery of my tiny town and have a cathartic grief experience. I knew almost everyone there: teachers, family friends, waitresses, janitors, attorneys, babies, doctors, parents of friends, friends my age who met untimely deaths. They were all there, waiting for someone to walk by and acknowledge them. It was a rock-hardened soul who could walk into her little town graveyard and not shed a tear or shake a bewildered head.

The Prairie View Cemetery lived up to its name. You could see the prairie for miles around, with the Sweet Grass Hills in the northern distance and the Rocky Mountains sixty miles to the west. Panoramic dramatic vistas, complete with cirrus clouds and red-tailed hawks. Breathtaking in spring and summer, desolate and biting cold in fall and winter. I was thankful Daddy died in the spring so that the ground was thawed and we could bury him right away. We had to store Grandma for four months before we could bury her, and it felt like pressing business unfinished until we had her in the ground.

It only took a minute to decide to plant my father to the left of Grandma. That way an empty plot would be to either side of them. More symmetrical and the view was wonderful from every vantage point. Daddy had chosen his final resting place well.

I had a Jewish girlfriend once who taught me the custom of placing a rock on any gravestone we visited. It's a practice I appreciated, so I searched around for a stone to put on Grandma's grave. As I put a golf ball–sized rock on her headstone, I heard a rumbling engine getting louder. I looked up in time to see a large motorcycle, driven by a black leather biker, barrel too fast down the road adjacent to the cemetery. A huge cloud of dust boiled up from the rear wheel, making the rider look far more dramatic than he deserved to.

"Asshole," I muttered. "Oh, sorry, Grandma. You know I've always had a potty mouth." Here I was, apologizing to Grandma's grave for swearing. Some things never change. But it pissed me off that the bike rider had no respect for the dead. Never mind I used to take that same road at death-defying speeds in my old Chevy.

On my way home from the graveyard, I got to thinking about the maps on Dad's worktable. His obsession with them bothered me. He usually bought land quickly and turned it over just as rapidly, making a tidy profit before he had to pour any maintenance money into the property. As far as I could tell, he'd been holding the Martin farm for almost a year and, during that time, poring over the maps.

Maybe he was holding on to the land because of the threatened suit by the Martin boys. As far as I knew, old man Martin had no quarrel with Daddy's purchase of his land. Farming wasn't lucrative around Prairie View anymore, so why were the boys so all-fired to get it back? And the big question for me: did I really care? Hell, I had no connection to that land. I could just sell it back to the Martins and be done with it. But my father was fascinated by it. Why? Those damn maps.

I decided to set the Martin mess aside until I had a meeting with my father's attorney after the funeral. I was really in no shape at that moment to think about or discuss business legalities.

CHAPTER TWELVE

The funeral events went as expected. Lots of familiar faces, some whose names I'd forgotten, came up to me and offered hugs and condolences. I went through all the motions tearless and numb. I twisted my dry hanky when Lauren Lindstrom, my father's goddaughter, sang *Ave Maria* because it was Daddy's favorite church song. Billy wrapped his arm around me while Annie lightly held my hand, and for once, her touch didn't distract me. Occasionally, I felt Connie's solid touch in between my shoulder blades because she sat directly behind me. There were at least three dozen flower arrangements besides the ones I ordered.

When we left the church after the funeral services, I noticed Sheriff Terabian, in dress uniform, holding court near her cruiser. Annie had hold of my arm, and I asked her why the sheriff was there.

"Oh, she's head of law enforcement for the entire county. She has to attend the funeral of our leading citizens." I shot Annie an annoyed glance. "It's expected. You know that. She's…a good person to have on your side…I suppose."

"Well, she's not on my side, Annie." Annie looked disturbed about my comment, but she didn't reply. I let the matter go, but for a brief moment, the sheriff caught my eye and gave a vague nod. I hoped she felt a little red-faced about writing me a ticket only a few days earlier. However, I was certain I'd never know how she felt about that. She was all uniform and business, and surprisingly that seemed unfortunate.

The sheriff's cruiser, lights flashing, led the procession to the cemetery. As the crowd gathered around the grave site, I held on to Connie and Billy. When the low voices of the mourners died down, the meadowlarks' song became the background music to the priest's prayers. I glanced around once and caught the sheriff looking at the crowd like a secret service agent watching a president's audience. What the hell was she looking for? An assassin? She needed to get a grip on her life. Her gray eyes met mine for a second and I looked down, feeling my ears burn. Annie moved in behind me, placed her hand on my shoulder, and I forgot all about the sheriff.

After the funeral, burial, and endless reception, I had Billy take me home. I couldn't face another well-meaning hug. I smelled like a women's restroom with all the secondhand perfume that had rubbed off from lacquered hair, floral lotions, and cologne. I wanted a shower, my sweats, a glass of wine, and some soft laughs with Billy.

Before returning to her home, Connie had beaten us to the house and stocked the kitchen with all kinds of food to supplement the ten or so casseroles now waiting in the freezer. You could trust folks of Prairie View to keep you fed in times of crisis. The problem was returning all those casserole dishes. Each one was labeled with the owner's name, implying that I should eat the food and return the dish with appropriate compliments to the chef. Billy saw it as a culinary windfall for himself.

"Oh, just take it. I can't eat all that stuff. How many hamburger casseroles can one gal eat anyway?"

"Don't you worry, dearie, we'll make use of this cornucopia of goodness while you're here, and you won't have to eat at the Grill all that often. I'll return all the containers myself. This food will save you from your own cooking."

"What do you mean? Connie's a great cook, and I don't intend to make her stop or anything."

"I guess your dad didn't tell you. Connie put her foot down a few years ago and told Dean she was only cooking once a day in this house. First of all, your father would often not show up when supper was ready. And then there's Connie's back."

"What about her back?" I was out of the loop in my own home. A self-imposed isolation from the day-to-day life of my father and Connie was a result of my disconnection when Grandma died. Prairie View, without Grandma, wasn't home anymore.

"Connie has a herniated disk. She really isn't supposed to work at all. But she's a workhorse. What is she going to do without this job?"

"Who says she's out of a job?" Then it dawned on me. Connie was out of a job, and it was my responsibility to make sure she would be okay. Wasn't it?

"Damn, Billy, this is all too much for me. Daddy's business, this house, its contents, Connie, the lawsuit, all that land. I don't even know anything about Daddy's land, except that stinkin' Martin farm."

"Look, your dad was on top of everything. He had good help. His managers are excellent. His attorney in Great Falls is well respected. Have you looked at your dad's files in his office yet? When it comes to business, I may be the queen, but he is the undisputed king of organization."

"I haven't gone through his stuff yet, and his office is just too… personal for right now. I'll get to it eventually. He knew he was in bad shape, Billy. Do you think he prepared for this, I mean legally?"

"I know he did, Jilly-bean. He told me he was readying everything in case you had to take over suddenly, and he knew you'd be pissed off about that. So he tried to make it as easy as possible. He didn't tell me about his bad heart, though."

My exhaustion was starting to pull me down. I felt its weight leaning on my sagging shoulders and drooping head. "Billy, do me a favor, would ya, hon? Open a bottle of wine, pour us some, and promise you'll go with me to see the Great Falls attorney on Tuesday. What's his name again?"

"Her. Her name is Sylvia McCutcheon, my tired pathetic friend. And of course, I'll go with you. I'm expected, too. Do you want anyone else to go with us?"

I assumed he was hinting that I could ask Annie to come, too. But I didn't like the feel of it. Annie and I had only just started reconnecting, and it didn't seem appropriate that she be there. Well, that's what I told myself, anyway. When I thought truthfully about it, I admitted that I was embarrassed by all that money I was getting. Annie worked hard in her little shop, probably not making much. And Wayne was an orderly at the hospital. Their two sons, barely a year apart, were in the military, probably in Iraq. Actually, Annie hadn't really told me where they were stationed, but that's the natural assumption you make for any member of the armed forces: either going to the Middle East, in the Middle East, or returning from the Middle East.

"Let's just make it an outing for the two of us, Billy. I don't have it to field any extra energy from anybody. Um, Annie and Wayne's marriage. How is it? I mean, are they happy together? Do you hear anything? They're together all the time, but I used to hear that it was tough between them." I know I sounded thirteen years old. I was also struck by a section of my heart that really didn't care about Annie and Wayne's marriage. When had that developed?

Billy, to his credit, didn't roll his eyes. With the palm of his hand, he rubbed his shaved head, making a sandpapery sound, and thought about my question. "I don't know, Jill. Usually, I have a bead on just about everybody, but Annie and Wayne keep to themselves, you know? They don't hit any of my watering holes. They don't attend any church regularly that I know of. On occasion, they come to the Elks Club for a special event, but don't stay long. I don't even see them in their yard on the weekends. They're private, a little rednecked."

Billy leaned both elbows on the kitchen island. "Their boys graduated from high school and were gone immediately into some branch of the military, but darned if I even know which one. Whatever trouble Annie and Wayne had, it was over years ago from the looks of things. I hope you aren't still toting that tarnished, sputtering torch for her, because I don't want to see you get into something messy."

"You should see the odd looks she gives me, Billy." Since Billy wasn't hopping to my wine request, I went into the pantry where Daddy had a wine storage cooler. I shouted from the pantry, "It's like she's sizing me up, or sometimes, like she has something important to say. Then her face gets neutral again. I feel fucked around by it." I used the corkscrew hanging from the pantry wall. The cork squeaked then popped out. I went back to find Billy glowering. "Hey, what's wrong?"

"I don't know. I have a feeling you're going to get soundly shafted again. You can't go back, you know. You're not seventeen anymore. She's married, and you are too sophisticated, not to mention too gay, to go after a small-town married woman. It's a bad idea. And while Wayne's pretty much of a nice guy, he does drink some and he hangs out with weirdos."

"Weirdos? Like who?"

"On the weekends, when he's not at the hospital, he hangs out with the hunting and fishing crowd."

"Oh, you little fairy, the whole town is the hunting and fishing crowd. Quit being so judgmental of the very people whose money you shovel into your fist several nights a week."

"No, I mean the rabid hunters. You know, the guys with the scary bumper stickers and gun racks in the back of their pickups. They even have a firing range up on the Martin farm where Wayne hangs out."

"The Martin farm? Why does that place have to plague every conversation I have? Are you saying Wayne is buddies with the low-life Martin boys? Nice old Wayne?"

"I'm not saying he's buddy-buddy with them, dearie, only that I've heard he goes and shoots at their private range. A place where only the Martins' select little crowd gets invited. Annie shoots, too, from what I've heard."

It was time for me to have that wine. Annie into guns and hanging out with the Martins? It didn't fit. I was sure there was more to the story, but figured if it was important, Annie would tell me one of these days. I poured two fingers of the Frog's Leap (Rutherford Cabernet, 1989) into two glasses. I handed Billy his and started swirling mine, curious to deconstruct the bouquet and taste. As I sniffed my wine I saw Billy slog back his glass without a thought to the amount of money that was in his mouth.

"Um, Billy, Daddy's whiskey cabinet is over there. Help yourself."

CHAPTER THIRTEEN

I spent the next two days after the funeral entertaining all kinds of folks who dropped by to offer condolences. I know most of them meant well, but by Monday afternoon, I was worn out. The only good thing was that Annie spent part of Sunday afternoon with me, helping to clean up the kitchen. I was happy Wayne was working at the hospital. Annie and I shared a few beers and frozen pizza around suppertime. We sat across from each other, the kitchen island between us, laughing about some of the local characters.

"So, Annie, tell me about the rumor I heard about you." Her neck stiffened, and as she turned her eyes to me, I noticed a guarded look that dropped away as her face became more open and inquisitive.

"Okay, what kind of baloney have they been saying about my boring little life?"

"That you're a pretty good shot. Billy said you like to go out to the Martins and play Annie Oakley, or is it more like Calamity Jane?" I hoped she knew it was just a friendly question, not an accusation. She looked relieved, so I wasn't off the mark.

She smiled, gave an offhand laugh, and said, "Oh, that little rumor. Well, it's true. I'm a gun-toting gal these days. Wayne and I took some lessons several years ago, where I fired all kinds of rifles, pistols, shotguns, and automatics. I got hooked. So I practice whenever I can get away from the store. And, guess what, I'm damned good at it. Kinda ticks Wayne off because I'm better than him, but it's one thing we can do together."

I felt a minor jolt of jealousy at hearing about Annie and Wayne's common hobby. But years of practice at hiding it came into play. "So why the Martins, Annie? I mean, no offense, but aren't they a little, um, hard to deal with?"

"Now you're just showing your O'Hara prejudice about the Martins. Really, they're nice guys; you just need to know how to understand them. Josh is an amazing man. This whole thing with your dad is a misunderstanding gone out of control." I had been admiring the late afternoon sun in her short, married-lady haircut but was miffed by the word "prejudice."

"A misunderstanding? I'm not sure what it is because I haven't met with the attorneys yet. What do you know about it?" While I hid my irritation, I could feel myself slip into the puzzled questioner mode, one of my favorite journalism tactics. Even my relationship with Annie wasn't immune to that.

"Oh, I don't want to talk about your father's misguided dealings, not with him so newly in the grave. Let's save it for another time."

"Why 'misguided'? Whatever has happened in that land deal, I need to know about it...from several perspectives. If you've got something to tell me, I want to know. The whole situation is confusing, and it seems my dad was really focused on it just before he died. If it was such a problem, then I'd like to fix things as soon as possible."

Annie reached over the island and grabbed my hand. The first thing I noticed was that her hand was sweaty, but then I felt barely discernable revulsion in my gut. She looked directly into my eyes. "Jill, I know you can be reasonable and fair. Your dad was more stubborn than you." She tightened her squeeze on my hand, then gradually let go, but didn't move her eyes from mine. I forced myself to focus on her words, trying to ignore my surprise reaction to her touch.

"Old man Martin was in no shape to be selling his land. He's old, has dementia. Your dad, well, I have to say, he took advantage of that. Fifty-six hundred acres, Jill, only half of it farmable. Why would your dad do such a thing? He took the Martins' legacy from them. Those boys grew up on that farm and expected to live on it all their lives. Now you own it, and—"

"Dad bought that land from a demented old man? Hey, I know my dad was, well, greedy, but I can't believe he would knowingly do that. He did have some ethics, and one of them was respect for farmers and their land."

Annie was shaking her head, appearing sadly perplexed. "Well, for whatever reason, he wouldn't change his mind and sell it back, even for a small profit. The Martins don't have much money, and now that the old man is in the nursing home, they're strapped. The money their dad made on the farm sale got eaten up by creditors. Josh told me." She grabbed my forearm, gave me one of those melt-away looks I cherished when we were in high school, and said, "You can fix it, Jilly, can't you? I hate the thought of your dad leaving this world putting a bad taste in everybody's mouth."

"I'll look into it, Annie. I don't want my father's legacy to be any more tarnished than I think it is. I'm meeting with the attorney this week. Let's see what fixing this would take."

And there it was, the smile that had kept me captive for all those years. As I led her to the front door, we held hands. Just before she let herself out, she took my face between both hands, slowly kissed each cheek, looked into my eyes, and said, "I'm glad you're home, Jilly." I was relieved when I closed the door behind her.

CHAPTER FOURTEEN

I love attorneys. They're right up there with nurses, librarians, and janitors as the most helpful professionals when you're in a pinch. I have several friends who are attorneys, and I'm not above keeping at least three on retainer at all times. In my line of work, between getting accused of libel and working my butt out of tight situations, I find having an attorney on call, at any hour of the day, to be comforting. Besides, I can afford it.

Attorney worship was one area where I had always believed I differed from Daddy. Come to find out, Daddy had an entire firm working for him out of Great Falls. With all I know about the way corporations work, it didn't dawn on me that my father, a major business owner, would have a bevy of attorneys working for his diverse interests. Five of them, to be exact, and that didn't include the secretaries and paralegals.

The renovated Victorian home that was McCutcheon, Benson, Torgerson, and Associates would have been classy even in Seattle. It was a flagrant showpiece in Great Falls, Montana. However, while the offices were well appointed in hardwood and leather, they were small, intimate, and comfortable. I was given a cordial introduction to everyone who was there that day, and I was briefed about the role each person had in my father's enterprises. To a person, they responded to me with a deference that is outside most reporters' experience. Reporters' common reception is laced with distaste and the acknowledgment that we are necessary evils.

By the time Sylvia McCutcheon closed her office door behind Billy and me, I was dizzied by the scope of Daddy's dealings. I was in over my head. Billy appeared to sense my dismay and held my hand for a few moments while we sat and waited for Sylvia to settle in for our meeting. When she offered us a glass of scotch, I took her up on it, and I hate the stuff. The nostril-flaring gag I stifled as I swallowed the scotch brought me to my senses and distracted me from the panic I felt. I was in charge of all this.

So I decided to give Ms. McCutcheon the once-over to see if she was an adversary or advocate. She wore a deep brown suit, well made, and a beige silk blouse, decorated by a feminized bolo tie. The round silver clasp looked to be inlaid with some sort of fancy agate. Rocks are not my expertise. McCutcheon looked to be pushing fifty, with just a little gray at the temples tincturing the short, styled black hair. She was definitely in good physical shape as evidenced by her trim physique. When she smiled, she won me over. Her whole face exuded an intelligent exuberance for life. Now I assumed she was too nice to be my father's attorney. It dawned on me she was a lesbian, a handsome one at that.

"Ms. O'Hara, let me begin by offering my and the entire firm's heartfelt condolences over your father's death. As you can imagine, it's a shock to us. I also want to give my apologies for not attending the funeral. It was always your father's wish that his association with us remain…less public."

"Thank you, Ms. McCutcheon. I guess my dad was successful in keeping this firm under wraps because I didn't even know about you." I turned to Billy. "Did you know about this, Billy?"

"Well, I…errr…was aware that Dean…your father…had attorneys in Great Falls, yes." Billy looked a little lame to me. I gave him a stare for a few moments before turning back to McCutcheon.

"So, what happens next? Is this the fabled reading of the will? Is my father leaving everything to an animal shelter or a bimbo mistress?" I was trying to inject humor but it came off as bitchy and suspicious. I knew my dad left me rich. O'Haras don't abandon O'Haras.

Poor Sylvia McCutcheon eyed me for a few nervous seconds, then grinned, a really cute grin. She reached for her intercom.

"Andrew, would you bring in all the files we've prepared for Ms. O'Hara? Oh, and could you order us a fruit plate from down the street?" A fruit plate? She noticed my surprise. "We have a lot to discuss and will need some fuel. Besides, I could tell the morning scotch wasn't to your liking."

"Was I that obvious?" From a door in the side wall, in came Andrew. I certainly hadn't met him yet. A cute little gay man, around thirty-five, blond, with a set of blue eyes that projected intelligence and compassion. I glanced at Billy and caught him out in a flagrant wink at Andrew. Andrew was beaming at him. "Hussy," I said under my breath to Billy.

Then I understood that my bone-deep heterosexual father had gay attorneys. Everyone watched my dawning awareness and started chuckling. I leaned back into my comfortable chair and knew I was in capable legal hands.

❖

Several years ago, I had a friend who learned I was from a small town, and she made the assumption that I was from a working- or lower-class family. She occasionally made reference to my lower-class roots, sometimes in her admiration that I had overcome such humble beginnings. I allowed her to persist in this illusion for months because I was too embarrassed to correct her. I didn't know what to say after so long. "Um, actually, I'm kind of wealthy. Sorry I didn't mention it before." I felt like there's no good way to tell her that I was privileged unless I derided my privilege at the same time. But it would have been dishonest of me to do so. I wasn't flashy, but I liked having money.

So here's a secret: in each of those stunted, dried-out towns that are passed over by the interstate, some rich people live there. They live in the groomed, or not so groomed, houses at the edge of town, while they generate capital exploiting everything the area has to offer. Most of them are community minded and help keep businesses and churches thriving. Others are ticks with their pincer heads buried under the skin of their hapless host, growing bloated and indifferent to their food source.

My family? Parasites with a conscience.

Chapter Fifteen

The wise ones say that even the most innocuous event has awakening potential. Something inexplicable jiggles our brains and, boom, we see the world through a completely different lens. I suppose that's true; far be it from me to argue with sages. But my enlightening events loom large in my memory, like the big inch marks on a ruler, giving all the smaller marks their meaning and place in space. Kissing Kathy Dolman in sixth grade was an inch mark, as well as that talk I had with Billy when he told me the truth about my family history. But the meeting with Sylvia McCutcheon was not just an inch mark, it was a whole twelve inches. One whole foot of you're-on-a-new-road-Jilly.

Of course, I walked out of that office an obscenely rich woman. I had expected wealth, just not the obscene part. Not only land, but the businesses, including casinos, vending machines, and a tristate beverage distributorship. The securities investments were almost uncountable, and I had controlling shares in many West Coast companies. My father, who portrayed himself as a silly, small town womanizer, was brilliant with the money Grandpa left him. He told me many times that money begets money, but he took that credo to extremes. Money harvesting had been happening all around me as I grew into adulthood. But awareness of my father's power and wealth slumbered in a holding tank part of the brain.

And here was the shocker: for the past three years, he had been grooming Billy to take over as general manager of this hidden rural empire. Billy. So much for his retiring-at-fifty-with-a-good-man plan, which he was already behind on. Anyhow, Billy and I were now business associates. Actually, I was his boss (causing me to snicker at him a few times) but he ran the show. And I promise you, it was a big fat relief for me. The last thing I wanted to do was crawl around that drudgy town and manage a financial empire. I had scandals to expose and stories to publish. I just didn't have to worry about getting paid for them anymore. Hell, I could buy my own newspaper and pay myself for my stories. But what's the fun in that?

I could feel the hot breeze thrashing my hair as Billy and I stood on the sidewalk, four hours later, outside the Great Falls law offices. I think I was looking a little dazed because Billy slid his arm around me and squeezed my shoulders.

"What do you need, little rich girl?" Billy was trying to lighten the moment, but it was a limp, irritating try.

"I think I need a drink and some food, Mr. Fat Cat, General Manager of *my* fortune. Then we need to devise a plan for getting everything done here, including the Martin mess, so I can head back to Seattle. I need my lattes, my friends, and some unambiguous gay culture."

"Okay, the Rose Room is a few blocks away. They have excellent, uh, decent drinks and bar food. Does that sound okay?" He started for the car acting all too pleased with himself. His pants fit his butt in a way that made me want to cup a cheek. Even I'm not immune to noticing Billy's delectable physique.

"Yeah, the Rose Room's okay. Where are you going?"

"To the car? To drive to the bar?"

"As I remember, the Rose Room is about three blocks away. Let's just walk, wimpbutt." And I started a determined stride toward Central Avenue.

Billy's puzzlement reminded me of something else peculiar about small-town folks: they rarely walked anywhere. Even if the destination was a few blocks away, you were considered dorky for walking there. The main street of Prairie View was four blocks long. And I could remember my grandma parking at one end to pick up a prescription and then driving two blocks down to go to the bank. If I asked her why she did that, she would answer with a look that said, "What a dumb question."

Okay, to give small towns credit, that behavior had improved in recent years. Now they may walk the four blocks, but that's the limit. I think walking is too vulnerable in small towns. Everyone can see you and judge. They stand in their windows and say, "Hey, Marge Shire is walking somewhere. Where the heck is she going? Should I offer her a ride? She sure could use the exercise, though. Holy buckets, just look at those thighs. Since that last baby…"

"C'mon, the walk will clear my head. Geez, you'd think I asked you to walk to Glacier Park."

I took a booth near the front of the air-conditioned bar, waited for my eyes to adjust to the gloom, then took a look around. A typical Montana tavern, smelling of rancid beer, cigarette butts, burnt pizza crust, and Pine-Sol. Colorful commemorative whiskey bottles lined the top shelf behind the bar. The bar stools and booths had recently undergone their periodic reupholstering, now covered in maroon Naugahyde with water buffalo grain. Squeaky when sat upon. A huge bowed and speckled print of a red rose leaned out from the wall above our booth, supplying a reason for the bar's name.

A stocky, platinum-chignoned bartender stared at us. Her tough face wore her years breaking up bar fights, and she carried herself like she should earn a Purple Heart medal for tavern wounds. She decided to give Billy the time of day and tossed him a grudging half-smile when he ordered our drinks and a couple mini-pizzas. He pointed to the cloudy pickled foods jars including pigs' feet, eggs, and sausages, and ordered a few of them.

"I'll get your drinks now, and call you when your food's ready. I gotta go in the back and get plates for the pickled stuff. Dishwasher didn't bring them out last night. Typical bullshit." She splashed together my gin and tonic and Billy's ditch (whiskey and water in Montana-ese) and clonked them on the bar before taking a suck off her cigarette, pressing it back into its ashtray, and strutting to the back room, shoulders cocked, chest out, and arms swinging.

"Thanks, Mavis," cheerful Billy called as he headed toward me with my drink made from the cheapest gin known to man and garnished with a brownish lime flopping from the rim.

"This isn't what I meant about food and drinks. Can't we go somewhere a little more, you know…healthier?"

"Oh, we will, Jilly-bean, we just need to have a private talk in a place where no one wants to listen to us. Mavis couldn't give a shit about us, as long as we tip and don't take swings at each other. And quit the urban snooty shit. You're of this place just as much as me and Mavis." I wanted to dispute that but figured it futile.

"Okay, Mr. Down-home, now that we're both rich pigs, I guess we can be generous with old Mavis, but she could at least cut a new lime." I was trying to wring out a few drops from last week's lime slice.

Billy shook his head and took a slurp of his ditch. I could tell he was thinking about what a wimp I was, but he was diplomatic enough not to say it. "Listen, I'm glad Sylvia McCutcheon offered to drive you around to all the land deals your dad had in the works. You need to understand them. But I really want you on top of this Martin problem. I can't handle taking over everything your dad does…did…and deal with the Martins, too."

"Would you quit worrying about your verb tenses? Damn, between you and Connie, I can't decide whether Daddy is dead or alive."

At that, we started to laugh and couldn't quit, until I remembered that Daddy really was dead. Then I started to cry, just a little sniffle, but enough to alert Mavis as she came out of the back. She eyed us, ready to bust up a fight. I wiped my eyes with the back of my hand, sniffed a little more, and sent Mavis a weak smile. She didn't respond, just stared for a few moments before putting our frozen, individual-sized pizzas, fresh from their Tombstone box, into the greasy little oven she kept off to the side. I pretended my drink wasn't vile and swallowed a few sips.

After Billy brought our food back from where Mavis plopped it on the bar, I was ready to discuss things. While I talked, I was busy picking off singed pizza crust from my crispy concave pepperoni pizza.

"Something is funky about this Martin thing. I was going to ask Sylvia about it, but my instincts tell me that she's clueless except about the superficial reasons for the lawsuit." I told Billy what Connie said about Dad always hanging over the maps after the lady sheriff had visited him. And that Dad had quit hounding around after "dollies," studying the maps instead.

"I have no idea what caught your dad's attention. But it sounds like the sheriff has some information. I think you should talk with her." He saw me make a gag look so he changed the subject. "Have you had a chance to go through your dad's files in his home office?"

"No, I've just looked at his maps, and they're all focused on the Martin farm. Do you know how big that place is? Over fifty-six hundred acres. And it's really close to the border, godforsaken, near Whitlash, cozied into the Sweetgrass Hills. Does anyone even live in Whitlash anymore?"

"Yeah. Your dad and I drove up there about a month ago. The one-room schoolhouse is still open. The play structure is bigger than the school, so there's some money floating around. The post office slash general store is open, and a few houses are still being lived in. The town is mostly used by farmers to get mail and a few necessities." Billy was gnawing the meat off a dripping pickled pig's foot.

"Did you go there to see the Martin place?"

"We did, but there's the problem. The boys told us to go away... at gunpoint. The Martins don't own the land anymore, but we can't get the boys to move off. The sheriff says it's out of her jurisdiction even though some of the land is in Taft County, her turf. The houses and buildings are located in Liberty County, patrolled by a completely different sheriff's department. Your dad and I went to see the Liberty County Sheriff, Dixon is his name, and he was polite but seemed disinterested. You know how political it is kicking people off their land. And for better or worse, the sheriff is an elected position."

"Shit, politics in the middle of nowhere. Oh hell, why don't we just sell the damn land back to the Martins? Then we'd be done with it and I can get back to Seattle. Not like we'd be made poorer for it."

"And there's the other problem, boss. The Martins claim your dad stole it from an old man who has dementia. They feel they should be entitled to reclaim the land plus keep some money for damages and legal costs."

"Call me 'boss' again and I'll have to top you and have my way with your body."

"Be still my quivering heart. That would add up to sexual harassment. I suppose you think I should make you coffee every morning, too." I loved it when he put on his swish talk.

"Only after you've gone out to fetch my fresh Danish." While Billy laughed and popped an entire pickled egg into his mouth, I used my finger to rock my curled pizza. "Was that farm such a moneymaker for them? I know times here have been rotten for farmers, and lots of them have cut their losses and run. Why do the Martin boys want that farm so badly when they could make enough money to set themselves up somewhere else?"

"That, my dear, is the mystery. But knowing the Martins a little, I'd bet Josh Martin is into something under the table. He has more brains than his younger brother Eric, who actually tried to storm the bank in Chester and take it over, not rob it, take over and call it his. You gotta admit, that's a little nuts. Since he didn't hurt anyone, he only sat in prison for a year. Got out about a year ago and lives on the farm with the others."

"Others?"

"Yup. They have a whole crew of crazies hanging out there, practicing their marksmanship, I suppose. There are at least three houses at the main farmstead plus all the outbuildings. Plenty of room to put up their friends and, if I'm guessing right, partners in crime."

Then I felt it. The telltale tingle. Across my upper back. Up my neck into my hairline. Down my spinal cord and, my favorite, the tops of my thighs. Secrets. My gaze focused on the curling smoke lazing its way above Mavis's ashtray, next to an open *People* magazine.

"Jill? Come back. Whoa, where'd you go just now?" Billy looked nervous and intrigued.

"Ya know, Billy-boy, I think I should take a drive up there. Look around, check out some of my holdings." Now I was gazing at the pressed tin ceiling, smudgy gray from decades of tobacco smoke.

"Wait a minute, Miss Brenda Starr, you are not going to that farm alone. And there is no way I have time right now to ride shotgun for you. Take Sylvia. She's one of your attorneys, after all, and could give you lots of information about the situation."

"Ah ah, Mr. CEO of my company. As much as I like having attorneys at my beck and call, this wouldn't be an appropriate excursion for Sylvia. I'm thinking some maps, topo and otherwise, satellite photos, and binoculars would be better companions. Not to mention my voice recorder and a sturdy pair of hiking boots, neither of which I brought from Seattle. We're stopping at the mall before we leave town." I took a bite out of the pickled sausage, relishing the snap of the skin and the spicy oil coating my tongue.

"No…Sylvia, cute as she is, smart, too, would not approve of my activities, I think. Lawyers work with the facts as given, finding the inconsistencies, the subtle twists of language that can help or hinder. They don't snoop. They let others do that for them. I'll be that other. I want this Martin thing off my back as soon as possible. Who better to figure out what they're doing than me? I might find something to give us leverage to settle the matter."

Billy shook his head, tore off a strip of burnt cheese from his pizza, and slid it into his mouth. "Want another gin and tonic?"

"Why not? No lime this time. Oh, and a couple more of those pigs' feet."

Chapter Sixteen

It was going to take a few days to be ready to drive up to the Whitlash area. I had to get online and study satellite maps and photos. I wanted to get a look at the Martin place from above and see how many buildings were at the farmstead. I needed to examine topographical and agricultural maps that pinpointed neighboring farms and other nearby landmarks like reservoirs, coulees, and roads. I also wanted familiarity with the surrounding terrain and what it was like between the Martin farm and the Canadian border. I was sure the border had something to do with why the Martins were clinging to their property.

From what I could learn from Billy, the farm hadn't been worked in at least eight years, since the old man had an accident while supervising high school boys who were picking rock on some isolated acres close to the Sweet Grass Hills. The pile of rocks on the flatbed truck came loose and a few toppled on old man Martin's back, permanently debilitating him. He was in his late sixties when the accident occurred. Farm work is the most dangerous profession out there, and to get away with over sixty years of work without serious injury or dismemberment is a miracle. I guess the old man's number was up.

His boys, however, didn't pick up where their father left off. They sold the best of the equipment and all their chickens, but did little else. They let their land go fallow, allowing the wheat to spring up wild and knapweed to move in.

Local folks took up discussing the Martins, shaking their heads and commenting, "What a waste of good farmland." But here's the truth: God never meant for the Hi-Line to be farmed in the first place. Humans being what they are, they attempted to farm there anyway.

Around the turn of the twentieth century, poor immigrants from all over the world were hoodwinked into believing that a homestead in Montana was the road to riches. So they flocked to their vision of honeyed land. The dream of owning a vast 320 acres became a hellish nightmare when the homesteaders awoke to the reality of their predicament. Nobody informed them that the temperature varied by 140 degrees within a year. It could be over 100 degrees in a grasshopper-infested summer and below 40 degrees in a winter blizzard.

By the 1930s and 40s, bitter and dismayed, the homesteaders abandoned their sweat-soaked properties, escaping to the small towns first, then farther west to Washington or Oregon. They sold their treacherous land to other farmers who were luckier, more wily, or less delusional. While small towns continued to cling to tenuous survival, the farmhouses and barns were emptied, along with skeletal windmills. Everything was left to dry rot in the sun and gripping cold.

Hence my bafflement at the Martins' grasping to their rock-strewn, dead wheat fields was not unfounded. It didn't make sense to want to keep something useless when they could have my money, maybe buy a business in Great Falls or relocate to Spokane and work in a warehouse or factory. Collect a paycheck, enjoy medical benefits, and save for retirement. No, something was off about it.

CHAPTER SEVENTEEN

Before I drove up to Whitlash and looked around, I needed to see a few people. I was hoping to get information about what the Martins were doing there on that wasteland of a farm. I knew Annie had been there, but I didn't trust her insight for some reason. Because of the lady sheriff's inexplicable visit with my father several months earlier, I figured she probably had some information. It was time to visit law and order.

"Sheriff Terabian is on the phone right now. So could you wait? Just go ahead and sit over there and... Hey, ain't you Jill O'Hara?"

"I am." I knew the face but the name had long ago been dumped into the delete file. "But you have to remind me of your name. It's been ages..." A polite but wounded frown looked back at me.

"Roberta Tate! Remember me now?"

Of course, I did finally, but, as usual, not before I had hurt her feelings.

"Damn, Roberta, wow, you look great." She looked like she'd been in a knock-down, drag-out with Father Time. "How's your family?" A surefire question for pulling out information to help me remember more about her.

"Well, you remember I married Jake Thomas, so we have three—"

A door to the right swung open, interrupting Roberta and revealing Taft County Sheriff Terabian. Thankfully, she had stopped the Roberta show.

Terabian didn't say anything at first, just stood in the doorway like a justice system goddess and inspected me. Had we been in the city,

I would have assumed she was checking me out, but in Prairie View that was unthinkable. Her uniform was impeccably pressed, just like the other times I had seen her. Gorgeous women are the one and only species that render me speechless. I was embarrassed by the newness of my hiking boots.

"Oh, Ms. O'Hara, are you here to discuss your traffic ticket? You could do that at the courthouse where you pay the fine." She had her dark hair in a French braid. I'm a pushover for French braids, the sexiest hairdo on the planet.

"The fine? Oh! No, no, not the fine. I'm here to talk about some property questions." I knew better than to discuss anything around Roberta. No doubt she went home at night and discussed her work in detail with whomever was drinking Bud Light with her.

"Well, come in, then. Roberta, I'll be unavailable for the next fifteen minutes." She stepped to the side, allowing me to enter her large, comfortless, office. There were two stiff gray government-issue chairs with forest green plastic seats facing her metal desk, so I took one of them. I noted her black leather office chair was the only cushy thing in the room. To the left was a bookshelf holding dozens of spiral notebooks, procedure manuals, and Montana law books. There was one framed picture of a German shepherd, the only personal thing in the room. She did, however, have a great view of the wind-swept prairie from her window.

When working with law enforcement officials, it was usually my tactic to start the conversation, thereby controlling it. Sheriff Terabian, with her precisely tweezed eyebrows and pressed pleats, was well acquainted with the rules of my game.

"Okay, Ms. O'Hara, tell me what sort of land issues you want to address. Your father has lots of property, which piece are you concerned about?" She eased herself into the good chair and leaned back, resting her elbows on the chair's arms.

"It's the Martin farm, Sheriff. I understand you visited my father last fall regarding the farm—"

She shook her head. "I don't recall speaking to your father last fall about the Martin farm. And I'm sure you understand that a large portion of my work must, for both legal and ethical reasons, remain confidential." Her eyes were impassive, indifferently interested.

"Okay then, what about when my father and Billy Stover visited you about a month ago and asked your help with getting the Martin boys off our…my…property. You refused to help because your jurisdictional area does not cover the farm buildings. I understand your, let's call it 'hesitation' at not wanting to inflame what could be a violent situation, but you didn't even offer to speak to the Liberty County Sheriff. It seems to me that it's your obligation to—"

"Excuse me, Ms. O'Hara, I doubt you understand exactly what my obligations are." Her eyes and mouth were steely.

"Maybe you've confused your obligations to the citizens of Taft County and to your boyfriend Josh Martin—"

"You've crossed a line now. I'm not a subject for one of your investigations." Her voice was getting edgy with a waver of anger underlying it. "At this point, we cannot do anything about removing the Martins from the property until you've directed your attorney to start legal proceedings. Those proceedings will have to be initiated in Liberty County, not my county. The law is a process, Ms. O'Hara, and I strongly suggest that you show it some respect and patience."

Her nostrils actually flared a little. God, I love that on a woman. But I wasn't there to ogle Josh Martin's girlfriend.

"Okay. It's clear that your office doesn't want to get involved… for whatever reason. So, yeah, I'll get my attorney involved, but there's more to this Martin deal than you want to tell me. I'm really good at finding out things, Sheriff, and sometimes what I learn gets particularly sticky for the authorities." I stood, pushing the demeaning chair away with the backs of my legs. She stood, too, and pressed one set of long fingers into the desktop.

"Ms. O'Hara, I have one more suggestion. Take your 'skills' elsewhere. To a third-world banana republic or a corporate board riddled with inside trading. Don't insinuate yourself in my jurisdiction…ever. Or you will find yourself in trouble beyond your wildest dreams."

"Is that a promise? A warning? A threat? I am by nature a curious woman, Sheriff. I have every legal right to protect my property. Montana law is damn serious about property owner rights, and I intend to exercise my rights. Thanks for your time, Sheriff. Have a lovely afternoon."

She was still pressing one hand into the desk when I walked out. She looked like carved and polished granite.

CHAPTER EIGHTEEN

H ey, Fitch, it's Jill."
"Ah, Miss Snoop and Tell, I've been missing you. So sorry about your dad, babe."

"Thanks, and I appreciated those flowers at the funeral. I felt your support all the way over here."

"No problem. You know I love you, but I have a feeling you called for something else. You have that 'I got a job for ya' tone."

Fitch and I had been friends so long we didn't waste too much time on small talk. She was also my extraordinary research geek. Frances Ingrid Czech, name shortened over the years to Fitch, could find more information in one day than the entire FBI in one week. And she did it all from her bizarre office in the bowels of her huge house on Mercer Island east of Seattle.

In the 1980s, she was one of the primary computer techs to help launch what is now a multinational software corporation. She got filthy rich filthy fast. By the mid 1990s, she was bored and unchallenged in her profession, feeling she couldn't possibly stuff another dollar into her myriad accounts. So she dropped out and went underground. That's when we met, in a bar, eying each other for the night's meat entrée.

She was in leathers, her hair black and spiked like it remained today...the black now occasionally revived from a bottle. Sex between Fitch and me couldn't really even be called sex. It was terrible. While I'm not opposed to a little kink in sex, Fitch wanted to take it to a place I've never been and don't aspire to be: her well-equipped, soundproof dungeon across the hall from her basement office. I declined her bind and gag offer; she pouted for a few minutes, then brought out a bottle of 1972 Gattinara. We bonded over wine and never broached sex again. It was the beginning of a lovely relationship.

Fitch and I spent the entire night discussing my career and her discarded one. It was then our collaboration started. During that time, I had become aware of the burgeoning Internet and all its possibilities for research. I didn't have the patience to sit and sift through the information attainable online, but Fitch was born to it.

Together Fitch and I hatched her new career as a researcher. Not just any researcher, but a researcher who had the knowledge and people connections to stretch her fingers deep into cyberspace. She didn't want money; she wanted information. Not only for power but for the sheer lust for knowledge. I paid her a fee, but she donated it to some cause or another. I'm pretty sure she had other clients who bought her "information services." And I'm also pretty sure she was the money behind several fetish Web sites I'd come across during my own Internet ramblings. They had particular Fitch fingerprints in their construction. I never asked about them and she never told. A perfect relationship.

"So who or what are we looking for today, O'Hara? A philandering politician or a corporation using unsuspecting human guinea pigs?"

"Nothing so dramatic or interesting, unfortunately. It's a cop, the Taft County Sheriff, to be exact. Her name is Rae Terabian. There's more to her story and I want to know what it is."

Fitch snorted. "In northern Montana? How interesting could she be? She was born out of wedlock and her daddy was really the married-with-six-kids preacher down the road? She's a closet Democrat? No, no, I know what it is; she's a vegetarian and worried she won't get re-elected when folks find out."

"Quit being an asshole and help me out, would you? Look, she doesn't fit, not on the Hi-Line, anyway. And any information about her is for personal curiosity, not journalism."

"You mean she's a babe."

"And she's a babe who knows something about my father and my land. Something's off and I want you to find anything you can about her. It may help me know how to play my hand."

"You mean the one sliding into her pants?"

"Would you stop? Damn, you have a dirty mind."

"Why, thank you. And my 'dirty mind' is wandering to my little room across the hall."

"You have a date? Why didn't you say something? How long has she been waiting?"

"In her current position? Let's see. About ninety minutes. Not long enough. Give me all the information on your sheriff so that I can return to my little project across the hall. She'll start screaming soon. I don't want to miss that part."

"Please, don't tell me anything more. Your activities give me nightmares."

"You know flattery will get you everywhere."

I used to feel sorry for Fitch's submissives until several years ago when I decided to interview a few of them. It changed my worldview when I learned they adored her, craved and begged for her rough treatment. Sex and personal proclivities are a mystery, and I'm not one to question them.

I gave Fitch all the pathetically little information I had on the sheriff and told her to only spend a few hours on it. After all, she was just the Taft County Sheriff. What could Fitch find?

CHAPTER NINETEEN

S o, tell me about your store." I glanced up from my dinner salad of iceberg lettuce, carrot shavings, and French dressing. Annie and I were at the Corral, a steakhouse about ten miles east of Prairie View on Highway 2. The only other building near the restaurant was the looming silver grain elevator across the highway.

"My store? What's there to say? T-shirts, trinkets, tourist stuff for Highway 2 travelers, and gifts for locals."

"So how did you get into it?"

"Well, I got into it because I hate working for anyone. Wayne and I got a loan from the bank and one from his dad. We fill a local need and stay afloat."

"That's it? No future goals?"

"To be honest, it's just a means for me to buy my next firearm." She noticed my surprise and smiled proudly. "What can I say? I'm officially a gun freak. I'm an excellent shot, Jill, and it makes me feel good about myself. Josh wants to train me for competitions."

"Josh Martin?" I didn't try to keep the derision out of my voice.

"I know you're having legal troubles with the Martins. Garsh almighty, I don't pretend to know all the details, but Josh has lots more going for him than most people give him credit for."

"Well, he sure as hell can't farm for shit. So why does he want to give me so much grief about land he doesn't care for? I looked at the money Daddy paid for that land, and it's twice the assessed value. I have no idea why Daddy paid so much for a piece of nowhere, but I'd think the Martin boys would want to walk quickly away and be done with it."

"Some things are beyond purchase. That's what Josh believes. That's what I believe, too. And people like your dad and others around here always think they can buy their way through life." I'm sure she included me in that stinging comment. But she let up and said, "I'm sorry, that was unnecessary. Let's not discuss that Martin thing right now, because I know you'll do the right thing by them. Besides, it's a rare evening I get out without Wayne breathing down my neck. And I never get an evening with you. I want to enjoy this." She reached across the table, grabbed my wrist, looked into my eyes, and said, "Just for tonight. Is that okay with you?"

Even with Annie's hand on my wrist, her eyes locked on mine, I noticed someone entering the restaurant. With care, I broke my gaze into Annie's eyes to see the sheriff enter the dining room. Two uniformed, armed deputies were behind her. She took a pitiless glance at Annie's hand on my wrist and claimed the table farthest from us, deputies trailing. As soon as they were seated, one of their radios squawked. After conferring together, the two deputies left the restaurant. The sheriff ordered her food, never acknowledging our presence.

I noticed Annie's hand was nowhere near me anymore. In fact, she looked a little queasy and embarrassed.

"Annie, don't worry about her. We weren't doing anything but having a friendly moment."

"Oh, she just makes me so uncomfortable. Something about her makes me feel like I'm under a microscope or something."

"Well, not to start another tiff, but I think that any law officer who is Josh Martin's girlfriend is—"

"She's not Josh's girlfriend. Probably wishes she is, but believe you me, she's not." Annie's vehemence was a little out of proportion. I decided to push a little.

"What do you mean 'not Josh's girlfriend'? I thought everybody… never mind."

Annie was white knuckling the edge of the table. Interesting, but time to change course.

"So, tell me some more about your store. I want to know all about it. How you chose it and why. Does it make you happy?" I knew I was on the right track when her face became relaxed.

Annie and I sat for another hour. She ate a steak sandwich, medium well. I swooned over a twelve-ounce slab of prime rib, medium rare.

We drank the "best" wine the restaurant had, some two-year-old Washington Cabernet. It was the closest I'd felt toward her since high school but different in a way that confused me.

The sheriff sat alone, nursing a club sandwich and drinking lots of black coffee. She covered several pages of a legal pad with her scribbling then switched to reading the *Great Falls Tribune*. Occasionally, she'd greet other customers with a brief hello. When we got up to leave, Annie stopped at another table to speak to some friends. I ambled over to the sheriff's table.

"Working overtime, Sheriff?"

"Aren't we all?" She glanced at Annie, tilted her head back, and looked into my eyes. From any angle, she was breathtaking. She tapped her fingers on the newspaper and scanned my face, like I was interesting or something. Then, for the first time, I saw her smile. It was restrained but still luminous. Perfection. My traitorous hand reached to pull out an empty chair so I could sit and gaze at her. Her smile wavered. I came to my senses and forgot the chair.

Stepping back from the table, I grinned, embarrassed. "Have a good evening. Um, see you around." I never say "um." My grandma wouldn't allow it in the house.

"Good night, Ms. O'Hara." She turned back to her newspaper and didn't look up again. On the way out, I picked up her dinner tab.

❖

When Annie and I pulled in front of her and Wayne's modest home, she turned to me, put the tips of her fingers on my knee, and asked, "Would you come in and spend some more time with me?" Thwarting every fantasy and daydream I ever had about Annie, I hesitated. My palms bled sweat all over the steering wheel when I thought of the possibilities. Mainly because a huge, bewildered part of me wanted to stay in that car. There was the long-imagined sexual tension in the air, but it felt warped somehow, not like the texture of my dreams.

Annie looked concerned. "Are you okay, sweetie? Come in and get a drink of water. I think you've had too much wine. I know I sure as heck have." She was nervous and laughing at the same time. I nodded and popped my door open before I chickened out. I even tripped on the curb as I stepped onto the sidewalk. Annie grabbed my arm, then put her arm around me and kissed my temple. "C'mon, you've been under too much strain. Let's relax for a bit before you head home. Wayne will be at the hospital all night and I hate being alone."

I glanced back at the Murano, my method of escape, and remembered when I was eight years old, I begged my grandma for a Tonka truck that was advertised on television. I pleaded for months, obsessed with getting that yellow toy truck. When I finally unwrapped it on my birthday, I was disappointed, angry even that the truck didn't make me feel like I'd expected. I never played with it. Instead of chastising me, Grandma told me that it's common for the desire to be more precious than the desired. And that's what happened to me when Annie unlocked her front door and gestured my entrance into her home. It was what I'd always wanted, and I didn't want to be there.

She turned on a small ginger jar lamp near the sofa, and I looked around the plain living room dominated by a bulky shuttered entertainment center. For more than twenty years, I had had thousands of fantasies of being in a dim room, alone with Annie. Now she gently pulled off my jacket from behind me. Her fingers trailed from my jaw to my collarbone. I wanted to bolt for the door, and I wanted to rip her clothes off.

"Would you like a beer or a Diet Pepsi or iced tea?"

I barely heard her questions because I was laboring to decide whether to run or to just go for it with her, get her out of my system, finally. When I looked at her, I didn't see desire, more like apprehension tinctured with excitement and maybe power. It didn't fit the situation and I was even more confused. I concluded that running away was not a good idea, not until I was completely sure of what Annie wanted and what we still meant to each other.

"I'd just like a glass of ice water if that's okay." I sat on the comfortably worn, plaid couch and stared at the reading material on the coffee table. Annie went to the kitchen while I pushed away the latest issue of *Guns & Ammo*. Underneath was a pile of newsletters. I caught a glimpse of a heading saying something about the IRS's fraud against America and another heading: "The USA aka the Corporations' Prostitute." Curious, I leaned closer to the cheaply produced newsletter so I could read it in the murky light. Annie set a round bar tray right on top of it before I could read any further.

She eased next to me, her shoulder a few inches from mine. Her hair in the muted light glistened burnished highlights. It was hair for touching. I resisted touching it because she started speaking. "I'm so sorry that you've had to handle so much lately. Your dad was an amazing man and did so much good in our community. You've always meant so much to me and I hate to see you so stressed." She shifted her body to face me. "You know, I don't think Prairie View is a good fit for you anymore."

I resisted my urge to look away from her. "I know. The way I live my life, well, there's really nó room for me here. Not that people treat me poorly or give me a hard time for being gay. That part of me people ignore, at least to my face and as long as I don't try to date anyone's sister. No, I just need more. More…stimulation, more resources. I don't really know how to say it without sounding like a total city asshole."

"You're not a city asshole. I know Prairie View doesn't offer enough to keep someone like you fulfilled. You're so much more than this town." She reached with her left hand and started playing with the hair at the side of my face and leaned against my shoulder. Her breast molded against my left arm. My heart was beating so stridently that I could hear my blood swooshing in my ears. I wanted to feel exhilarated, turned on. Instead, I was terrified.

She gave my cheekbone a brushing kiss and said, "I miss you in my life, Jill. I miss what we had. I wish things had come out different, but at least we're here now. I understand you want to be happy." Her blue eyes were only inches away, seeming concerned and confident. Was she so sure I wanted her? Because, for the first time, I wasn't sure. She must have noticed my vacillation, but it didn't stop her from wetting my cheek with more kisses, going from chaste to come-on. She was grazing her lips across my ear.

I was like a virgin on her first date. "Maybe this isn't a good idea right now. There's so much to sort through, years of different lives…" And then she tilted her head and licked my lips, just like she used to. I was panting for two reasons—involuntary desire and panic. "You're married…and…"

Her hand left my hair, slid down my neck and across my collarbone, and covered my right breast, rolling the unmistakable rhythm of sex. Her open lips covered mine, sucking on them. Her tongue found its way into my mouth. She moved up and straddled my lap, a position that's always my undoing. I could feel her hair fall against my temples as she gave me a blazing kiss, not from a teenager, but from a mature woman, a woman who knows how to be in charge this way. I realized my hands had not gone around her yet; they lay at my sides, fisted. I told myself that this was my chance. My chance to finally have Annie in every way. Every way? Wayne's face came to mind. I glanced sideways to spy graduation portraits of two blond men, her sons.

"Jill, please, this is our chance…let's…" Her right hand was rubbing my belly, which was twitching in reaction. "I can feel your want."

"I…I'm kinda nervous. It's been so long…you know?" I gasped those words. She pulled back a few inches and looked at me.

"You, the city girl, the famous world-traveling writer, scared? I think you just have too much on your plate, too much. Let it all go. Forget the Martins, your dad's business, and let go…now, with me. I'll take care of you tonight." She was now rocking against me and whispering in my ear, her lips brushing breathless. My hands grasped her softly thrusting hips and stilled her.

"We have to stop this, Annie. It feels too soon. Actually, it feels off base. You're married and I'm…not able to offer you anything."

"You can offer me tonight. Just one time—"

A slam rattled the back of the house. Annie hauled off me and strode to the kitchen while pulling her hair behind her ears. "Wayne, I'm so glad you're here. Guess who's visiting…" I couldn't hear anything else except their muffled voices in the kitchen and then Wayne came in, smiling.

"Hey, Jill, good to see you. Keeping Annie company tonight? I'm glad. I hate leaving her alone at night. We got lucky, though. We overstaffed the shift, so I got to get out of there." I hoped he didn't notice my shock, my swollen mouth, or the shroud of miserable guilt enveloping me.

And that's how the next half hour went. The three of us having a meaningless conversation with me sitting in torment. Annie didn't break a sweat. That disturbed me.

It was the night of my liberation: the night when I realized I wasn't in love with Annie anymore. Oh, I loved her, on some level, but the compelling need that once ruled my life, defining all other relationships, had dissolved. In one dinner, one aborted make-out session, and one shallow conversation, I understood that Annie was not the Annie I had loved. The Annie I loved was a seventeen-year-old girl with no husband or kids. A nonexistent person.

"Fuck, fuck, fuck..." were the only words I could mutter as I drove the short distance up the hill to Daddy's house. I had the whole situation intellectually mastered.

CHAPTER TWENTY

The next morning, with an almost desperate need to get out of town, I loaded my fancy SUV with all the "observation" equipment I'd need to visit the Whitlash area where the Martin, check that, *my* farm was located. I wanted out of Prairie View and all its memories. I figured a drive in the country, whatever information it produced, would be a balm for my agitation. I also called Sylvia McCutcheon, my lawyer in Great Falls, to get an update on the status of the legal process surrounding the Martin mess.

Sylvia assured me things were moving, glacially, but they were moving, with a court date scheduled for eight weeks hence.

"I don't want to be here for another eight weeks. I was hoping to get back to Seattle in two, maybe three weeks, at the most." I think I heard either an exasperated sigh or a choked chuckle on the other end.

"Ms. O'Hara, I know—"

"Call me Jill, Sylvia."

"Okay, Jill, I know you have a timeline, but the judicial system has its own timeline. And that's something even God can't push. What I can do, however, is make an assessment and determine how much of your participation is necessary. In the meantime, my roommate and I would like to invite you for dinner."

And there it was, the clue to handsome and distinguished Sylvia's availability. And I was slightly disappointed. "Roommate" is intimation for "lover or partner," terms which were avoided by in-the-closet dykes. Closeted lesbians made good friends, to a point, but have snubbed me in public places. I was too "open" according to them, a threat to their equanimity.

"Your roommate? Do you mean your girlfriend?"

"No, he's my housemate and a fabulous cook. I don't have a live-in girlfriend at the moment, but we're working on it. My lover is an attorney for the Air Force, stationed here at the base. She's in Korea right now and won't be back for another month. You can meet her then, well, after we've had a few days of 'debriefing.'" That cleared things up for me. Sylvia was not homophobic, unlike many rural professional dykes. She had earned my trust.

"Sounds great, Counselor. We'll arrange dinner. Now, what do you know about the goings-on at the Martin place? I get the feeling there's more there than we know about." I waited several seconds for her reply, which finally came, circumspectly worded.

"Jill, as your legal advisor, I'm encouraging you to eschew any intentions of investigating that farm. If there are activities on the farm that are questionable, the less you know about it, the better. You are the legal owner and liable, but deniability can help you in a court of law. We must remove the Martins from the property with the full force of the law supporting us. It's possible it could be dangerous, otherwise. Have you discussed anything with the sheriff?"

"Well, um, I did have a visit with her, but it didn't go very well." I felt like a kid caught picking the neighbors' flowers without permission. "She's holding back information about the Martins. I can't trust her, can I? Talk about conflict of interests, her diddling around with Josh Martin."

"Sheriff Terabian is a law officer to her core. Whatever her… relationship is with the Martins, I doubt it will cloud her judgment. In fact, I don't think the rumors are true. I just hope you haven't alienated her, because she can be useful."

"It sounds like you know more. Care to let me in?"

"Like I said, deniability is your shield, and let's leave it at that."

I ended our conversation with a hearty promise to drive down to Great Falls for supper in a few weeks and a leaden promise to stay out of the Martin mess. My leaden promises are meaningless. My instincts screamed, "Story!" and I was loath to let any part of the Martin situation get away from me. If I was going to be stuck on the Hi-Line for a few weeks, I might as well be doing something amusing.

CHAPTER TWENTY-ONE

It was a brilliant day for a drive on the Hi-Line. Late spring is the season that tricks even the old-timers into believing this to be a benevolent land. The tender, precious green of new growth displayed itself in uniform rows of the wheat fields. The smokier green of new sage flourished in the areas where no crops were planted. Ephemeral wildflowers including delicate bachelor's buttons, miniature daisies with vulnerable middles, a random Indian paintbrush spattered innocent colors here and there. The meadowlarks' burbling call provided a jingling soundtrack, and the smell of ancient sage, dust, and sunlight accompanied the wind brushing its hand across the prairie.

Driving east on Highway 2, I made a left onto Highway 409 and headed north into one of the most remote areas in the lower forty-eight states. Highway 409 was a rollicking strip of tarmac, this day already melting under the torching sun. It led to a forgotten, little-used border crossing into Canada. Eight miles before I got there, though, I encountered Whitlash, a former boomtown now reduced to a despairing one-room schoolhouse, general store, and rambling hotel turned private home. A deserted grange loomed at the edge of town, a few flecks of its final paint job hanging on for their last bit of glory.

I couldn't see people moving around the little town, but I wanted to avoid talking to anyone. I didn't want the Martins to have any idea I was in their neighborhood. One person recognizing me could alert them, even though their farm—my farm—was another seven or so miles to the northwest.

Out of Whitlash, I drove west on Gold Butte Road, looking for Strawberry Road, which would take me north and, finally, near the

Martin place. As I made the turn to the graveled Strawberry Road, a storming plume of dust barreled head-on toward me. As it neared, I realized it was a motorcycle going far too fast for safety on farm roads. When it reached me, it slowed, and I discerned a monstrous black BMW and rider, chalky from dust. The ebony rider was helmeted, leather clad, and ominous in his anonymity. The opaque mask turned to me for one brief look, then he sped to his right going west toward Gold Butte. Right then I realized how alone I was and that I had forgotten to call Billy to tell him where I was going.

I pulled my cell phone out of the cup holder and flipped it on. The little searchlight on its screen circled several times then morphed onto the words "No Service."

"Shit," I whispered and considered going back and giving Billy a call from Whitlash. Efficiency prevailed over common sense as I reasoned I was just looking around and not trying to go onto the property. I was searching for a hill that overlooked the farm buildings, so I could get some idea how many people were there and to what purpose. I had purchased some high-powered binoculars in Great Falls, only to find my father had even better military binocs that would give me greater clarity at a distance.

From aerial photos of the farm, I perceived what looked like three houses, several smaller outbuildings, a large barn, two aluminum grain silos, a van, at least three pickups, and a two three-quarter-ton farm trucks. But what really captured my attention were the hanger-sized metal building that looked almost new and, most curious, the eighteen-wheel semi-truck. This was clearly a farm that had something happening, not the lifelessness one expected of a non-producing farm.

I knew I was close to the Martin place by the proximity of the most eastern Sweetgrass Hill. After setting my odometer to zero so that I could use my maps to locate myself somewhat precisely, I continued north on Strawberry Road, noticing lots of unmapped farm access roads snaking to my right and left. They were never more than ruts, really, but I knew they were occasionally used and could be treacherous if taken in anything less than an SUV. Another illusion about the terrain was that it looked flat, both to the eye and to the map; it was anything but flat. Ditches, gullies, coulees, dry creek beds were among the sometimes hair-raising obstacles that farm roads navigated. It was these roads that took you to the ubiquitous abandoned farms with their tottering windmills, monuments to despair.

Within five minutes, my imperfect navigation system suggested I was nearing the Martin farm. It should have been due northwest of my location, so I turned left onto a couple ruts and started to bounce across the land. I was hoping to get between two low hills to be out of sight, stop the Murano, and climb to a possible vantage point.

To avoid getting spotted by a farmer, I slowed to creeping speed, minimizing dust kick-up. My now powder-dusted SUV rocked and creaked over small boulders. At one point, one rut was six inches higher than its sister, and my vehicle swayed so far to the left side, I found myself leaning far to the right in an unconscious effort to keep the vehicle on four wheels. Several jagged rocks rose up to challenge me and I eased around each one without blowing a tire, my biggest worry, second only to the getting caught worry. At one point, I had to inch down the trail along the edge of a gully. The trail was slightly washed out and crumbly. This time the Murano leaned to the right and easily could have toppled had I not paid close attention and found the sturdiest sections of the ruts. My neck and back were sopping wet from nervous sweat.

I finally reached the bottom of the gully and stopped the SUV. I rolled down my window and turned off the engine. For a while I sat there, cooling off and calming down. I listened to the land and heard the crackle of grasshoppers and the breeze riffling the wild wheat and sage. The smell of pungent savory sage dominated everything. About two hundred yards to the west was a buckling old barn and part of a rotten corral. The house had been removed decades ago or maybe was never built. I paid a quick homage to the souls who started a new life here but ended up elsewhere, hopefully in a more fulfilling endeavor.

My topography map led me to believe that the gully wall looming to my right would take me to the top of a hill that would supply a good vantage position to study my quarry. I reached for my new backpack and checked the contents: maps, water, ball cap, binocs, some energy bars, sun screen, first aid supplies, and a snakebite kit.

A snakebite kit was a primitive affair, changing little in all the years people had thought to market them: a tiny razor knife for slicing the fang punctures, a worthless suction cup for sucking out the venom, some disinfectant swabs, and a few Band-Aids. The ineffective suction cup was just a reminder that you wanted the rattlesnake to bite you where you could get your mouth so that you could suck out the poison after you've sliced a cross into your wound with the razor knife. If the snake bit you in an unreachable spot, you hoped you had a friend with you who was willing to suck away at the blood and poison. If you were alone, you should stay calm, try not to pass out, and remember to pray.

I left the SUV sitting on two level ruts, adjusted the backpack, slapped on the ball cap, and started up a game trail that scored the hill in front of me. About a hundred feet from the car, I started to sweat again and looked forward to reaching the top so the wind could dry me off. My new hiking boots, stiff but comfortable, slid backward whenever I'd step on a loose pebble, but they gave my ankles welcome support and a little protection if I should incite a rattler to strike at me.

Hills being what they are, it took me longer than expected to reach its top. Every time I thought I was almost there, more of it appeared ahead, as if it grew while I climbed. The sun's scorch was mitigated by the buffeting breeze that I knew would steady itself once I reached the summit. Puffing but triumphant, I fumbled to the top of the hill but didn't stand up straight. Instead, I crouched and skittered to the other side of the summit. The view was jaw dropping. The Sweetgrass Hills, three sentinels of the vast desolation of northern Montana and southern Alberta, lay around me.

Perfect. I had an unimpeded one hundred and eighty degree view due north. Far to my left, West Butte loomed. Closer to me and a little south was the middle Sweetgrass Hill, Gold Butte. It was a prairie oddity; she was an extinct volcano rising out of the desolate land. East Butte to my right was baring her delicate springtime chest to the relentless wind. A climber to the top of any of these three sisters could see one hundred fifty miles north, east, and south. The view west was obstructed by the eastern face of the northern Rocky Mountains, sixty miles away.

I didn't need the one-hundred-fifty-mile vista, though. I just needed to see the land spread in front of me, the Martin farm, or to be technically correct, my farm. I was struck by the ludicrous situation, me spying on my property.

I stayed crouched and made my way to a flat rock that was covered by an ancient collection of brick red lichen. It made gravelly sounds as I skootched my denim-covered butt onto it.

The area I surveyed was sheathed in spring greens but there were several signs of human occupation. Nearest me, a quarter of a mile away, were what looked like several junked cars and a school bus; three hundred yards beyond them were piles of abandoned farm machinery. A few miles to the north and a little to my right, I could see the metal roof of a large building, and I assumed that was the monster I had seen in the satellite photos. That was the farm compound; most of it was hidden in the coulee in which it was built.

It took me a few minutes of fiddling with the military binoculars to get them adjusted for my vision. I chose the abandoned cars as the point to practice focusing. When I finally got them cued in, I jerked. "Jesus!" First, I was startled by the closeness of the objects. Then I was stricken by the objects themselves. The ground around the rusty vehicles was littered with dismembered human body parts.

Legs and arms were sticking out of the cars and the school bus windows. A torso spilled from the open rear door of a green Impala. A few bodiless heads were mingled into the ghoulish mess. Near one head with staring eyes, a severed hand rested near the ear. I panted and my stomach began to back up.

After taking my eyes away for a moment to calm my gag reflex, I raised the binocs for another look.

Something was unnatural about those scattered limbs and torsos. No blood. No bones. No decomposition. I cracked a nervous titter when I realized they were mannequin parts. Upon closer inspection, I could see nicks and pock holes in the dummy parts and hundreds of small dents in the vehicles. The Martins were using the vehicles and the mannequins for target practice.

When my heart settled down, I moved my binocs to look at the rusty farm machinery farther on. There were a few corroded trucks and tractors, a disintegrating swather and moldering combine. All of them were covered with bullet pocks, too.

"Looks like a fucking military training ground," I muttered. I swung my binocs to the right, scanning areas that looked empty. It took me a few minutes but I found them, two to be precise. They were dug into the sides of a gully, cement fascias were painted in pale greens and grays for camouflage. Each had three one-foot square holes, one each to the right and left and one in the middle. I couldn't make out the entrances but assumed they were somewhere in the dirt that covered the roofs. I had seen too many of these in my travels.

"Military bunkers. Holy shit." I was whispering because I now understood that I was in an extremely dangerous spot. Fully exposed, I was in range to become an enticing moving mannequin and a source of twisted fun for gun nuts. "Time to go, Jilly old girl."

Then I noticed a large farm truck, painted in the same camouflage as the bunkers, with high wooden bed sides, also camouflaged. It was moving west, across my view, between me and the large metal building at the farm. Then it turned to its right and disappeared, probably down the road that headed into the gully that cradled the farm. The Martins were clearly running a paramilitary training camp, but for what purpose? Forming an army to fight who? I remembered the extremist newsletters on Annie's coffee table.

Keeping my eyes on the spot where the truck disappeared, I packed my binocs, hoisted the pack onto my back, and crept away to the other side of the hill and out of sight, hopefully, of the farm. Even though I couldn't be seen from the shooting range anymore, I still felt exposed and my back twitched with the feeling of having been seen.

The sun was flashing off the roof of the Murano as I half slid, half trotted down the game trail. I was a vulnerable target and decided that going back to Strawberry Road the way I came could place me into the shooting gallery. I had no reason to believe that the Martins wouldn't shoot me as a trespasser, later pleading ignorance as to my identity. People in Montana really did shoot at trespassers, and the law often protected their right to do so.

I mulled over the evidence that the Martins were running a paramilitary camp on my property. Montana seemed to attract militaristic survivalist loonies because of its remoteness. But in recent years, the groups had taken a more sinister turn, espousing neo-Nazi hate rants, American isolationism, warped Christianity, white-man patriotism, and guns. Lots of guns. I'd read articles about the Montana Freemen who had their own private stand-off with the Feds. The Freemen even created their own "township" so they could develop their own laws. The Martins were reading the Freemen's playbook.

I threw my backpack into the front passenger seat, clicked on the car battery, and rolled down the windows. My hands trembled when I rested them on the steering wheel. I studied the tumbling old barn and corral in front of me and noticed that if I followed the trail, I could head the car out of the coulee and toward the south. What was to the left, beyond my line of sight, was anybody's guess. Then I remembered the topography map, retrieved it from my backpack, and attempted to locate my position, all the while listening for any approaching vehicle or footsteps. I was doused in yet another bath of sweat, but this one was drawn by fear.

The map divulged that I was approximately on the boundary of the Martin place. All I had to do was get one hundred feet south and I'd be on someone else's land, hopefully someone not prone to shooting at trespassing Muranos. I started the SUV and picked my way along the lopsided and broken trail ruts. Stiff, unbending fingers of rigid sage scraped the sides of my vehicle reminding me of nails on a chalkboard. I was certain car paint was being left on the ends of those bushes. I sent a silent apology to the rental company.

As I neared the decomposing barn, the trail curved left and around the southern arm of the coulee. The trail headed south, slightly curving left as it cut across the prairie. I followed it without pressing the gas any farther. Moving too fast on these types of trails could cause anything from broken axles to high centering the chassis, both mishaps I'd experienced in my less careful past. I passed another pile of abandoned farm equipment, but none of it was full of bullet dents. I took that as a good sign. The trail started to move uphill and was curving back to Strawberry Road. At one point, I reached the corner of someone's fenced property and the trail became better maintained.

Several minutes later, I saw Strawberry Road a half mile in front of me. I sped up, relieved to be near a more public location. A hundred feet before reaching the road, a jagged rock reared up from the packed trail dirt. My left front tire hit it dead on. "Damn!"

I hauled onto Strawberry Road and pulled my car over to check for damage. My fear distorted to rage when I squatted to look at the damage and heard the telltale pizz of air escaping the tire. "Motherfuck," I said about twenty times while kicking gravel across the road.

After allowing my rant to fizzle out, I talked myself into calming enough to get some help. Since my cellular plan didn't stretch to

Nowhere Montana, I looked around for a farm I could hike to. Nothing. "Okay, then I'll just have to change it myself," I said to a chittering gopher.

I made a mental review of all the steps for changing a tire. Changing a tire was one of the skills I was most proud of and had used many times in different foreign backwaters. I had a butchy girlfriend in college, Gloria, who took it upon herself to improve my self-reliance. She was a vicious bitch, but I came out of that six-month affair able to change a tire and motor oil, install faucets, hammer a nail and not bend it, saw a board with a power saw, and use a shovel without looking foolish. I saw my relationship with Gloria as a kind of lesbian Outward Bound.

I pulled up the floor of the cargo area in the Murano and tugged out the spare tire, the jack, and tire iron. Next I found a couple rocks to block the rear tires, secured the jack under the dust-encrusted car frame without lifting the car, popped off the lacey hub cap, and muttered Gloria's all-purpose mantra "lefty loosey, righty tighty" to help me remember which way to throw my weight on reluctant lug nuts.

I positioned the tire tool on the first nut and gave it quick push downward. Nothing, except a wincing jerk to my shoulder. "Okay, I'll just have to use force, then," I threatened the nut. I stood, focused, brought my foot up, and smashed my boot heel down on the iron. "Goddamn it!" Blinding pain. My heel and my knee vibrated from the shock of impact. The nut hadn't moved.

A deep-toned rumbling distracted me from my pain and the immovable nut. I peered north and saw the massive black motorcycle and rider approaching at barely controlled speed, road dust rolling behind him. He was coming too fast to prevent the dust from filling my eyes, nose, and mouth. I pulled the collar of my T-shirt up over my mouth and nose, turned away from the bike, squeezed my eyes tight, and prayed for him to pass and not stop. I needed help, but not from this guy. I waited for the dust to settle.

Since my luck already sucked that day, it didn't surprise me to see him slow down as he disappeared over a small rise in the road. My blood banged my eardrums as he approached me at a sane speed. He stopped his bike about fifty feet behind my SUV and sat there, waiting for the dust to dissipate. I still held my T-shirt over my mouth, breathing heavily, trying to decide how to handle him. I figured my best ploy would be the helpless, innocent girlie strategy and silent fervent prayer. However, I dropped my hold on my T-shirt, reached down, and plucked the tire iron off the nut and gripped it.

He didn't move or speak for an entire minute, just sat there and watched me through that opaque helmet visor. He was so dusty that it looked like he'd been riding in a snow blizzard. The burble of a nearby meadowlark pulled me out of the stare-fest and set my mouth into motion.

"Hi? Uh...I uh, seem to be having a problem with my tire here. I sorta know how to do it myself, but the darn lug nut..."

He stood, straddled the gigantic bike for a moment then swung his right leg over and got off. The dust rolled off his black leather chaps in rivulets, appearing liquid. It streamed off his leather jacket, and I realized he was a lot taller than me. I also saw he was skinny, so I knew a solid smack from the tire iron could break his wrist, even with his fingerless biking gloves for protection. His approach was careful, barely making a crunch in the gravel with his cumbersome steel-toe boots.

He stopped about six feet from me, just out of reach of a possible swinging tire iron, and regarded me. I couldn't take my eyes off his visor, but I used my peripheral vision to watch his body movements. His right hand crawled up across his body. I grasped the tire iron inching my right shoulder back, readying for a sturdy swing. His hand pushed something on the side of his helmet and a chin strap dropped down. His other hand moved up, and both his hands cupped the helmet on each side. He inched off the black helmet. A dust-crusted ponytail flopped over his shoulder. When I saw his face, I dropped the tire iron.

"Jesus H. Christ, Sheriff! You could've identified yourself."

"And spoil that little bit of fun?" She had the guts to grin down at me.

"Why are you here, anyway? Aren't you a little out of your jurisdiction? I thought you didn't meddle in Liberty County cases."

"I don't. I'm riding my bike. A hobby."

"Well, out here, on gravel roads, in the middle of nowhere, is a pretty dangerous place for that hobby." Then I remembered her connection to Josh Martin and felt uneasy again. "Oh yeah, you're out here visiting your boyfriend. I forgot."

She scanned my face, dropped the grin, but didn't show any of the anger I had witnessed in her office. "Speaking of being in a dangerous place, need someone to change your tire for you?"

"I know how to do it. I just can't get the lug nuts loose."

She exhaled a patronizing huff and picked up the tire iron, handing me her helmet. Her leathers squeaked when she squatted and looked at the nuts. I stepped back a few paces in case she decided to use the tire iron on me instead of the lug nuts.

She fit the iron back onto the lug nut. "If I can't budge these, I'll call in for help."

She stood, brought her right boot up, and slammed it on the tire iron. The nut let out a grinding scream and moved. She threw a short smile at me and continued to the next lug nut and finally worked her way through all of them, getting them loose enough for removal.

"I guess I coulda done that if I'd tried harder." My independent lesbian credentials were plummeting into disrepute.

"I guess you could have, but why bother, huh?" I'd never seen a smile that could so change an unyielding face into a captivating one, but this gal had it, for a few seconds anyway. Her face became serious. Then she stepped toward me, stopped a foot away, looked down, and inspected my face. She smelled of leather, gasoline, and peppermint. "Do you always believe every rumor that comes out of that little town?"

"Which rumor do you mean, Sheriff?"

"Oh, and be careful which hills you choose for spying. The watcher becomes the watched."

Without another word, she ran her index finger down my dusty nose, turned, and sauntered on those endless legs back to her bike. That's when I grew my own smile. "Holymarymotherofgod," I gasped under my breath. The chaps. The legs. From behind. It's indecent to flash an image like that at someone like me. And she knew it. I saw smile lines on the sides of her eyes just before she replaced her helmet.

I couldn't remove my eyes from her rear until she climbed back on her BMW. She turned her beast-of-a-bike around and sped down the road toward the Martins. She was lost to me in a blur of road dust.

I remembered the tire. She didn't stay to help me finish changing the tire. "That bitch!" But I wasn't all that mad. And I didn't feel all that scared even though I knew she had been watching me spy on the Martins. I went back to work on my tire and proudly finished it on my own, without any bloody knuckles, and with only one ragged fingernail.

Later, when I was back on Highway 2, heading west toward Prairie View, I saw the black rider in my rearview mirror. It reminded me that I still had that vexing traffic ticket to settle. She buzzed alongside my SUV, rode there for a few seconds, lifted one finger off the handle and sped ahead, breaking the speed limit. "Some cop," I said to her back, evaporating into the glare of the setting sun. Yeah, some cop.

CHAPTER TWENTY-TWO

My escapade in the country left me agitated and hungry, but I wasn't in the mood for another thawed funeral dish. I parked on Main Street and went into the Stockmans Bar, figuring there would be plenty of bar food, a glass of beer, and maybe someone to visit with. It was early enough that I was the only customer except for one lone male body at the far end of the bar. After the blinding sun, it was too dark for me to figure out if I knew the other patron, so I sat at the opposite end. I wanted to avoid any pitiful drunk who decided I was pick-up material.

The bar stool felt like home, the padded edge of the bar pushing just underneath my breasts, my elbows leaning on the cool wood-grained Formica. Some venues just felt right, and sitting at a bar was like that to me. I cozied to the smell of old tobacco, sweat, and beer. I always wanted to rub the velvety thick paper coasters sloppily slid under my sweating drink. No band, jukebox only. None of my friends in Seattle understood this about me, but some of my finest conversations and laughs have occurred while sitting at a bar—not at the tables, but right there at the bar. I could appreciate the lure for folks who spent their days sitting there, nursing a few drinks and talking with whoever showed up. It really did help with loneliness. The only reason I didn't hang out at bars very often was because they were too comfortable, and I was likely to want to drink my life away.

"That you, Jill?" The other customer was speaking to me. "It's me, Mike Hassett. You blind or something?"

"I kinda am at the moment, Mike." I grabbed my beer and walked to a stool next to Mike's. "How's my old boyfriend gone bad?" I asked as I hugged him and kissed his whiskery cheek.

"'Bout the same. How's my old girlfriend gone gay?" He always enjoyed teasing me about that. He turned to the bartender. "Jeff, get this lady another of what she's drinking, wouldja?"

"Thanks, Mike. And, Jeff, give me two of those beer sausages, some mustard, and a bag of honey peanuts. I'm starving." I saw Mike starting to rally to offer going out for dinner but I waylaid him. "I have no desire for a restaurant. This is the only place I want to be right now, so let's have a visit."

To be honest, Mike was the perfect person for me to run into. He had his little U.S./Canadian border drug-running business and knew the Whitlash area better than anyone else I could think of. I was patient, though, and went through a relaxing hour of pleasantries and gossip before I homed in on the information I wanted.

"So what's going on with the Martin boys? You know my dad bought their land from the old man, but those boys don't want to give it up. It's pissin' me off because it's keeping me tied up here." I was staring into my beer glass trying to be less interested than I was.

"Ho boy, the Martins. I'm not sure what I know, or if what I know is true. It's weird, though, and I suggest you just walk away from it, Jill. They're trouble."

"How could they be trouble? It seems like they just hang out on that sad old farm out there and produce nothing. What's in it for them?"

Mike glanced to make sure the bartender was far away. "Well, you know how I make my living, right?" I nodded, hoping he'd see I accepted his path in life. "I know all the roads that cross the border between Interstate 15 and Highway 232, and some of them aren't on any map. Some lead to perfect stash or hiding places, others get you to main highways without being noticed."

"Yeah, I remember all the times we partied out on those roads."

Mike gave me a fond grin. "We did, didn't we? Anyhow, about six months ago, middle of the night, I had just made a pickup and was heading south through Whitlash. But a few miles before I hit the town, two pickups were parked sideways in the road, acting as a roadblock. Like cops or something. All I could see in front of me was twenty years in prison, then I realized it wasn't cops. It was the Martins, Josh and Eric, and about five other folks was all I could see 'cuz of the dark. All of them were holding big nasty-looking guns."

"Jesus, are they nuts?"

"They might be, but they're dangerous nuts. I was sure they wanted to steal my shipment, and that would've got me in huge trouble, too. I'm not sure what I'm more scared of: prison or the group that gets me my shipments."

Mike was looking pretty shaken, so I twirled my upright finger at the bartender to order another round.

"So did they take your dru…uh, shipment?"

"No, they made me give them all my cash, a grand plus, all I had left after paying my suppliers. Josh said something like they were the legal posse of that area and in charge of all the tolls."

"Posse? Tolls? Legal? What the hell, Mike?"

"What could I do? Call the cops? And besides, I heard that lady sheriff is mixed up with Josh, somehow. People saw her and him having a heated exchange at the Elks Club a few weeks ago and other times they've been seen off alone, talking." Mike downed half a glass of beer and went on. "So now I have to avoid that whole area. It's been limiting my crossing options, and my supply group on the other side of the border is on me about it. They think I'm slacking when it's just that I have to use more of my time being on the road. It's really fucked up."

"Yeah, it is." I had to digest what he said for a minute. "What did you mean about tolls and posse?"

"I'm not sure. But that's what they said, and with all that firepower behind them, I wasn't going to argue. In the meantime, I'm driving ten extra hours a week just to avoid them."

Mike didn't seem to want to go on with that part of our conversation, so I visited another thirty minutes, made sure Mike had a full beer in front of him, and went back to Daddy's house.

My body was aching like it does when I've spent a whole day embedded with the military. The dust, sun, heat, stress, fear, and too much beer encouraged me to run a bath in Dad's giant bathtub, built for his size. I spied some of his hair in the tub and pulled down the sprayer to wash it down before drawing the water. I cried a little, understanding that I was washing what little was left of him down a drain. Then the absurdity of the thought hit me, and I started laughing. I could feel Daddy laughing with me, even hear him somewhere in that spot in your memory that stores the voices of people who are gone.

While the tub was filling, I put on my bathrobe and went downstairs for a glass of milk. While I sipped, I flipped through the mail Connie had piled on the table in the hall. Bills (was I supposed to pay them?), advertisements, condolence cards, and a hand-addressed personal letter for me in a business envelope. I figured it was a condolence card, and whoever sent it had run out of the right-sized envelopes. There was no return address. I decided to read it first. I unfolded the letter, and a smaller piece of paper fluttered to the floor. When I picked it up and recognized it, I almost choked on my milk. It was a business check from somewhere called the Eagle Township for $650,000.00.

The letter had an official-looking seal at the top. It was round with stars inside the border. In the middle was a faintly printed American eagle. Superimposed on top of the eagle in bold print was "Eagle Township." In the left top corner was a small American flag, underneath the flag, in small print, "Our Only Allegiance." Bottom center was a picture of an open book with "Holy Bible" printed across it.

A chill tortured my spine as I read the letter.

Dear Miss O'Hara,

> *The free Township of Eagle has decided to forgo our rightful and lawful complaint regarding your family's theft of our land. We do this on good faith of accord and satisfaction that the refund of the counterfeit money, also known as the American dollar, with which you unlawfully confiscated our sovereign land, is now returned to you as paid in full.*

> *Any further action against the sovereign Township of Eagle will be considered an act of war and will be responded to accordingly.*

Sincerely,
Joshua J. Martin, Duly Elected Sheriff of Eagle Township

It took several readings to make sure I understood the bastardized legalese, but the point was made, especially in that last sentence. Milk forgotten, I stood in the hall as the evidence started to chink into place and memories of an old story nudged me. "Oh. My. God." Then I remembered the running bath water and charged upstairs.

The water was a few inches from the top, and I rushed to twist it off. After letting out several wasted gallons, I took off my robe and sank to the chin into the blessed hot water. I heard the phone ring several times but let the voicemail handle whoever was calling. I had some thinking to do and needed to plan my next moves carefully. There was a story here, a delicious one, and for once, I was living on the inside. I was an integral part of it. Whatever I did would affect the story. I wasn't on the outside, trying to expose and analyze all the angles to piece the truth together. I was in it, and I was thrilled. Then I remembered the cashier's check, $50,000 short of what Daddy paid for that woebegone property, but I wasn't going to quibble. Maybe there was a way I could keep the money, devise a marketable story, and get my ass back to Seattle.

CHAPTER TWENTY-THREE

The next day was Sunday and I realized Daddy had been dead almost two weeks. On top of that, I'd been made ridiculously wealthy and in charge of Daddy's ventures. In addition, as always, there was Annie. Only this time it was different. There was no bittersweet longing. Instead, there was the sort of bafflement one feels when playing blind man's bluff. Blindfolded, you're spun around and around, but you are clever and certain you know the lay of the room and where all the other players are. When someone rips off the blindfold, you are befuddled because nothing is where it should be. You look around, blinking, relearning your bearings. That scene in Annie's living room was my decades-old blindfold being torn off. I needed to realign myself with reality. Everything was there as I had left it, but now it was in the wrong spot. Or I was in the wrong spot.

And then there was the memory of the sheriff in those chaps.

After making coffee, I decided to check the voicemail I had ignored the night before. There were two messages.

"Jilly-bean, oh, I mean...boss! We have a company to run, and I need to discuss a few issues with you. Nothing earth-shaking but I want them out of the way by Monday. Can I see you tomorrow? Call me. Bye."

As much as I didn't want to face business matters with Billy, I did want to talk with him about that cashier's check. He needed to know I was going to take the money and back off the Martins. Not because of the "act of war" silliness, but because I wanted more of their goodwill so that I could develop my story unimpeded by legalities.

The next message was from Annie. I winced when I heard her hesitant voice.

"Hi, Jill. It's Annie. Um…I need to apologize for the other night. I had no idea Wayne was coming home. I hope you believe me about that. Could we…uh, talk sometime soon? I'll be gone all day tomorrow, Sunday. But we could talk on Monday, if that's convenient for you. Call me? Please?"

Compelled but simultaneously repelled, I called Annie's number to leave a message. I didn't want to talk to her, not yet. Instead of voicemail, however, Wayne picked up. I forced myself not to hang up since everybody has that damnable caller ID feature these days.

"Hey, Wayne, it's Jill. I know Annie isn't around but I wanted to leave her a message."

"Hey, Jill, you're right. She's not around. Doing her target practice, I guess. She's…well, she's not around on Sundays." Wayne sounded a little down, maybe hungover, and that gave me an excuse to keep it short.

"Okay, well, tell her I'll get a hold of her sometime tomorrow, would you?"

"Sure, no problem. Um, there's something else I need to tell you." Just hearing his voice made me feel so guilty. I felt like I needed to head to the church and the confessional, which I hadn't done in twenty-five years.

"What's that, Wayne?"

"I did a shift at the nursing home last night, substituting for a sick nurse's aide. You know old man Martin is a resident there, right?"

"I'd heard it mentioned. He's that senile?"

"Actually, I don't think he's all that senile. His mind seems fairly sound, but his body is shot to hell. Pretty typical for these old farmers. He sure as shootin' knew your dad passed away. Folks with dementia don't keep tabs on who's alive and who's dead. Anyhow, he asked me several times to call you and get you over there to talk to him. The other aides said he's been asking for you for a couple days now, but they figured he just wanted to cuss you out over the land deal. So they've ignored him."

I rubbed my eyes thinking that even the hospital staff knew about my business. The joys of small-town living.

"Well, what's your hit? Is he just out to tell me off?"

"I kinda don't think so. He whispered to me that he wants to tell you something about the farm and he looked sane as you or me. I thought I should give you the option to decide whether you want to see him or not." Wayne sounded as puzzled as I was.

"Wow, thanks, Wayne. It's weird and might conflict with the legal battle, but I'll seriously consider it. I'm meeting with Billy today to discuss business and we'll kick the idea around. I appreciate you passing the message along. Anyhow, tell Annie I'll talk to her tomorrow."

"Sure, and, Jill, just so you know…Annie and me…we, well… we lead pretty separate lives these days. So…just so you know that, okay?"

"Oh? Okay, Wayne. She never said such a thing to me, but okay. Hey, I'll see you later." I couldn't get off that phone soon enough after that little confession from Wayne.

When I set the phone down after talking to Wayne, I sank to the floor and sat there hugging my guilty anguished belly. Even though I'd done nothing much with Annie, I had spent years fantasizing delectable sexual encounters with her, years imagining myself whisking into Prairie View and rescuing her from her tepid marriage. Had any of this harmed Wayne? Hardly. But I wanted some sanctimonious, fervent-eyed zealot to flog the culpable dickens out of me. That was my favorite guilt-cleansing fantasy, flogging. Was that Catholic or what? I was the most adept mental flagellator in the world.

After several minutes of cerebral self-abuse, I returned to the land of the reasonable and called Billy to set up a meeting. He wanted to come over for a working lunch, mostly, I suspect, to have yet another thawed casserole. I rummaged in the freezer and found one labeled "Thursday Night Special" that came from Mrs. Calendora. Billy could return the Pyrex pan, I decided, and he would sincerely be able to report to her that the food was "yummy," something I wasn't sure I could do.

CHAPTER TWENTY-FOUR

With the aroma of hamburger and tomato sauce wafting through the house, Billy and I decided to start talking business before the casserole was heated, and we planned to continue business while eating. Billy droned on, wanting me to approve some shifting of responsibilities in management at the beer/wine distributorship, and he had some niggling concerns about a casino in eastern Washington that was balking at a contract for our poker machines. I was appalled. What could be more deathly dreary than those issues?

"Maybe I'm being wishful here, but aren't you the one who is supposed to care about this shit? I sure don't. Make the decisions, Billy. That's what Dad apparently wanted you to do." Billy looked relieved, and I had just made my first executive decision: delegate. I could handle this.

"Let's talk about something more interesting, like six hundred and fifty grand." I showed a bewildered Billy the envelope from Josh Martin and loosened the enclosed letter and check. Billy glanced at the check, blinked a few times, read the letter, then read it several times more. He had as much trouble comprehending it as I did.

"I don't like this," Billy said, "and we should tear up this piece-of-shit check and flush it down the can."

"What! Are you kidding me? If it's a legit check, it's our chance to get our rear ends clear of this. Plus, it gives me a better position from which to figure out what's going on up at that farm, without them gunning for me."

"Look, in the end, it's your decision but I have a rotten feeling about it, that's all. These are not nice people, Jill. They won't let you off the hook just like that. They're out to get anyone they deem dangerous to their idea of a perfect society. Listen, just last night, one of my regular customers, who has a big farm east of the Martins, said they have posted a warrant for the arrest of all 'counterfeit' law officers."

"Posted a warrant? What are you talking about? Where?"

"Apparently, their Eagle Township has a warrant out for all law officers who are subverting the American Constitution. They've papered Whitlash with them and pounded them into area electricity poles and fence posts. They don't name names, but the gist is that Eagle Township is now above county, state, and federal laws."

"That's definitely squirrelly, but here's my angle: if they pay me back the money, they're free to establish their little utopia without my interference, and I'm no longer the big bad establishment. What's the problem? That way, I can visit their little burg, under protection as a member of the press, and write an insightful piece about them. My guess is they'd love the publicity. Everyone wins."

"Is that all you do, see the world as one big story source?" He looked even more perturbed when my response was to shrug. "Suit yourself, but you know my opinion, anyway. Let's move on to that other topic you wanted to discuss."

"Oh yeah, I almost forgot…" And I told him about Wayne's message from old man Martin. "So I'm wondering whether I should go see the old guy. I suppose my trusted attorneys would advise against it, but I have a feeling it would be…illuminating. What do you think?" I was sure Billy would nix that idea, too, but he didn't, not entirely.

"You know, your dad and Martin had an odd friendship. More of a mutual self-respect. In his day, the old man was an excellent farmer. He had to be to make a living off that sorry place. Too bad his sons couldn't take after him. In truth, he was the real owner of the farm, but his sons have put him under guardianship after he sold to your dad. He has no real legal rights to make decisions anymore."

"So my visiting him wouldn't make any difference legally?"

"I don't think so. Not if you were visiting him at his request. But what do I know? I think you should call Sylvia McCutcheon and get her opinion before you go running over to the nursing home."

"Hey, Sylvia is smart and a capable attorney, but I don't want her interfering with my idea of fun. I can plead stupidity if my visit causes a hassle. I think the old guy deserves a Sunday visitor."

"You might be making a dodgy situation even worse, Jilly-girl."
"Or I might be making an old man happy in his twilight days."

❖

Bravado aside, I did not like nursing homes. I wasn't heartless, but I did not know anyone who enjoyed entering a grim reminder of their future. I gathered myself as I drove into the parking lot of the one-story, sprawling building that served the area's most difficult and poignant geriatric cases. One long wing attached to the hospital when I was young had grown to three wings, fanning out under the gray, bald hill looming behind. One of the few successful businesses on the Hi-Line: geriatric care. Someday that, too, will decline as fewer people grow old in that ungracious terrain.

I opened the front door and tucked under my arm a $12.99 one-pound box of the best milk chocolates I could find at the drugstore. Immediately in front of me was a prominently displayed reader-board designed to allow efficient name removal as each resident "vacated" the facility. I steadied myself at the shock when I read that Melvin Martin was in room 309 of the Margaret O'Hara wing. My grandmother's name. My father must have funded the construction of that wing so that it would be named after Grandma. I didn't know he'd done that. A balloon of loss exploded within me, and I had to lean against the wall while I endured piercing grief that both Daddy and Grandma were gone, and I was alone.

The odors of institutional food, disinfectant, and dilapidated humans finally brought me out of my agonizing moment. This was going to be harder than I thought. Another part of me wondered if I would be footing the bill for the fourth wing of the nursing home. I couldn't see my father wanting his name on a hospital wing, but I was beginning to wonder if everything I knew about Dad was a misperceived notion planted either by him or my youthful righteousness.

Forcing my original mission back into focus, I scurried past the empty nursing station, relieved at not being seen and, therefore, recognized. A television was playing in what appeared to be a recreation room that could be viewed through a large plate glass window. Over the backs of two wheelchairs, there were two sets of gray hair listing over to the side, obviously dozing in front of a ranting televangelist.

The O'Hara wing was farthest to the left, and room 309, by my reckoning, would be a third of the way down. At the head of the hallway was a vinyl waiting-room couch with a decrepit woman in her flannel nightgown, white-blue eyes vacant, mouth ajar, and spotted skin folding over wrinkled fold. She was clutching a plastic baby doll to her chest. It took me several seconds, but I recognized her: Mrs. Racine, my freshman English teacher.

"Hi, Mrs. Racine," I said almost under my breath as I edged past. No response. Just as well, I thought.

The door to 309 was closed, unlike all the other doors that were wide open, emitting a soft cacophony of television, quiet conversation, and an unnerving "arrgghh" of a resident's dementia. It was my chance to leave, get out before the place swallowed me whole. This was scarier than the time I had to interview a group of imprisoned women who were describing, in detail, how they had beaten, almost to death, a particularly offensive guard. Those were some hard-core, angry women. Okay, I reasoned, if I could do that prison interview, I could interview one sickly old man.

A rattling distracted me, and I looked up to see a nurse's aide pushing a supply cart toward me.

"Are you here to see Melvin?" the plump, kind-faced aide asked. With my nod, she said, "Well, he's having his bath right now, but I'm sure he'll be done in a few minutes or so. You don't mind waiting, do you?" I shook my head. "Gee, it's so nice to see he has a visitor, and with chocolate too. That'll make him happy."

"H-he doesn't get many visitors?" My vocal cords were scraping for sound. "Not even his boys?"

She hesitated and glanced around. "I never have seen 'em here. 'Course, I don't work twenty-four hours a day, so... Anyhow, just wait a few minutes and I'm sure he'll be all cleaned up and ready for company. I'd better get down the hall. You heard Mrs. Torgersen died this morning?"

"No, I d-didn't know."

"Well, she did, and now it's my job to swamp out the room. Sad, ya know? But her kids and grandkids were all around her at the end. Guess that's not too bad."

"No, sounds like a pretty good way to go, I suppose."

Just then the door to 309 swung open, and I turned to face a towering male nurse, Native American, with "Vernon" stitched on the pocket of his green smock. "Yeah?" He glowered down at me. His black hair hung to his shoulders, and I noticed that his lips were full, sexy, like a woman's. His body, however, was all man, strong enough to lift limp, fragile bodies from wheelchair, to commode, back to wheelchair, then into bed, all without a single huff or puff. Clearly, Vernon was a force.

"Uh, I'm here to see Mr. Mar…uh…Melvin. Is he free now?" I sounded cowed but, to be truthful, I was cowed. Cowed by Vernon, Mrs. Racine's doll, the smells, the grunting from another room, the sheer despair and pervasive grief in that place.

"A visitor?" Vernon's face changed from bored efficiency to delight, and he turned his head back into the room. "Ay, Melvin, you got a visitor, and a pretty one, too, you old coyote. You been snaggin' on the girls while I wasn't looking?" Vernon stepped back, out of my way, and there, sitting upright in a blue recliner, was old man Martin, a toothless half-smile on his weather-freckled face. His thin white hair was slicked back from his bath. His hands rested on each chair arm and his feet were covered with thick sheepskin slippers. There was not a lick of dementia in his eyes as he narrowed them and inspected me with slightly lecherous but genuine approval. I couldn't begrudge him a little lechery, given his current situation.

"Are you the O'Hara girl?" His voice was raspy but with a softness that reminded me of wind blowing through full-grown wheat. Again, my voice wanted to disappear, so I nodded and offered a hesitant smile.

"Yes, sir, Mr. Martin." I felt like a ten-year-old being inspected by a barely familiar, aging uncle.

"Ya look mostly like your old man. Spindly, same nose and chin. Eyes and hair color more like your mother, though. She was a nice-lookin' gal, too."

"My mother? Honest to God, Mr. Martin, that's the first time in my life anyone has compared me to my mother." In fact, I didn't know anyone who knew my mother. My dismay must have been evident.

"Oh, yeah, I'm sure the topic of your mother is a sore subject. Best leave off that and move on to why I want to see you."

"No. Uh, no, Mr. Martin. Please feel free to tell me about my mother. I…I don't know much about her, you know."

"We can talk about Eva later. She's long gone anyway. Nobody's heard from her in years. But I'm going to call you Little Dean. You're just too much like your daddy not to." He was still grinning toothlessly, but sweetly now. This was not the conversation I had expected from this person, in this place. He had full control of how it was going to go, and I was willing to let him have that control.

"Okay, Mr. Martin, I can live with that. I'll consider it a compliment." And I was surprised that I actually did consider it a compliment.

"Call me Melvin. Dean's kid should call me Melvin." I nodded agreement and he said, "Let's discuss my old farmstead, okay?" He turned to Vernon. "I'll let you know if I need you again, Vernon." Vernon passed me a concerned look that I knew meant concern for Melvin, not concern for me. Then Vernon left with a nod to Melvin.

"Vernon's a good boy, for an Indian." Another thoughtless reminder of the racism in northern Montana, unabashed and unapologetic, a tightly woven piece of the fabric, barely noticed. Some of the nicest people would spew it unblinking. I was the same way until I moved away and could look back at it with cringing shame. It brought me many anguished hours of self-debasing. I had to force myself to look past Melvin's comment and move on with the conversation. This didn't feel like the time for the stock "power and privilege" lecture to Melvin Martin. He'd get his when he finally climbed the big grain elevator in the sky.

"I don't want my boys to have the farm. Your dad promised he'd keep it away from them, and I expect you to honor his promise."

First he mentioned my mother; then he contradicted everything I've been told about the farm deal.

"I'm not sure I understand—"

"'Course ya don't. You've been fed a line of bull pucky from my prevaricatin' family. Those chocolates for me?" I handed him the chocolates, and he proceeded to rip the cellophane off the yellow box. When he finally got the lid open, he poked a chocolate to see the middle, moved to another and poked it, too. The second one met his approval and he popped it in his mouth, making beastly slurping sounds.

"I don't care what the boys are sayin' about your dad. He agreed to buy the farm, and for a good price, too. Way more than a goddamn realtor would've got me." His hands squeezed into fists and pressed on each chair arm while he slurped over his chocolate.

"You want me to keep the farm? But that's not what the attorneys and your sons are thinking. I'm confused here."

"Get one of those chairs over there and sit down. I don't like women staring down at me." Like an obedient woman, I unfolded one of the chairs leaning against the wall and settled my rear onto its cold metal seat. He pushed another chocolate in his mouth. He hadn't swallowed the first one yet.

"Those boys of mine don't deserve to own one rattlesnake on that land. Them and their crooked friends are nothing but poison. Now I hear A-rabs are out there." His speaking was muffled. There were wads of brown chocolate spit gathering at the corners of his mouth.

"Arabs? Tell me what happened, Melvin." He stalled as he shoved another chocolate in his mouth.

He smacked and gummed his chocolate and finally swallowed. "It's them people there, the ones squattin' on my land. They got no respect, no understanding for what's important. They don't care how much Martin sweat and blood is soaked into the soil. Hell, my dad died out there, just fell over dead, workin' that land. And my Effie's buried there, my wife. My boys and those people don't give a shit." His jaw was jittering and he was tearing up. I hated it when men cried because it made me so weak.

"I'm not sure I understand who you mean by 'those people.'" I was getting the whiff of possibly excellent information.

"Them fake military types. That's who I mean. One of them even has those Nazi signs on both his arms. Our soldiers fought those bastards sixty years ago and now they're livin' on my land. And they call themselves 'Patriots.' They're making my farm into a military base. Hell, they even built some bunkers on the ridge. Bunkers…like that big piece of empty land was going to be attacked." He glanced out the window as if expecting someone to be spying on him. I looked, too, and noted Melvin's room overlooked the hospital emergency entrance.

"Why do you think they were doing that?"

"They're pretendin' to be soldiers." He returned his gaze to me. "They even have obstacle courses out there. They'd set up half a dozen shootin' ranges, made it so I couldn't even get on the tractor anymore 'cuz I was likely to get shot."

"When did all this start?" I was trying not to push him too far, worried he would stop talking.

"Oh…more'n three years ago now. It just got worse and worse. Then, oh, more than a year back, I caught those sons-a-bitches shooting at the gravestones." Here he stopped, hid his face with both veined, calloused hands, and began to sob. His bony shoulders heaved against the back of his shirt.

I felt ashamed watching his misery. "The gravestones, Melvin?"

"They was shooting at our family graves. Our little cemetery. My ma and pa are buried there and my sweet Effie, the mother of those things called my sons. And those ungrateful sons were allowin' their friends to shoot up the graves of their mother and grandparents. Their own flesh and blood." He covered his eyes again, his voice breaking. "I built those markers myself. Built them to last and burned the names in." And he melted into another desolate fit of crying. I grabbed a box of tissue from his bedside and placed it next to him. He ignored it.

"I grabbed my shotgun and pumped buckshot into their butts. Instead of standing up for me and Effie's grave, my boys tackled me and locked me in the house."

"They locked you in? For how long?"

"For a couple weeks, at least. When I finally understood they wasn't going to let me out, I called that lady sheriff. My boys are so dumb they forgot I knew how to use the phone. So they—"

"Wait, you called the sheriff? Sheriff Terabian?"

"Well, that's the only lady sheriff I know of. And a lot of good she did too. Minute after she got there, she was yucking it up with the Nazi guy and Josh. Came in to see me and told me, all serious and such, that she'd make sure I was safe. Then went back outside and did some target practice with Josh." Melvin's eye was twitching and his breathing had gotten labored. My time with him was limited.

"They let me out, though. Even let me go drive to the store in Whitlash to get supplies. That's where I called your dad from. It took a few trips and some good old subterfuge, but a week or so later, your dad had all the papers at the store, ready for me to sell him the farm. I signed 'em and he had the money transferred to my bank account, lickety split.

"This is a terrible story, Melvin. What happened then?"

"Sheriff came back a week after the sale with papers declaring me a danger to myself and others. My boys and her committed me to this… this…hellhole. My own boys…" He was weeping into his weathered hands again. After a few minutes, he pulled a cloth handkerchief out of his back pocket and purged the wet contents of his nose. I was hoping he'd wipe the chocolate spittle from his mouth, but he didn't. "So that's why, Little Dean, you gotta keep that land. It's a good farm when someone works it. My boys, they ain't farmers. They're goddamn criminals." His breath was coming in ever shorter gasps, and I suspected he needed reconnection to the oxygen machine waiting by his bed.

"Okay, relax now. I'm going to call Vernon. Is there anything else you need to tell me?"

Through ragged breaths and hiccup-like coughs, he said, "Don't let me and your dad down. We had an agreement. He was always my friend. And don't trust my boys. That's the saddest thing I've ever said." His coughing and wheezing were frightening me, and we hadn't had that talk about my mother.

"I want to come back and visit you again, Melvin. Maybe talk about my mother. Would that be okay?" He managed a few pained nods.

I got up and pressed the call button hanging down the side of his chair. Vernon must have been waiting because he was there in seconds reattaching the oxygen hoses to Melvin's nose. I waited to see that the old man would be okay. He wasn't the most likable character, but my father trusted him and that's all I needed to know.

I left the room when Vernon did and followed him down the hall. "Excuse me, Vernon, but you seem to have a pretty good relationship with Mr. Martin."

Vernon's face was unreadable as he thought about my statement. "We understand each other, me and Melvin. Why?"

"My guess is he's in here without resources for a little comfort. I want to help make this place better for him. What does he need?"

Vernon looked at me with a little more regard. "He needs a good easy chair, one that helps him stand up. And a small television, too. Most of all, though, he just needs visitors."

"Okay, I'll take care of the first two, but don't know what can be done about visitors." I circled my cell number on my business card. "Call me if he needs anything else that wouldn't interfere in family responsibility. And could we keep it between us for now?"

Vernon nodded, tucked the card in his shirt pocket, and sauntered down the hall. "You bet," he said over his shoulder.

CHAPTER TWENTY-FIVE

I lingered in my SUV and pondered what I had learned. Melvin Martin wanted my father to buy the land. Daddy obliged. The Martin boys were making the farm into a town. Was that legally possible? Not on my land. The so-called town was issuing, at least in my case, sizable cashier's checks. Was the check bogus? Probably. If not, where were they getting those kinds of funds? The "town" was well armed and willing to use the weapons to forestall anyone nearing their "borders." Where were they getting the weapons, and how could they get away with "policing" the roads? The sheriff was involved and so was Annie, at least peripherally. Who could I trust?

I was avoiding my father's filing cabinets in his home office. Going through his private papers still felt felonious, against ancient household rules. I could hear his voice in one of the few times he admonished me, "Jillian, never, never play in my office. That's where Daddy works, and if I catch you in there, I'll have to spank you." He didn't scare me with his blustery threat, but he did impress upon me the importance of the rule.

With resigned dread, I accepted that I was now head of my father's business affairs. I was in charge of everything and I didn't want the stinking responsibility. Still, there was nothing to do about it. I resolved that, when I got back to my father's home office, I was going to start searching his files.

He must have known something about what was going on at that farm, or he wouldn't have been so obsessed with the situation before he died. Buying and selling real estate was an offhanded event for him.

The funeral casserole I'd shared with Billy had worn off, and I found myself ravenous as I left the nursing home parking lot. Instead of going to a restaurant right in town, I decided to drive out to the Corral Steakhouse, where Annie and I had eaten a few days before, when I was still under the fragile delusion that I was in love with her. Since that night, I felt lighter, as if I'd cleaned an old sludge buildup from my heart. And I didn't feel so angry at Prairie View and everyone connected to it.

❖

The Corral parking lot was full of gun-racked pickups, portly American cars, and one imposing black BMW motorcycle parked by itself at the far end. Perfect, the sheriff off duty. Across the highway towered the Galata grain elevator, the only thing left, besides the Corral Steakhouse, of another unnecessary town the rail barons built. The evening sun cast its yellow-gold light onto the dilapidated metal walls of the elevator. Rust stains drooled from the rivets, giving it the look of a weeping baby skyscraper. The wind was buffeting something near the top because I could hear banging metal over the dim *thump-thump* of the bar's jukebox.

I gauged the Corral, trying to decide whether I should enter the bar first or go straight into the dining room. The bar door burst open and crashed against the wall. A body flew out the door and landed flat on its back in the gravel. It was Wayne. Another smaller and wiry body stumbled out and fell face-down. His white blond hair helped me identify him. He got to his hands and knees and looked up with a spit-spewing, "Fuckin' losers!" It was Josh Martin.

I stepped behind my SUV, an instinctive self-protective reaction. I was fifty feet away, but I had an unimpeded view if I peeked my head around the back corner of the Murano. From his sitting position, Wayne kicked Josh in the side. Josh dove on top of Wayne and began punching his face. Annie rushed out of the bar crying, "Stop it! Stop it!" But Wayne and Josh continued rolling around in the dirt, battering the shit out of each other.

I was about to reveal myself to help Annie when she reached into her purse, pulled out a small handgun, and blasted it into the dirt near the men's heads. They kept pummeling each other. Annie fired again and put the barrel of the gun to first Josh's head and then Wayne's. Her hands were trembling.

I stayed hidden. I'd spent enough years in battlefields to know when to avoid being shot, and hiding was a prudent response.

Josh and Wayne's faces were bloodied and Josh spit a line of blood into the dirt. They kept their eyes on Annie as they disentangled and pulled themselves up. Tears were streaking Annie's face. Both men approached her, and Wayne put his hand out for the gun. Annie backed up, shaking her head. Wayne said something I couldn't hear, reached for the gun again, and loosened it from Annie's hand.

A lanky, leather-jacketed figure appeared in the open bar door and leaned against the frame, hands in jeans pockets, watching the scene. Wayne, Josh, and Annie turned to look at the sheriff, who was standing as if she were watching a sports event, attentive and entertained.

Without a word, Josh and Wayne flanked Annie, wrapped their arms around her, and led her to an army green pickup. Josh opened the driver's door, Annie crawled into the middle, and Wayne took the passenger's seat. Josh threw a hostile glance to the sheriff and gunned the truck onto the highway, heading east.

I turned to the bar door, and the sheriff was looking at me.

"Did you get your tire repaired, Ms. O'Hara?"

"What? Oh, yeah, it's fine." She was a cool one, throwing in a non sequitur after what we just witnessed. "Hey, aren't you going after them?" I pointed down the highway. "Someone could have been seriously hurt."

She studied the east-going highway for a few moments, then looked at me. "Josh has his own brand of the law. I wouldn't want to interfere. Not yet. My business is a lot like yours, don't you think? Don't reporters have to wait around a lot? Wait for the right things to happen? Then, when all the ducks are in line, pounce, and the whole story reveals itself. Isn't that how it works?"

For a few moments I considered her question. "I suppose you're right, Sheriff...kind of." I approached the bar door. "Care to have dinner with me?" She was staring at me, considering my offer. "Or maybe having dinner on the Hi-Line with an open lesbian would risk your reelection." That was low, I knew. She didn't blink.

"If I want to be reelected, I'll be reelected, no matter who my dinner companions are. It's just that I like to have dinner with pleasant company. Are you capable of pleasantness for an hour?" She had me. Considering all my fractious encounters with her, it was evident that I usually ignited the fireworks.

"I could be pleasant if you ditch the 'Ms. O'Hara' tag and call me Jill. Oh, and buy me a gin and tonic with a fresh lime wedge."

She straightened up and gave me one of those stunning, if rare, smiles but didn't move so I could enter the bar. "Call me Rae," she said as I pushed by her, the minimal clearance forcing me to make tight contact with her arm. She still smelled like leather and peppermint.

Over the years, I have shared meals with menacing terrorists, white-collar criminals, oily murderers, imposing senators, a U.S. vice president, CEOs of large corporations, and fabulous movie stars. I handled those tense interviews with poise because I had a goal: to gain their confidence and mine their insecurities, their secrets. But when I was in the company of the rare woman who had animal presence, coupled with shadowy beauty, I lost all my carefully constructed edge. I became an inarticulate twelve-year-old, stumbling over easy words and forgetting my drift in the middle of a sentence. The sheriff was starting to have that effect on me. I didn't feel mad at her anymore, and that made me worry that I'd lost my edge.

We chose a table that could seat four and sat on opposite sides. Salt, pepper, and a tent ad for tropical drinks separated us. I refrained from nervously tapping my fingers on the red and white checked tablecloth. She handed me a menu. "Are you a vegetarian, Jill? People seem to leave Montana and become vegetarians. Have you joined the carrot-consuming ex-Montanan horde?"

The good-humored insight relaxed me. "I hate to wreck your hypothesis, but I'm here for a giant bloody slab of prime rib. I can't imagine life without beef. I literally cut my teeth on it and intended using it to strengthen my bridge work until the day I die."

She gave me a thrilling look of approval. "I'm a T-bone, medium rare, girl myself. Baked potato, sour cream with bacon bits, and a glass of beer, pie for dessert." Her mouth, when pronouncing *B*, pushed together in a way that reminded me of light, tender kisses.

"That's a red-blooded appetite you have there, Sher…uh, Rae." The strange thing was, despite my nerves, I knew I'd enjoy talking to her about herself. I decided to dig a little, waiting until after we ordered food and my gin and tonic arrived, with a fresh lime wedge. I took that as a positive omen.

"So tell me." I leaned my elbows on the table and gazed at her, an agreeable pastime. There was a thin white scar, about half an inch long running vertically from the corner of her lip toward her eye. It felt personal and made her more vulnerable. "Your name is Terabian, right? Is that Greek?"

She was fiddling with her sweating glass of beer. "No, Armenian, actually."

"What's an Armenian girl doing in northern Montana? I mean, this area doesn't normally attract people of your ethnic descent. Oh, unless that's a married name." Her eyes narrowed. She knew a prying question from a naturally curious question. What she didn't know was that I didn't know which kind it was. She was more interesting to me than any interview subject.

"I've had the name Terabian my entire life. I'm from Michigan. I've been in law enforcement for more than eighteen years, and I've been sheriff here for two of those years. I came here because I like Montana." Okay, I wasn't going to get her to go on and on about herself.

"Yeah, but, north central Montana isn't the Montana the rest of the country fantasizes about. No mountains, no big game, no snow sports, no fly fishing, no backcountry frolics. There's nothing here except wind, rattlers, and graveyards. Oh, and Republicans in droves."

"It's those 'Republicans in droves' that voted me, a woman, into the office of Taft County Sheriff. And the wind here is refreshing, the rattlers…atmospheric, but the graveyards are depressing." There was an upturn on the scarred side of her mouth. She was playing with me without divulging the object of the game.

"I'm curious. Why did you, the county sheriff, stop me for a measly traffic violation? Isn't that something you delegate to your deputy underlings?" She leaned back, glanced over my shoulder, then at the wall before looking back to me. She hadn't expected that question.

"Like you, I'm curious. First, an unfamiliar vehicle of a make not usually seen in Detroit-is-God land. Second, the vehicle is driven confidently as if the driver knows the town. And, third, the driver herself."

"Care to elaborate on that last criterion?"

"No, I don't."

"You seem pretty familiar with reporter interviews, Rae, but I'm not a reporter right now, just a dinner companion."

"Are you? You have no other motive to have dinner with me other than let's-get-to-know-each-other girl talk?"

"I don't think either one of us is capable of, or interested in, girl talk. But I do find you…interesting…out of the norm for these parts."

She stared at me for several moments. "Out of the norm…hmm… seems I've never been in the norm anywhere, so I'm comfortable with that. But you could hardly say that you're the norm for these parts. How do you deal with that?"

"I'm a part of the fabric of Prairie View. Granted, a privileged part, but a part nonetheless. Because of that, my being gay is a part of the fabric, maybe not appreciated by everyone, but accepted, like the snakes. Nobody hassles me, and what they say about me behind my back is none of my business. Now, if a nice Jewish dyke couple from Hoboken, New Jersey, moved into town, opened a little ethnic restaurant, I'm not sure they'd have such an easy time. But I could be mistaken. Maybe their excellent food would garner some forgiveness from the locals, but let them step out of line and…"

I could have been wrong, but I swore she glanced at my breasts. An astonishing non–Prairie View behavior for a woman, so I took a brief look at the front of my shirt to make sure there were no errant gin dribbles on it. Clean.

Our salads were flopped down in front of us, chunks of iceberg lettuce resting in stained wooden bowls. Oily orange French dressing was drizzled over the pale green clumps. I think I saw a shred of red cabbage in mine. One, probably tasteless, cherry tomato rested off to the side. The waitress, some "dolly" I didn't know, gave Rae a colossal grin and wink. Rae winked back, although a little more soberly. Where the hell was I? All my years on the Hi-Line and I'd never seen two women flirt with each other. Could it be I never noticed, or was this a new cultural development?

Rae sensed my bewilderment, grinned, and dove into her salad. I couldn't muster a single word, so I tackled my salad with the same gusto Rae tackled hers. The dressing was tasty.

When our meat platters arrived, positioned on our paper placemats with more reverence than was accorded the salad, the waitress, bending low, asked Rae if her meat was the way she liked it. The wench didn't even glance at me, and I wasn't bad looking, probably even a few years younger than the sheriff. My lesbian ego was taking a battering. On top of that, I suffered unfamiliar twitches of jealousy. I rarely experienced jealousy because I'd never found anyone I cared to be jealous over, besides Annie, of course. But that was finished and tucked into my thank-God file. An exuberant buzz of release breezed across my heart. In that single expansive moment, I knew, I was free.

I must have appeared exalted because Rae was eying me. "What?" she asked.

"Oh, just a major revelation over my bloody beef," I said.

"Care to elaborate?"

"No, I don't."

Content to keep our little secrets private, we spent the next thirty minutes wielding steak knives, chewing, and discussing Montana politics, the Seattle theater scene, and the Mariners. The sheriff was an avid Mariners fan. Finally, something personal to get my fishing hooks into.

"Sooo, if you like the Mariners so much, do you prefer any other Seattle teams? The Seahawks? The Storm, maybe?" That last question about the Storm was important code. It was the 'Could you be gay?' query. Women's professional basketball games were better termed Dyke-o-rama.

Rae set her fork in her platter, leaned back, and said, "The Storm? Huh. Is that basketball?" I gave a hopeful nod, but she replied, "Basketball's not my game unless it's live or I'm playing it myself. So, no to the Storm." She gave a self-satisfied grin and started sawing on her perfectly medium-rare T-bone. Montana may have lacked in the vegetarian cuisine department, but beef was always first rate in a steakhouse. It was either fry it right or close the kitchen.

We ate every piece of meat on our respective platters, dabbed at our greasy mouths with napkins, and regarded each other. She appeared to be enjoying my company. At least, I found myself hoping that's what her look meant. Of course, I had to ruin the peaceful moment with my next question.

"What's going on up at my farm, Sheriff?"

Disappointment, then anger and resignation crossed her face

within a second. As a journalist, I had to learn to read the emotions my questions elicit. In my next career, I thought, I'll be a wealthy New York shrink.

"Are you always prone to bring business into pleasure, Ms. O'Hara?" The little lip scar had a faint twitch. She was even hotter when she was pissed.

"Touché on the name thing, Rae. Sorry. Look, I'm having an enjoyable time, too, but I just saw something deeply disturbing an hour ago. Annie Robison is…an old friend, and I'm interested in what's going on with her. She's hanging out with Josh Martin, who's beating on her husband. She fired a gun…twice…in a public parking lot. You, the law and order around here, chose to ignore it. And the town thinks you're involved with Josh and his…group, a rumor I find difficult to believe, by the way."

"Ah, the reporter's instincts." Now the little scar was bending along with a sneer. I waited for her to say more, but she only glared at me.

"C'mon. I'm in a tough place here. I have a pending court battle with these Martin jokers. Their old man wants me to keep the place, contrary to the story being floated around town. And the Martin boys are plying me with—probably a rubber—six hundred and fifty grand check to give up and walk away. On top of that, they're declaring my farm, *my* farm, is now something called Eagle Township. I need some reliable information!" A few geriatric parties were watching us now. I gave the room an apologetic smile and waited until everyone turned back to their food.

In a lower voice I said, "I think you took my dad into your confidence. I think he had an idea about what's going on at that farm, and, somehow, he was in cahoots with you. You don't trust me because I've come from the big city and my profession makes you suspicious. But I know this place every bit as well as you do. I may not know all the players anymore, but I do know the rules of the game." She was looking at my hand, and I realized I was pointing at her with my bloody steak knife. I set it on my platter.

The wench came to the table and asked if we wanted dessert. We both said "rhubarb pie," at the same time. The wench flounced off.

"The rules," she said, watching me closely. "There are no rules in the Martin game. Let me amend that. The Martin rules are made up as they go, to benefit the Martins and their buddies."

"So where do Annie and Wayne fit in? Are they part of that Eagle Township fantasy?" For all my inner revelations regarding Annie, I didn't want her mixed up in something that could hurt her. I thought about my conversations with her, how she hinted that I should give the Martins their land. Did her seduction attempt have more behind it than a simple itch that needed scratching?

"Honestly," the sheriff said, "I'm not sure of the extent of the Robisons' involvement. They're in it to some extent, though."

"In what? What is happening up there? You're avoiding the question."

She let out a decisive sigh. "Feel like a windy ride?"

"A what?"

"My bike. I want to show you something, and it would be best if your car isn't seen in front of the sheriff's department."

I would never turn down a ride on an enormous bike with a babe, even in Prairie View. So I agreed to go to her office, knowing I'd have to wrap my arms around her all the way there. Was it worth the matted hair? I still needed to confirm that she was not involved with Josh Martin, and I was willing to do more research on the question.

The wench brought the check and scowled at me when the sheriff paid the bill.

CHAPTER TWENTY-SIX

When we stepped out to the parking lot, the wind was blowing about twenty miles per hour, and we would be riding straight into it. Rae was unfazed and handed me one of those little helmets that looked like a World War I combat helmet. It didn't make me feel all that protected, but I wasn't going to wimp out on her. I acted like I got on the back of giant bikes with strange women all the time. I was terrified, both by the exposure of being on a motorcycle and by touching Rae. Gorgeous as she was, there was a remoteness that made her unavailable for touching.

I strapped the ridiculous helmet to my head while she waited impassively. She backed the bike out, fired it up, and pointed to the places where she wanted me to rest my feet. The bike's engine surprised me with its low noise, and that helped me feel less intimidated when I climbed on. I wondered what she was waiting for as I sat there looking at the back of her helmet. Then I realized she was waiting to feel my arms around her waist. I couldn't bring myself to do it. I put my hands on either side of her belt.

About half a second after she gunned that beast, I understood that not wrapping my arms around her was a death wish. Not only did I cling like a koala to her waist, but I buried my face between her shoulder blades to keep the blistering wind out of my eyes.

Leather, peppermint, and the heat from her body were the only sensations I knew until she slowed as we entered town. We reached her office by taking darkened residential streets. With my face hidden behind her back, we made it to the rear entrance of the building without my being recognized. By that time, I didn't want to take my arms away from her. I wanted to believe she liked me there, too.

The front of the building was manned for the night by a lone dispatcher who monitored, via closed circuit video, the few pathetic souls sitting in the jail cells while she dispatched emergency calls to the officers patrolling Taft County. After Rae unlocked the back door, we moved down a dimmed hallway to her office. She unlocked the door and gestured me in.

"Wait a minute while I go tell Janet, the night dispatcher, that I'm here. Otherwise we'll scare the hell out of her if she hears us talking."

I flipped on the light switch next to the door and entered her impersonal office space. Since the dog picture was the only warmth in the room, I went to look at it. A majestic German shepherd, eyes alight with intelligence, looked into the distance as if spotting deer on the run. I heard the office door close behind me.

"That your dog?"

"She was my girl for twelve years. Her name was Bess." Rae moved next to me and looked at the picture with poignant affection. Our shoulders were an inch apart.

"Not with us anymore, huh?"

"Nope, she's chasing squirrels in the forests of dog heaven. It's been four years, and I still miss her." It was the first real emotion I'd seen in the sheriff. I liked how it looked on her.

"Okay, Sheriff, why am I in your office at night? Are you going to finally answer my questions or put me in lockup?" I sat in one of the stiff visitors' chairs. She went around her desk and dragged out a plain cardboard box, the size that books get packed in. Poking out of the top were several lengthy rolled-up maps, like the ones in my father's office.

"I'm going to tell you what I told your father. However, much of what I'm going to tell you is highly confidential." She gave me a pointed look. I nodded and she continued. "Since you are the legal owner of the Martin property, it is within your rights to know that the farm is under federal investigation." She was rolling out one of the oversized maps over the top of her immaculate desk.

"Federal investigation?" I tried to act appalled but, to be truthful, I was thrilled. A story on my li'l ole piece of property. How lucky can a girl get? Of course, I felt I had to cover my excitement with a façade of appropriate landowner concern and dismay.

I didn't fool her because she said, "Look, I don't want you to think this is a story to sink your reporter's teeth into. Not only is the information I'm giving you classified, but it's dangerous. We're not talking about some two-bit Mike Hassett drug-running scam."

"You know about Mike?"

Her scornful glance made me understand she knew a lot about everything going on in Taft County. She returned her attention to the map that was of the Sweetgrass Hills and Whitlash area. The Martin farm was outlined with yellow marker, and a penciled *X* marked the approximate position of the farm houses and outbuildings. A few roads were highlighted in yellow. One road ran into West Butte of the Sweetgrass Hills, another yellow line went straight across the Canadian border to the top of the map, and one other highlighted road ran west, closely paralleling the border, across Interstate 15, and ending with another penciled *X* at nowhere. I looked closer and realized I knew exactly where that *X* was sitting.

"Jerusalem Rocks? What's so interesting about Jerusalem Rocks except that they look like Dr. Seuss's backyard? Plus, they're thirty miles west of the Martin farm. And they happen to be owned by my father, er...me."

Actually, Jerusalem Rocks were terrifically interesting and surprisingly unknown. The people of the Hi-Line liked to keep it that way. That's why Dad never sold the property that had been in my family for ninety years: to protect it from human degradation.

Possibly the most captivating geological formations in the state, the obscure sandstone cut-outs rose like mushrooms out of a south-facing ridge. They stretched for miles, east, and west, looking like a topsy-turvy twisted city. When I was a kid, Dad would take me, along with one or two of my friends, to explore the place. Nobody could ever take a sizable group of kids because the place was treacherous with sudden drop-offs and loose rocks. Watching two or three kids tumble through the stony make-believe city would give any grown-up a long day of liability-laced anxiety. The place was always eerily empty of sightseers and, oddly, nobody had ever seen a rattlesnake there. The wind blew like an icy son of a bitch, but that accounted for the bizarre rock formations.

"Hey, bootleggers in the nineteen thirties hid their stashes there." I knew that because my great-grandfather was one of those bootleggers. Remembering that helped me understand why Rae had drawn an *X* there on the map.

"Maybe, but let's look at the farm first, okay?" She pressed her finger on the *X* in the middle of the farmland. Her fingernails were short and perfectly manicured. I forgot the map for a moment and admired her strong hand, which had an old jagged scar stretching from the thumb knuckle to her wrist. I pictured running my finger down that scar and then up her arm. Focus, you fool, I thought.

"So, what about the farm and a federal investigation?" We were standing as close as two people could without touching. I heard her breathing and smelled her familiar scent, which was becoming addictive. I pushed my hands on the edge of the desk to force my attention away from her and back to the map. "I know they think they're patriots and are running a paramilitary training camp. I saw some evidence of it the day you sort of helped me with my tire. So they're running guns across the border. Why not just bust them and shut down their operation? You'll have no complaints from the landowner."

"What we have going at the Martin place is far more worrisome and risky."

"Wait a minute. What federal agency is investigating my property? Is it the ATF, the FBI? Who?"

"I'm sorry, but I'm not at liberty to divulge that information, and not only because you're a reporter. I can't compromise the work we've devoted to this investigation, and in good conscience, I can't place you in harm's way." She turned her head and looked directly into my eyes.

"I've been in harm's way before. I've covered two wars, crawled around the streets of Bagdad, been embedded with troops…" I found her probing look overwhelming.

"It doesn't matter." Her face had softened, then she turned back to the map and appeared to gather herself. "It doesn't matter what your previous experience is or how trustworthy you are. If this case gets compromised in any way, at the very least, people could die, and we'll have a national scandal on our hands. All I want is for you to understand a few things." She stepped away from the desk, away from me, and gazed at the closed blinds behind my head.

"Okay, like what? That the feds have control over my property?

That my ownership rights over the Martin farm and Jerusalem Rocks no longer matter? And, by the way, just who are you working for, Rae? The people of Taft County or Big Brother Uncle Sam?" Of course, her words "national scandal" were like waving a banana split under my nose.

Her face hardened. "I am an officer of the law. It's my duty to protect the people of this county, including you." Red was creeping up her neck, and I was certain she was going to hit me. I pushed the back of my legs against the desk, ready to parry whatever was coming.

She squeezed her eyes shut, and when she opened them, I caught a glimpse of deep fatigue. I wanted to touch her face, but was afraid of her response. She was unreachable, isolated. Comfort was not what she sought, but I knew it was what she needed. I shoved my hands into my pockets.

"Okay, Rae, tell me more. Tell me what you can. But you have to understand that I will ask questions. It's my nature."

"As long as you understand that it's my nature to not answer questions."

"Fair enough. Should we continue with the map?" I was taking full breaths again.

Returning to the desk and map, she said, "There are at least eighty people living on your property."

"Eighty! How the hell can that place house eighty people?" Then I remembered the enormous metal building, the bunkers, the three houses, and all those outbuildings. It was possible.

"You were spying on that land the other day. What did you see?"

"What makes you think I was spying? It's my property, isn't it? You were following me, weren't you?"

"You really do ask a lot of questions."

I laughed. "Okay, I'll tell you what I saw, but you have to tell me why I was seeing it." She didn't reply but grinned at me, expecting me to tell her about my little field trip to the Martin place. So I did, including the macabre mannequins, bullet-riddled vehicles, and military bunkers. None of it surprised her.

"So tell me, Sheriff, what are the Martins doing building bunkers on my land?"

She looked at the far wall. It appeared she was weighing what and how much she was going to tell me. "You've figured out that the Martins are running a paramilitary operation up there." I nodded, waiting for more. There was nothing new about gun and survival nuts living in remote areas of Montana. "Well, they're drawing their group members from several survivalist-type organizations that have existed in Montana for decades."

"You mean like the Montana Freemen?"

"And Posse Comitatus and other militia-type groups, some neo-Nazis, only the Martins are trying to take it to a new level of domestic threat."

"Domestic threat? You mean domestic terrorism? Like Tim McVeigh kind of crap?" I almost told her about Melvin Martin's bit of information about the Arabs, but didn't want to share my knowledge of that juicy bit.

"We think it's highly likely but maybe more severe. They're better organized and funded. They have enough operatives to present a terrible threat to, well, to our country."

"Are we talking bombs here? What's there to bomb in this godforsaken place?"

"Think, Jill. Think about how ideal this desolate area of the country is for national defense."

"There's nothing here to defend except some cows, sheep, a few people and..." Then came the terrible realization. "Oh, holy shit. ICBMs. Minuteman missiles." I staggered back and thunked my butt into the inflexible visitors' chair. "I forget they're here. We all do. The silos are just part of the landscape now. Have been for decades, my whole life, really. Nobody thinks about them."

"And that's what makes them so valuable and potentially vulnerable. The missile silos are buried and almost invisible on the landscape. The local population barely notices them, except when a crew from the Air Force base at Great Falls makes their rounds. When was the last time you even looked at one?"

"We've been trained to ignore them. Okay, once, during high school, we had a few too many beers and threw all the bottles over the fence. We wanted to see if the cameras worked. We were always told there were cameras watching the silos, all the time. We wanted to see what would happen, but got scared. So we went a few roads away, hid the car, climbed a little hill to watch, and waited. It took about forty-five minutes for security to show up."

"Actually, the security devices are more like highly sophisticated motion detectors, and they do work." Rae was facing me, leaning her rear on her desk. "Unfortunately, security is located in Great Falls, and there are around two hundred of those suckers to patrol. And they aren't centralized. They're spread in a shallow U-shape from Prairie View, through Great Falls, and over to the Lewistown area. That's the size of a small country. On top of that, there are three hundred more in other Plains states and—"

"Wait, wait, wait! Are you trying to tell me that Josh Martin, his crazy brother Eric, and their buddies are going to blow up intercontinental ballistic missile silos? God, I can hardly say it, much less fathom the idea. Bombing nukes? They're just yahoos, Rae! They haven't got that kind of power, do they?"

"Let's just say they're connected yahoos."

"You mean there're more of them somewhere else, like terrorists?"

"These groups, in the past few years, have gotten more organized. The Internet has helped them immeasurably. They have international connections with groups that are salivating to pop off a nuclear bomb anywhere inside our borders. Better yet, they'd love to fire one off to Russia, starting an all-out war between us and the Russians. Disrupting and harming the United States has become a highly prized goal. Most of us just do our little lives, not thinking about it, hoping someone else is making sure we're safe, not understanding just how vulnerable we are in remote places like northern Montana."

"I can't believe the hayseed Martins are—"

"Let's just say the Martins are guilty, but unwitting, puppets of others. I can't tell you any more than that."

It was never good to tell a journalist that she only got to hear part of the story. Rae just committed a little error. Now I wanted to get the rest of the story, like who was manipulating and funding the crazy Martins. What about the Arabs Melvin Martin alluded to? What were their tactics? And for me, what did Annie and Wayne Robison have to do with it?

"One other thing, Rae. These missiles, aren't they fairly deep in the ground, well protected by, I don't know, steel or cement? I can't imagine that there's a bomb that could penetrate and then set them off. That seems pretty impossible." Tense as the conversation was, I still noticed how long her legs were in those black jeans. I wished she had worn her chaps. I wanted one more look at her derriere in those things. Her resigned sigh pulled my attention back to the serious discussion.

"Okay, look at this." She reached into the map box again and pulled out another oversized map. I joined her at the desk as she rolled out a wrinkled map of central Montana. There were little dots all over the map, not correlated to any town, as far as I could tell.

"These are all the ICBMs in Montana, all two hundred of them."

"Jeez, it looks like scatter shot. There's no pattern, is there?"

"Not visibly, no. But they are strategically placed so that a group of ten missiles can be controlled by a localized launch control center responsible for just those ten missiles. Since there are two hundred missiles in Montana, that makes twenty launch control centers."

"Are they manned?"

"No, but they're equipped to be manned by a missile combat crew within minutes of an order from Strategic Air Command. That crew will be in charge of their ten missiles, but in an extreme situation, and with the correct codes, the crew can commandeer forty more missiles and launch them."

"So, conceivably, a small crew can be in charge of fifty nuclear warheads? And launch them?"

"It's possible if they're supplied with the correct information. The missile targets are limited to Russia or North Korea but, as we know, one nuke, hitting any target anywhere, is all it could take to start a full-scale nuclear war. Some of those babies have a range of seven thousand miles."

"And this is called national security," I muttered.

Somehow, while we'd been gazing at the locations of Minuteman missiles, our shoulders had drifted together. I was pleased that she was pressing as hard as I. Then the heat ignited. I looked at her strong, slender right hand, pushing on top of the map, holding her weight. It was automatic. I reached and brushed my fingers on hers. My index finger smoothed the scar on her thumb.

Rae straightened up, taking her hand away from mine. I suffered a rush of embarrassed disappointment. She grabbed my shoulder, moved me to face her, and used her other hand to squeeze my jaw and force me to look at her.

"Rae, I'm sor—"

"Shh, don't." Still holding my jaw, she leaned down and gave me the sweetest kiss. Tender, light, and awash in sensuality. We repeated those progressively carnal kisses over and over. Then her mouth opened wider and our tongues got down to business. That's when my arms remembered to wrap around her and pull her rangy body tight into mine. Her strenuous breathing and the smell of her leather jacket erased my reason. My pelvis started pushing rhythmically against the top of her thigh.

She forced my backside to the desk and straddled me, pressing her demanding center into my belly. What could I do but what I did next? I lay back on top of those missile silos and pulled her on top of me, never breaking our kiss. Her crotch was banging against me, probably causing wrinkles and tears in the maps, but who cared?

We were both groaning with pulsing need. I pushed her jacket to the side, unbuckled her belt, and worked down her zipper. Pulling her shirt out, I caught a glimpse of black lace panties. That sight amplified my urgency. She could do anything to me.

"Please, please…" I was begging for her to take me.

She jerked my T-shirt above my breasts and ripped one bra cup down. It pushed my burning, taut nipple into cool air. Her warm, moist mouth covered my entire breast. I almost passed out from sensation while my crotch nearly bucked her off the desk. She worked my shirt over my head until my arms were stretching against my ears. When she got the shirt to my elbows, she twisted it with one hand, pinning my arms. I was helpless and I loved it.

She went to work on my other breast, pulling the other cup down. Both breasts were now straining with ache. I was panting and whimpering.

"Sheriff!" Knock, knock. "Sheriff Terabian, it's me…Janet. Are you in there?"

"Shit!" She fell on me, winded, her hips still moving. "What, Janet?" Her voice was shaky, gravelly.

"Uh, I just received a call from the mini-mart. A robbery and shooting. The suspect has left the premises. I've dispatched a car, but I'm sure they'll need you if someone was injured. Um, are you okay?"

"I'll be…right there and, yeah, I'm okay."

She was okay, too, because she lay there on top of me, winded and shuddering. Without much effort on my part, she had come in her jeans. Well, she had one up on me. My whole lower region was soaked, swollen, and unfinished.

"Sorry. I have to go." She was still lying on top of me, our faces a few inches apart.

"Oh God, can't they investigate without you?" I was ready to debase myself in any way that would get her to stay.

"You have no idea how much I want to finish what we started, but it'll have to wait. Really, I'm so sorry. Ride with me to the crime scene, and I'll get one of the deputies to give you a lift to your car."

I accepted the honest regret in her eyes as she inched my bra over my breasts, helped me sit up, and returned my crimped shirt to its former position. She was gentle, almost reverent with me.

I helped her straighten her appearance and watched her retrieve her badge and gun belt from a cabinet. Seeing her strap on that gun belt made me hot for her all over again. If that wasn't bad enough, I had to re-straddle her vibrating bike. This time I wasn't shy about wrapping myself around her. I know her speed was erratic because my hands on her stomach were a distraction.

When I got off her bike, I said something new for me: "Please don't tell me this is the end of it."

I received one of those incendiary smiles. "We've barely started, Ms. O'Hara." Just then two more sheriff's cruisers pulled into the parking lot. "Your ride is here. I'll see you later." She turned, composed, and strode into the mini-mart.

"Yes, Sheriff, you will see me later." My only satisfaction was that she had to investigate a homicide with her lacy panties soaking wet.

Chapter Twenty-seven

When I got home, the impact of recent disclosures, and desktop humping, had me wired. I opened a bottle of a Portuguese Douro, inexpensive but yummy, stepped into Daddy's office, and slumped against the doorway. I mulled what Rae's role was in this Martin mess. Why would she share obviously sensitive information with me, a reporter? Wasn't that irresponsible? Was she setting me up? Yes, I was impossibly attracted to her, but I wondered if I had just been used as a pawn in a bigger game. "Well, I can play chess, too, Sheriff."

I turned on the office ceiling light and stood at the doorway, picturing my father looking up from his work, reading glasses on his nose, and smiling at me.

"Oh, Daddy, what did you leave for me to clean up? I need some help here." I spoke to my mental image of him. I saw him give me that look that always said, "You're Daddy's girl and capable of greatness. Just do the next thing."

So that's what I did. I took a large sip of wine and sat at his desk. His oversized chair cradled me. The smell of cherry pipe tobacco was comforting. The stuffed elk and jackalope served as buddies while I studied the room's art and finished the entire glass of the Douro. Then I considered the desk drawers.

There were five drawers in the desk, a belly drawer that held pens, pencils, paper clips, rubber bands, and various items that have no category: a convention name tag, button from a shirt, comb, fridge magnets with advertising, other things of no interest as far as I could tell, except what looked like a filing cabinet key in the far right dish.

The top drawer on the left held a ragged Rolodex, an address book, and an almost new BlackBerry. I pulled the BlackBerry out and set it on the desk in case I had to refer to it later.

The top drawer on the right held an old pistol I'd seen and fired many times in my life. It was a little Ruger Bearcat .22. An ineffectual little piece, but cute, with an engraved bear and cat on the barrel. It had belonged to my grandmother. She was the one who took me into the country and taught me to fire it. We'd save up empty pop cans and, every few weeks, go shooting. I could still feel her arms around my nine-year-old body, helping me point and aim the little gun. It had hardly any recoil, so I became a successful shooter in one lesson with that pistol. The pop cans made short hops when the bullets hit them, and each successful shot was a spur to continue to practice. Later, I would graduate to larger handguns, then rifles, shotguns, semi-automatics. Eventually, I could handle any gun my father owned, and he owned a mini arsenal, all stored in the basement of the house. My affection for firearms was something I'd used many times over the years to provoke tedious, politically correct lesbians. It had even ended a couple of dates on a sour note. Somehow, that made me gleeful.

There was nothing else but bullets in the Ruger drawer, so I brushed my hand along the gun barrel. I checked to see if it was loaded; it was. And I whispered thanks to Daddy for keeping it to remember his mother. I vowed to do the same.

Underneath the Ruger drawer was a file drawer. This one was important because it held Dad's insurance plans, including plans for himself, Connie, and me. There were also files for current assets and one for outstanding bills, which was empty, to my relief.

The top left drawer had a series of files lying flat. They were performance review files for all my father's managers. Confidential but best saved for Billy's eyes. The final drawer, to the bottom left, was another file drawer, but instead of standing files, there were several fat brown manila envelopes. Each envelope was dated in two-year increments in Dad's round cursive handwriting. They weren't sealed, so it seemed he was using them for storage only. I chose one dated 1995–1997. It held newspaper clippings, about two dozen of them. My work. He'd been collecting everything I'd had published from every newspaper that printed my writing.

I cried. For a long time, I sat with those old stories spread before me, and I let the tears wet the top of my shirt. I used the bottom of my shirt to wipe my nose and eyes. When the tears were done, I poured another glass of the wine and took the filing cabinet key from the belly drawer and went to the corner of the office where Daddy's filing cabinet was.

As I braced myself for whatever I'd find, exhaustion rolled down my frame. I steadied myself by leaning my shoulder into the wall. I couldn't do it. Not yet. Every part of me was fatigued in a way I'd never experienced before, even after days of Iraq battle coverage. Too many emotions, memories, and revelations for one day.

"I'm going to bed, but I'll see you in the morning," I said to the accusatory filing cabinet. I grabbed my wineglass and bottle, pocketed the cabinet key, and went upstairs to start a bath before bed. I was looking forward to using the relaxing water and my right hand to relieve the tension from my encounter with Ms. Law and Order.

❖

I awoke to the sound of a rumbling vacuum cleaner bonking against walls and furniture. "Connie," I groaned into my pillow. I remembered I hadn't yet worked out her terms for further employment, but she was still here, doing what she'd done for years: vacuuming on Monday morning. Time for me to get up and do the next thing. "Connie, then the filing cabinet," I whispered.

Connie was just wrapping up the vacuum cord when I descended the stairs.

"Mornin', Connie. Any of your evil coffee ready yet?" It was an unnecessary question as the aroma of fresh coffee enticed me toward the kitchen.

"Now don't you start, Jillian," she said as she gave me a quick, wrenching one-armed hug around my waist. "One of these days, an O'Hara is going to appreciate my coffee, and I'm countin' on you being the one."

"Well, I'm going to finally disclose a family secret: we all have loved your coffee. Better to be teased by an O'Hara than not."

"Don't I know it," Connie said with a rueful head shake.

"Connie, come in here while I drink my coffee. We need to talk."
I entered the kitchen and made straight for the coffeepot. I turned to see
her watch me with curiosity and anxiety.

"Okay, but today I gotta get that powder room cleaned up from all
the after-funeral guests." I could tell she knew what our conversation
was going to be about.

I motioned for her to sit at the counter, and I took up post on the
other side. I knew this was going to be a grown-up conversation, and I
didn't know how I wanted it to end except that I wanted Connie to be
happy with the outcome.

"We need to discuss your staying on with us. That is, if you want
to stay on."

"Good Lord, what else would I do at my age? But I know that your
daddy now being with the angels changes things. And I don't want you
to keep me here as a charity case. My husband makes enough now for
us to be okay. And in a few years, retirement…"

"I need you, Connie." We were both surprised at my confession.
"I need you to keep this house up." And right then, I found the perfect
solution. "I need you to take care of Billy, too. He will be working
more than he ever has before, and I need you to look to his household
needs. He's a typical bachelor, like Daddy, and I'm going to offer this
house for him to live in. That way he will have the space to entertain
when he needs to, a private office to work out of, and you to make sure
the house runs smoothly. Besides, it's still my home, too." My voice
was pleading and persuasive. She and Billy were the only family I still
had. Somehow, bundling them into one house seemed an appropriate
solution. I could tell Connie liked the idea, but now I would have to
sell it to Billy, a minor detail. And I wouldn't have to liquidate the
taxidermy.

"Okay, I like that idea. The cooking, though, I can't do that
anymore. It's all I can do to keep this house looking good." She held up
her hands that were faintly warped from arthritis, and I knew her back
hurt, too.

"Okay, it's a deal, except one thing."

"What's that?"

"You be honest with me about what's too much, and I'll get more
help for you. We'll let Billy figure out his own meals. Maybe you can
find someone to cook for him." She grinned and nodded. "I noticed last

night that Daddy has insurance for you but I didn't read the file. Is it enough to cover you and your husband?"

"Oh, sweetie, it sure is. More than enough. Your father was too generous with me being just his housekeeper, but I always made sure I did a good job, stayed loyal, and kept my mouth shut. Well, I kept it shut more often than not, I guess." We both laughed, knowing Connie interjected her opinions whenever she thought it important, which was frequently. "My garsh, he even bought us plots in the cemetery. That one kinda scared me, I have to say. I wasn't really ready to start thinking about gophers using my nose for a golf tee." That got me laughing, then I grabbed her hard old hand.

"So we have an agreement?" I asked.

"We have an agreement, dear. Now, can I get to that nasty powder room?"

I nodded. "I'll be in Daddy's office going through the filing cabinet if you need me."

She looked worried. "I suppose you'll find some interesting things in there."

"What do you mean?" I wondered if she knew about the goings-on with the Martin place.

"Just that your daddy was a man with secrets. I don't know where he kept them, mostly in his head I expect. But there are bound to be a few in those drawers. And I'm wondering if some of them are better left right there in that cabinet."

"Well, you're probably right about that, but what choice do I have?"

"None, sweetie, none," she said as she patted my arm. "I got work to do." She turned and left me with my half-cold cup of coffee.

❖

A few minutes later, with a fresh cup of hot coffee, I opened the drapes to let in the light and glanced at the sagebrush on the prairie outside the office window. The view was gorgeous and barren. My cell phone vibrated in my pocket. It was Fitch.

"Hey, I called you on the cell because your sheriff, as you predicted, might be a little more than Miss Podunk. I don't want anyone hearing our calls, not that cells are much safer."

"What, you mean my father's phone is tapped? Get real." Fitch was famously paranoid.

"It probably isn't, but I don't want anyone tracing me to his phone while she's the law around there. I hope you kept your hands out of her pants." When I answered with guilty silence, I heard Fitch whisper, "Shit."

"Would you just tell me what you've found? I'm not in the mood for lectures, especially from you."

"Okay, but for starters, I want you to watch your back. That sheriff has about twenty years' history in law enforcement, much of it is hard to define. Hazy."

"Hazy?"

"Well, my evidence is circumstantial because I'd need more time and would have to call in favors. I don't want to waste either unless directed by you."

"Let's hear what you have and I'll decide."

I heard Fitch settle into her chair, slurp some coffee, and tap on her keyboard. "Okay…Ramela Azad Terabian. Thirty-seven years old. She grew up in Detroit, Armenian family, father an auto worker, mother a travel agent. One brother, Alek, two years older—"

"Do I need all this? Give me the bottom line here."

"Yes, you need all this and I won't give you the fluff, okay? Except you should see her in her college volleyball uniform. Perfectly hot. I'll send you a link when all this is over. University of Michigan, by the way. Graduated with a degree in sociology and criminal justice and became a police officer in Chicago."

"Hmm. So what brings her to outback Montana?"

"Murky. But let me tell you a bit more history. She serves, with distinction, as a cop in Chicago for several years, then nine eleven happens. And this is the tough part. Her brother was on that plane that plowed into the Pentagon. Apparently on a business trip for his law firm."

"How'd you learn about that?" My heart hurt for Rae and her family.

"Read it in *The Armenian Weekly*, of course. September 14, 2001, edition. It's a national news rag for the Armenian American community. Not surprising, the *Weekly* doesn't mention the name of his law firm or branch of law he practiced, just calls him an attorney, then goes on about the loss to his family and the Armenian community."

"So where does Rae, um, the sheriff, fit into all this?"

"Tell me about her handcuffs and I'll tell you more."

"Knock it off. I'm really not in the mood."

"Okay, sorry, just can't resist the uniform angle. Anyhow, after that, any record of Rae dries up until she was hired as a deputy by the Taft County Sheriff's department and within eighteen months is elected sheriff. Curious, don't you think? I thought that was a good ol' boy's job."

"Nah, women in Montana have been doing men's jobs forever. What's curious is her getting elected so fast. People around here don't usually vote for unknown quantities." Then I remembered Rae telling me, while standing at the Corral door, that she could get elected sheriff any time she wants. "What's your hit about her, Fitch?"

"Can't tell. She could be legitimate law enforcement, all right, or she could have gone rogue. Personal tragedies do funny things to people's brains sometimes. Anyhow, all trace of her disappears from the Web until she shows up in Prairie View, a town that defines nowhere."

"I'd be insulted if it weren't halfway true, but there's more to this place than census count or location can ever convey, trust me. Anything else you can tell me?"

"Probably, if you want me to spend the time and make a few private requests."

"I think not. My guess is I can get the rest out of her eventually."

"Well, sweetie, I have all the implements you need for information extraction."

"I'm sure you do, but I'll use my own methods, thank you. I'll call you in a few days." Trading a few love barbs, we ended the conversation.

❖

I fidgeted at my father's desk, digesting the information about Rae, then decided to save it for later musings. I moved in front of the filing cabinet again. There were four drawers, each labeled with a different category. The bottom drawer was labeled "Real Estate Transactions:

Complete." The next drawer above, "Real Estate Transactions: Current." Above that, "Legal Proceedings." And the top drawer, "Personal." Clearly, my father's other business files were stored in his office down at the distributorship. I figured those would be Billy's headache, but the files in this office were mine.

"Oh fuck, it's too much!" I slapped the key on top of the filing cabinet and strode to Daddy's desk. I couldn't do it, not yet. Instead, I fired up the BlackBerry, found the number, and called Sylvia, the attorney.

"Jillian, I'm glad you contacted me. We need to discuss several real estate deals you father was in the middle of before he left us." At least she was speaking in past tense.

"Would his documents be kept here, in his office at the house? Because that's why I called, Sylvia. Oh, and to discuss having dinner with you and your roommate, of course." She had a sweet laugh. I knew I would be friends with this woman, and I had a one-second fantasy of a double date with Sylvia, her partner, Rae, and me.

"We'll get to dinner, but let's talk business first. I feel so…Monday morning, you know? What are your questions?"

"I see that my father has a filing cabinet with a drawer for current real estate transactions. What should I be looking at currently?" I was hoping this would lead her to the Martin questions, but I was wrong. She briefly discussed three deals that she and my father had in the works. Those were the files she wanted me to read before we met.

"Okay, and what about the drawer that has Legal Proceedings for a label?" Sylvia went on about several legal issues my father was involved in, none of them dire, except the Martin farm. Actually, most of them were cases where my father was gifting land or money to people and organizations. I was beginning to feel pride for my father. But I needed to get the conversation to the Martins, and I couldn't wait anymore.

"Can we talk about the Martin place now?" Sylvia was quiet while I heard papers moving around her desk. Then she cleared her throat.

"Sure, what do you want to know?"

"They sent me a check for six hundred fifty thousand dollars, just to leave them alone. I'm tempted, but I met Melvin Martin yesterday and with the sheriff last night—"

"Wait, wait. You met with a member of the plaintiff's side without me in attendance? Jillian, what were you thinking? You could compromise so much!"

"I don't think so. Get this, he wants me to keep the land. The old man doesn't want his sons to have it. The people they have on the land scare the old guy. And he's not off his rocker, like the boys are saying. He's as sane as you or me."

I heard Sylvia take a deep breath. "Okay, now I have to play the attorney card. You must stay away from him, Jill. No matter what his wishes are, you can no longer meet with him. However, his wishes and state of mind are important to our case, so I want you to let me handle the rest of this. Maybe we can get a doctor's diagnosis and a statement from Mr. Martin regarding his wishes. But we have to do it within legal bounds or anything we get from him will be tainted and inadmissible. Got it?"

"I do, but you have to know that 'legal bounds' carry no weight with the Martin boys and their crowd. They've turned the farm into a township, a well-armed township. They have threatened me with war, and I'm sure you will be one of their targets. So I'm thinking other routes, besides the courts, are necessary here. We're talking dangerous people who are a threat." I didn't want to tell Sylvia about the domestic terrorism threat. For some reason, I felt the sheriff wouldn't want me to. A meddling attorney probably wasn't something Rae wanted to deal with. Neither did I, actually.

"Look," I said, "this situation is way more complicated, not to mention interesting, than I ever imagined. I have no idea where this is going, but I need to know that my attorney won't undermine me. Can I count on you for that?"

"From what I know about you as a journalist, my guess is you have all kinds of information and ulterior motives that you won't share with me. So I suppose I get to be caught with my pants down." She was starting to sound receptive. I liked receptive in a woman. "Okay, my life needs more excitement, at least until my girlfriend gets back from Korea next month."

"My reporter's instincts have a feeling things are about to escalate, so no worries about your reunion honeymoon." I felt my belly drop as a twinge of envy tweaked me. I wasn't envious of Sylvia's girlfriend;

I was envious that I didn't have someone waiting for me in Seattle. My aloneness in the world had become a lurking presence in my inner landscape. Then I thought about Rae, her hands, that little scar by her mouth, and I felt better, settled somehow, and aroused.

CHAPTER TWENTY-EIGHT

I had no intention of immediately reading the files Sylvia suggested in preparation for our next meeting. So I ignored the bottom three drawers of the cabinet, and after unlocking it, I opened the top drawer labeled "Personal." It was almost empty.

There was a thick file in the front marked "Old Maps." Another thinner file was labeled "Medical." Another thin one labeled "Jillian." And a fourth fat one, in the back of the drawer was labeled "Meeker and Meeker." I grabbed the maps file first, thinking it would be the least personal and less likely to drag me into tears. As soon as I opened it, I knew I had the key to Daddy's thoughts as he studied the farm maps just before his death.

I took the file over to the work table in the middle of the room and spread out its contents. "Wow!" I whispered to the jackalope overseeing the room. Folded into the file were three old maps: two were old farm maps dated 1917, and the other was a map of Montana, ripped out of what appeared to be a 1923 road atlas.

Underneath the three maps was a yellowed pencil drawing on decrepit stationery. It had been folded for many years but now was smoothed flat. The creases made it look intentionally quartered. The lines on the drawing were faint, but the subject was unmistakable. It was a rendition of a specific formation at Jerusalem Rocks. Since Jerusalem Rocks snaked for miles east and west, I couldn't begin to decipher which formation it was. But it must have been important to my father.

I spread both farm maps on the table. One was of the land that now comprised the Martin farm and several other large farms. A dark circle was drawn around the town of Gold Butte, a place that no longer survived in contemporary times but was still a mining town back in 1917. The gold ran out and people abandoned the town. The ranchers who owned the land leveled the entire town in the late 1960s. They were tired of their livestock getting stuck and injured in the abandoned buildings. Daddy took me to visit the still extant graveyard once. The map also showed old roads, ones that I was sure were no longer used but still existed at least as trails.

The other farm map included the properties around Jerusalem Rocks. A faint *X* was placed toward the northern end of the formations. I recalled my grandma telling me that it was the north end of Jerusalem Rocks that held the bootlegger caves. Daddy always made me stay at the southern end of the formation, claiming the northern end wasn't safe to play in.

The theme for the *Magnificent Seven* filled the room and broke my concentration. "Damn! Connie!" I shouted. "Could you grab the phone, please?"

"Oh, sweetie, my hands are covered with disinfectant. I'm sorry." I heard her voice echoing from the main floor bathroom.

"No problem." I grabbed the phone without checking caller ID first. "Hello?" Someone was laughing. "Who is this?" I checked ID readout which read "no data."

"Did you cash the check?" It was a man with a gravelly soft voice.

"What check? Who's calling?" I hated these kinds of calls, and I had to admit that I'd had several in my time.

"So you're too good to take the money? Is that it?"

"So what happens if I don't cash the check?" The sound of a rock hitting the office window startled me. The jackalope made a noise. Its glass eye was shattered. I dropped to the floor. The fuckers were shooting at me.

Rolling on my back, I put the phone back to my ear. "You assholes!" He had hung up.

Connie burst in. "Jillian, what in the world..."

"Down! Now!" I had to hand it to her, she dropped without hesitation.

"What's going on?" She was looking at me through chair and table legs.

"Shit, Connie, someone just shot at me."

"Call the police, Jill. Now."

I dialed 911 and told the dispatcher what happened. And I told her, no, I didn't know if the shooter was still out there. And I wasn't about to take a peek to find out. She kept me on the phone while she dispatched officers.

❖

Four squad cars were lined in my driveway, lights flashing, making a cinematic scene. I had just finished explaining the incident, omitting the phone call, when Rae's car pulled up. Seeing her uniformed presence rise out of that car was so distracting that I almost forgot the gravity of the incident. She had her game face on, however, and that helped me to focus.

"Sheriff, can I speak with you privately for a moment?" I asked as she approached.

"Not yet, Ms. O'Hara, I need to inspect the crime scene first. Would you repeat your story to the officer, just to make sure you give him every detail? Standard procedure." I could tell she was pissed and worried. "I'll find you in about thirty minutes." I had no choice but to wait to tell her about the phone call. I believed that part of the story was for her ears only, and I believed explaining it to a rank-and-file sheriff's deputy would cost way more time than I wanted to spend.

Within a few more minutes, Annie pulled up in her decade-old Buick. As I retold my story to the deputy, I watched her scan the yard, appearing to weigh whether she wanted to interrupt the police proceedings. Then she used a cell phone, talking for only a minute and catching my eye while she spoke. She lifted her hand in acknowledgment, said a few more sentences into the phone, and closed it. She was clearly wavering about something.

She waited to the side, listening, while I finished telling my short story to the deputy. When I was done, I walked over to Annie and was surprised when she put her arms around me and held me close for a moment longer than was seemly for Prairie View women. Then she let go and backed off like a duty had been completed—at least that's how it felt to me.

"Are you okay, Jill? What happened? Did I hear you say something about a shooter?" She did look concerned. I'll give her that.

"I'm okay, but I'm worried about Connie. It was terrifying, Annie. One moment I'm on the phone, the next I'm on the floor and then Connie is down there with me, telling me to call nine-one-one." I saw fear cross Annie's face. "Don't worry. Nobody is hurt, just rattled. C'mon, let's go inside."

She kept her arm stiffly around my shoulders as we entered the house. I saw Connie in the living room, speaking to another deputy. Most of the action was in Dad's office, and I caught a glimpse of Rae looking out the window and pointing while speaking to one of her officers. Annie steered me to the kitchen, and I followed her lead, deciding to put coffee on for the officers.

Annie watched me make coffee while I told her an abridged version of the shooting. She grabbed my forearm, just as I was hitting the on switch on the coffeemaker.

"You have to let this go, Jill." She was almost glaring at me.

"Let what go?"

"This whole 'I'm the big landowner, so don't cross me' game you're playing."

"Uh, game? I didn't know I was competing. So who's my opponent?"

"I think you know, and I think your stubbornness is half the cause of what happened this morning."

"What the hell are you talking about? I'm going to assume that you're alluding to the Martins. And I also have to assume, from what you just said, that you feel they're justified in shooting at me. Is that what you're saying, Annie? Is it?"

She realized she had gone too far. "No, I'm sorry. I didn't mean it like that. It's just that, well, if you'd give them what they want, they'd probably leave you alone."

"Annie, I saw you last night." She tilted her head, puzzled. "At the Corral, I was in the parking lot."

Boy oh boy, did I have her then. Realization played across her lovely features.

"I think you're here for them, not me. You're here for Josh and maybe Wayne and for whoever else is slithering around the Martin farm, which, by the way, is now *my* farm."

"You have it wrong." She was looking at her feet, tapping her hand against her leg. Then she nodded to herself, looked at me, her blue eyes conciliatory. "Look, let's not get into it right now, okay? We have a crew of cops who need coffee." She started glancing around the kitchen. "How do you want to serve it?" It was like she turned the channel inside, and now I was watching a whole different show.

Discomfited, I set out a dozen coffee mugs and got another pot going while Annie went to inform everyone that there was coffee in the kitchen. Connie followed her back into the kitchen and pulled frozen funeral cookies out of the freezer. Daddy's death, the feeder of multitudes.

For the next hour, cops filtered in and out of the kitchen, grabbing cookies and slurping coffee. I marveled how my near death had become their party. I wandered into the hall to find Rae, but looking into the office, I saw she wasn't there. I caught a metallic glint out the window and spied her outside, the sun casting rays off the handcuffs on her belt. She was about one hundred yards from the house, walking with eyes cast to the ground, looking for evidence. Inside the office the cops were gone and so was the jackalope. One piece of taxidermy I wouldn't have to worry about.

Back in the kitchen, I found Connie wrapping up the few remaining cookies. For the first time in my life, I thought she looked old.

"Connie, Annie and I will clean up here. I want you to go home now."

"Those darn cops undid all the work I done in the powder room. I'm glad they're gone." I could see her heart really wasn't into the tidiness of the powder room.

"Well, you have plenty of other days to get the damn thing clean. I never use it, and I won't be having any guests around this week, unless you can count that slob Billy. He wouldn't notice a dying rat twitching in the corner. Take the day, please. It would make me feel better."

"I don't want you alone here…"

"I'll stay with Jill…until she feels safe, Connie." Annie's offer appeared genuine, at least enough so that Connie was appeased. And that's all I really cared about. Connie got her purse, gave me a long hug and a sloppy cheek kiss, and let herself out the side door.

As soon as the door clicked shut behind Connie, I turned to wipe down the counter. Annie's hand slid up my back and onto my shoulder. She pushed me to face her and pressed the small of my back into the counter. She was inches away from me, too deep into my personal space.

"Maybe this isn't perfect timing, but I feel cheated that we didn't get to finish what we started the other night." Annie's eyes were hooded, but her arms around my waist were stiff, reluctant. I nudged her away from me a few inches, feeling claustrophobic. Her perfume smelled cheap to me, probably was cheap.

"Um, I don't think it was *we*, Annie. It was you."

"Do you remember what we once had? Don't tell me it doesn't mean anything to you now. I've watched you over the years. How you look at me."

"Well, maybe for a while I thought about you, maybe a lot even."

"And now?" She was rubbing my belly and kneading her fingernails into me, something she used to do frequently, twenty-three years ago.

"And now the past stays where it belongs. There's nothing but ancient history between us, and that's all, Annie."

She drew back and her hooded eyes opened. The hand on my belly stilled. I logged the emotions passing over her face: disdain, defeat, disappointment, and, finally, anger. Behind her, Rae moved into the doorway. I didn't know how long she had been listening.

"Are you saying you don't want what I'm offering?" Her voice made it sound as if I were making an unforgivable mistake.

"Yeah." I glanced over at Rae's gray inquiring eyes. "Yeah, Annie, I'm going to take a pass on what you're offering." I looked back to Annie. "It's better that way."

"That's the biggest bullshit line I've ever heard." She pushed me away. It was the first time I'd ever heard her swear.

With that, she turned to leave, knocking past Rae, who was watching me now with compassion and admiration. Rae waited in silence until we heard Annie's car door slam and the guttural sound of the car's engine drift away.

"A fine-looking woman you're turning down there, Ms. O'Hara. Is there more to this story that I need to know about?"

"She's nice to look at, Sheriff, but a little too…confusing, for lack of a kinder word. And, yes, there is an old story, a fairy tale for me when

I was young, but I think we just read 'The End' with no 'happily ever after' attached to it."

Rae, lean and groomed in her uniform, stood in that doorway, every lesbian's fantasy. I took the few steps toward her that put me within touching distance and moved my fingers on her full lips.

"So, will you tell me the fairy tale of that luscious scar?"

She grinned, making the scar lift and tempt. "Not much to tell. A street fight. A boot in the mouth…"

"And the owner of the boot?"

"Let's just say the ankle of the foot that belonged in the boot is still walking around with pins in it." Her eyes, growing heavy, bored into me with ferocity. Her hand covered mine, which was still at her mouth, and she licked my palm. Just once.

"Would you like to go upstairs so we can make our own fairy tales in private, Ms. O'Hara?"

"I'd like nothing better, Sheriff. But first, we need to discuss what happened before the shooting this morning. Then you can lick my palm again."

She parked herself on a stool and watched me. I poured each of us some coffee, distracted, knowing we were close to finishing what we'd started in her office the night before. My poor crotch was throbbing in protest at the delay.

"I didn't feel it was a bright idea to tell your deputy everything. Besides, it seemed too much work." Nodding approval, Rae leaned her elbows onto the kitchen counter and kept quiet while I scrambled onto my own stool and told her about the maps and the phone call that interrupted everything. I also told her about the Jerusalem Rocks drawing.

When I concluded, I said, "We can look at those things later when we've completed our other, more interesting, transaction. And I have a question and want an honest answer." She appeared willing to answer anything, but I had to remember she was a cop. "So, did my father show you the maps and drawing?"

Rae shook her head. "All your father told me was that my department could have full access to the Rocks, even though he seemed nervous about it. We sent an investigator out there, but to tell the truth, the formations were too extensive and the weather so uncooperative that we had to postpone further investigations there until we had more manpower and better weather. And your father's drawing, that could just be a nostalgic sketch from some day hiker, your father as a kid, maybe, or even your grandmother."

"I want to go out there and look around," I said, hoping to sound less journalistic and more like a concerned landowner. She didn't fall for it for a second.

"Oh no, I can't let you do that, Jill. Until the area is searched and secured, even you, the owner, can't go to Jerusalem Rocks. I have no idea who or what is out there. You snooping around there could call attention to my investigation or get you hurt."

"Sheriff, are you forbidding me from entering my own property?" She had no idea how she had just challenged me.

"Not forever, just for now." She grinned, stood, stepped toward me, and placed a leg between mine. Her hand snaked around my neck and stroked the underside of my hair. Lips only inches from mine, she said, "I have to make a few phone calls. Reschedule a few things…"

"Time's a-wasting," I said and I ran my tongue along her lower lip. I unclasped the cell phone case from her belt, pulled out the phone, and slid it into her hand. "Make your calls."

I knew that she was attempting to draw my attention away from Jerusalem Rocks. But while she played cop and spoke into her phone, I played journalist and made a mental list of what I needed to visit the Rocks. A story this immense never falls into a reporter's lap. Just as she was compelled to serve and protect, I was compelled to snoop and inform. In the meantime, there was one more compulsion I needed to quench first: getting Prairie View's law enforcement between my legs.

CHAPTER TWENTY-NINE

By the time Rae closed her cell phone, I was so hot for her that I grabbed the front of her belt and dragged her out of the kitchen and upstairs to my room. I was savoring how passive she was, a uniformed woman allowing me to call the shots. When I glanced back at her, her eyes were already glazed and her mouth was open just a little. My guess was she wasn't getting much of this kind of action in Prairie View. This was going to be superb.

I shut the bedroom door and pushed her into the middle of the room. She didn't touch me, but let me take the lead. I stood several inches away from her and gorged myself on the visual feast of Rae. Her height, more pronounced from the effect of the uniform, forced me to look up into her eyes. Her shirt was tight across her chest that was moving her badge up and down double time. Her breathing was labored and erratic. It caught when I reached around her neck and released the black clip that held her hair. I arranged her long, black hair around her shoulders. Then I undid the uniform tie and placed it on the dresser for later possible activities.

I was puzzled by her acquiescence but didn't want to spend time questioning what was happening. I stepped back again to consider my options. There was no way I was going to rush this. It was an unprecedented opportunity. And if I was anything, I was an opportunist.

"I don't know where to start, Sheriff. Everything here looks so delicious. Would you like to suggest what I should taste first?"

"It depends upon what you like for an appetizer, Ms. O'Hara."

"Well, then, I'll peruse the choices."

I placed my left hand on her belt and took my time pacing round her long frame. I played my fingers against the hardware hanging from the belt: gun holster, radio, flashlight, cell phone case, knife sheath, and her handcuffs. I circled my index finger in the *O* of the cuffs. I could feel the wet gathering between my legs and imagined her sumptuous black hair spread across my thighs as she explored me with her tongue. I almost came just thinking about it and found myself rubbing my breasts across her back. I told myself to slow down because I realized we didn't even have our clothes off yet.

"I saw a morsel last night that triggered my appetite, but I didn't get a taste," I said, standing on my toes and moving my lips against the back of her neck.

"And that was?" Rae's voice was strained.

I moved around and unbuckled her belt, loosened the button at the top of her pants, and inched down the zipper. There they were, another pair of black lacy underpants.

"Those," I whispered, "hiding under that staid uniform."

Her eyes were heavy-lidded. Her voice, low and raspy. "Well, they seem to bring results. Are you going to respond like you did last night and fall on your back?"

"Oh, don't think I'm that predictable." I slid my hand into the front of her pants and cupped her on the outside of the moist panties. She started shivering. I pushed aside the material separating my hand from her wetness and ran a middle finger once through her folds, then used it to moisten her mouth.

I was licking her wetness from her open lips when I said, "Delectable appetizer. Perfectly prepared with a hint of salt and Chardonnay."

Rae was panting. She gave up on passivity, grabbed my waist, and pulled me into her, kissing me hotly, blending our moans. I explored her tongue as it rhythmically pushed into my mouth. My crotch pushed into her leg in time with her tongue.

"Time for the main course, Ms. O'Hara."

"Call me Jill and you'll get dessert." Our lips were an inch apart.

We both stepped back and kicked off our shoes. I unbuttoned the top of her shirt while she loosened my pullover from my jeans. When her hand touched my belly, I felt an unexpected wash of moisture between my legs and knew this would seep through my pants. I kept loosening her shirt buttons, exposing, to my delight, a matching bra. This girl knew what a woman liked.

"Is that standard issue for sheriff uniforms? If so, sign me up."

"Hmm, only when the sheriff has special duty. And I am a dutiful woman." She freed the button at the top of my jeans, lowered the zipper, and fell onto her knees. If this was duty, I was all for it.

She licked my belly just under my navel while she pulled my pants over my hips and down to the floor. I watched her rub her face into my sodden panties, an intoxicating sight, as her long fingers kneaded my ass. I pushed myself into her, a silent plea for her to remove the flimsy panties. Instead, she pressed her tongue into the fabric and against my swollen clit, causing me to gasp and thrust.

She stood, nostrils flaring, eyes determined and dilated. "Get on the bed," she ordered, leaving no room for disobedience. Wonderful, I had found myself a top, right there in good old Prairie View.

I edged around the mission-style bed frame, kicking away my jeans. "I need for you to take off your pants. I want to see more of you," I said as I sat on the bed. "Let me help."

She hesitated, then stepped in front of me and allowed me to push her uniform pants down her endless legs to the floor. The aroma of her arousal besotted me and I heard myself groan. I leaned forward and kissed the front of her as if I were tongue-kissing her mouth. She was swollen under the thin, wet silk and I longed to take her into my mouth without fabric separating us. Her breath was coming in short gasps, and she rocked herself against my tongue.

She grabbed my shoulders and shoved me onto my back, leaving my legs hanging over the bedside. Back on her knees again, she grabbed my underpants in both hands and ripped them apart, heedless that they were a pricey item. I was ecstatic.

"Stay there," she commanded. I watched her remove her panties and finish unbuttoning her shirt without removing it. Her hair was wild around her shoulders as she bent over me to pull off my shirt and bra. The sight of her unbuttoned shirt, revealing perfect silk-cupped breasts and glistening wetness between her legs, undid me. She straddled one of my thighs and rubbed her engorged sex in a rhythm that was hers, never looking away from my eyes. "Touch me now," she gasped. Her hands were holding her up on either side of my head.

I put my hand between her burning folds and my thigh, finding her distended and ready. She cried out and moved faster on my hand. In a few seconds, she came all over me, gushing fluids. Just when she was ending her orgasm, I pushed two fingers inside her. My thrust made her come again. I never saw anything so sexy as Rae, bending over me, climaxing and moaning.

She fell to her knees in front of me, breathless. Grabbing my rear and pulling me toward her, she used her shoulders to nudge and spread me wide. Without preamble, she took me with her mouth. Her savage tongue plunged into every valley and crevice. I could feel it searching, plundering, savoring. When it settled on my pleading clit, her tongue pulsated while she sucked me. Then she slammed three long fingers into me and I went over. My contractions around her fingers drew the orgasm out into one long scream.

She wasn't done. Grabbing me beneath my limp arms, she pulled me to the middle of the bed, then to the top, resting my head on the pillows. Again, she spread my legs as wide as they would go and rose up on her knees in front of me. "Hold on to the bed and don't let go," she said.

With her fingers, she opened her lower lips and placed her dripping center on my already excited clit. With small, precise movements, our wet, hard centers touching, she brought both of us to another climax, first her and in seconds, me. She fell on top of me, winded and shuddering. I closed my eyes and reveled in the kisses she covered my face and neck with. I realized they were the kind of kisses given a lover, not a one-night fling. They were sublime and I welcomed them.

"You're exquisite," she whispered several times. Her hair brushed my neck and collarbone.

"That was the hottest thing I have ever experienced," I told her. It was true.

We rested, eyes closed. Minutes later, I felt her move off me and heard the clinking of something metal. Then I felt her kissing my left arm, moving it above my head while she licked. I opened blurry eyes to see hands moving so fast I couldn't catch what they were doing. But I felt cold metal around my wrist and heard two clicks. I focused my eyes enough to see that she'd handcuffed me to the wooden slat in the head board.

"Don't be afraid, but I have to keep you safe," she whispered in my ear and she got off the bed. She was buttoning up her shirt. Her eyes were pleading and guilty. "You mean more to me than you know." She glanced at my bedside phone. "It's unplugged, sorry."

"What? What are you doing?" She was gathering her clothes, belt, and shoes.

She moved to the doorway. Her mouth was resolute, but her eyes were filled with regret. "Forgive me. I can't let you interfere or get hurt." She was gone.

"What the fuck? Rae! Don't leave me!"

I pled for a few minutes but heard the front door slam, her car start, and the crunch of the gravel in the driveway.

"Fuck!"

CHAPTER THIRTY

It took me a several minutes to calm myself and assess my predicament. The strange thing was that I wasn't raving mad at Rae. Oh, I was angry about her tactic of locking me to the bed, but I was a lot to blame. I had told her I wanted to go to Jerusalem Rocks to poke around and she said I couldn't. She was a cop and knew reporters well enough to not trust my obedience to her orders, regardless of the fact we had just made love.

Made love. Yeah, this felt like more than a hump and run, despite the handcuff cutting into my wrist. I even grinned at that point and offered rueful admiration to her resourcefulness. I pulled myself into a sitting position, trying to keep my left arm from cramping. I noticed a bite mark at the top of my breast.

"She could have lied to me and said nothing of importance is going on up at the Rocks," I said to the walls.

It was getting darker in the room as late afternoon was passing by. I knew Rae would release me when she felt it was safe, meaning she would free me when it was too late for me to get the story.

I wanted to get up to Jerusalem Rocks and find the location on the drawing in my father's office. I knew those formations as well as anyone and knew there were caves in the Rocks. Daddy would never let me go in them when I was a kid. But I remembered they were located at the west end of the Rocks. A little climbing around and I'd find them. I was willing to bet Ms. Amazon Cop didn't even know where the caves were.

"She doesn't really think I'd just lie here and nap." I pouted, watching the green light blinking on Rae's uniform tie left on my dresser. The green light. Blink. Blink. "My cell phone!" It was lying next to Rae's tie, its on light reflecting off the metal clip.

I glanced at my cuffed wrist and started planning my movements. Because I was buck naked, there was nothing dignified in what I had to do next. I hoped I was strong enough. I slid off the bed to my right and flopped over on my stomach. I grabbed a headboard slat with my trapped left hand. I planted both feet on the floor and used the strength in my legs and right arm to push the entire bed toward the dresser. It was excruciating, and I was a little embarrassed at the thought of my bare hiney pushed into the air. But I wasn't one to stand on decorum when faced with a challenge.

It took a full thirty minutes for me to inch that massive bed across the wood floor. I would push the bed an inch, then flop facedown and rest, then repeat. I knew the floor was damaged by the screeches every time the bed moved. I had no idea how I would explain that to Connie. During each rest, I cussed Rae and I made a mental list of items to pack in my car for the trip to Jerusalem Rocks.

The last several pushes, I was too tired to even look at my progress. Then, to my relief, because it butted the dresser, the bed couldn't move any farther. But then, neither could I. I lay there shaking, my body half off the bed, face buried in the covers. I felt the fabric beneath my face dampen with tears and drool. I was mortified at having been cuffed to a bed by my lover, left naked to fend for myself, and spending all my energy pushing several hundred pounds across the floor. Well, by the time the tears stopped, I was just plain pissed off. Pissed off and determined.

I crawled back onto the bed and stretched my right arm to the dresser. "Fuck!" I screamed. My arms were too short. "Goddamn you to hell, Rae Terabian!"

I stopped straining and sat for a moment to review my options and to get the cramp out of my left shoulder. Then it was clear what I had to do. It was crude but simple. I lay down on the bed. I blessed my yoga teacher as I stretched my cuffed arm straight above me and reached my left foot to the top of the dresser. My heel rooted around for the cell phone. I felt it. Then I rested my heel on top of the phone, careful not to use so much weight as to damage it. With a quick backward jerk, the phone shot off the dresser and onto the bed, right at the base of my butt.

I reached between my exhausted legs, snatched the phone, flipped it open, and speed-dialed Billy.

"Well, I guess you're over the assassination attempt," he said instead of saying hello.

"No jokes right now, I need you." I heard my voice trembling and took a breath to calm it. I didn't want Billy to think me overly rattled. I just wanted him to get me free from the bed and then leave me alone. If he thought me upset, he would stay with me all night, if necessary, until I was composed. Given my current situation, it would take all my dramatic abilities to convince him to leave me alone for the evening. I wanted to be at the Rocks before dawn.

"You need me? Why? To process your close encounter with the law?"

"What do you mean?"

"I mean, dearie, that I went to your house as soon as Connie called to tell me you'd been shot at and that the jackalope got the worst of it. I thought you'd need some male energy, you know. Protection? A shoulder? But what do I hear upon entering? Humma humma sounds from the peanut gallery. And the only car in front of your house was the sheriff's cruiser. I'm not betting that one of her manly-kinda-men deputies was upstairs giving you a strong shoulder."

"Shit," I muttered. I didn't need this now.

"That's not what you were screaming when I walked in. It was more along the lines of appealing for salvation from the deity."

"Look, now's not the time. I'll fill you in later. Right now I need for you to get here fast. You do have a house key, right?"

"Your dad kept every spare key right here in the office. What do you need?"

"I need for you to go into the garage, unlock his tool cabinet, get the electric Sawzall, and come up to my room." I'm sure he heard my veiled panic.

"Sweetie, are you okay?"

"I will be when you get here with the Sawzall. Oh, and for God's sake, keep this to yourself."

"As if. But don't worry, babe, I'm on my way." He hung up and I knew I was going to be fine.

Half an hour later, after suffering a few sniggers and verbal jabs at my unclad condition, I explained to Billy about Rae's concern that

I'd interfere with an investigation. He graciously turned his back as I dressed.

"And, of course, you are going to heed her oh-so-obvious warning and stay home, right?" His light tone was belied by his tense shoulders.

"Billy, I think it's pretty clear that I'm not welcome in her work. So, yeah, I'll stay here and get some sleep tonight. Today was tough." I was rubbing my wrist where it had been rubbed raw, first from moving the bed and then from Billy's rough but efficient work of sawing off the cuff.

"Well, that kind of tough we should all have. That sheriff is a no-slouch woman. Unfortunately, I'm not convinced that a girl who leaves her girl cuffed to a bed is something to sink your teeth into. But I have no idea what little kinkies you favor, honey, and choose not to think about it."

"Fine, my girly-man, you just put those thoughts out of your pretty head. Leave me to have an evening of rest and I'll call you tomorrow. I promise." I could tell he was unconvinced, but I also knew he had his tables running that night and was still breaking in his new front man. He was a loyal bastard but he was also a businessman. My father had made an excellent choice in Billy. Billy left about twenty minutes later, after making sure the house was sealed tight in defense against another attack.

CHAPTER THIRTY-ONE

I spent the evening gathering what I needed for scouting Jerusalem Rocks. From my father's office, I packed the maps and the enigmatic drawing of rock formations. For superstitious reasons, I grabbed the silly little Ruger .22 Bearcat and its box of bullets. I wanted Grandma with me in some form and figured her pistol was the tough side of her I might need.

I bagged a variety of portable food from the kitchen: granola bars, fruit, cookies, chocolate, and a couple bottles of water. From the storage room: a decrepit frame backpack, sleeping bag, thermal blanket, flashlight, folding hunter's knife, small first aid kit, and safety goggles to protect my eyes from the stinging wind.

And then came the hard part. My father's digital outdoor thermometer read forty-two degrees and the wind was blowing. I required warm clothes and hadn't brought enough from Seattle. I needed to go into Daddy's bedroom and find warm things that would come close to fitting me. Connie and I had avoided that room so far, and I had hoped to continue to do so indefinitely. Somebody, Connie I presumed, had closed his bedroom door and, by unspoken consent, it remained closed. Each of us was waiting for the other to broach the subject of cleaning it out. We were both avoidance queens, and I assumed I had a good year or two before facing that heartbreaking project.

While I lingered in the kitchen, postponing my entry into my father's bedroom by eating toast and drinking hot chocolate, I obsessed about the reasons Rae had not come back to free me. Did I read her wrong? Was she off somewhere chortling over her sadistic trick? Did she simply forget me? Was she too busy and reluctant to send someone else to witness my pathetic circumstances? I remembered the look in her eyes as she left. She appeared convinced she would be back and felt terrible about leaving me there. Okay, so where was she? Forcing my questions to rest for the time being, I headed toward Daddy's bedroom.

The door hadn't been opened in weeks, probably since Connie chose the suit he wore to his funeral. When I opened the door, a blast of bedroom odors assaulted me. Used sheets, hair oil, socks, and his pipe tobacco. The air was close and fetid. Holding my breath, I moved to open a window but remembered that standing close to a window wasn't the safest idea and worse now that it was dark. Instead, I swung the door back and forth several times to fan a few whiffs of fresh air into the room.

It was a large, masculine room, just like his office, furnished with heavy mahogany dressers and night tables. Bedside lamps with various ranch brands on the shades occupied each side of the bed. Only in this room, there was no taxidermy. That relieved me. The idea of a dead animal in a dead man's bedroom gave me the willies. Everything was as if he were downstairs, watching TV before going to bed. I was nine years old again, Harriet the Spy, sneaking into his private space, searching for clues. I have no idea what clues I was looking for back then, but I'm sure I overlooked most of the good ones.

I waited in the middle of the room for the grief to press like a compactor. For whatever reason, I was spared the impact for the moment. All I felt was mournful longing. I realized that longing is one of the leavening ingredients in the grief recipe. Okay, I could live with longing. In fact, it was familiar. There it was, the sure knowledge that this loss, too, I would survive.

"Shit, Daddy, you have to help me. I can feel you around." And I did. He was with me, in the unknowable but palpable form the dead take. His presence soothed me and I calmed to the point where I could enter his walk-in closet and take stock of his clothes. Because I knew he was present, my heart didn't break. I knew it would another day, but not just then. To the left hung all his jackets and coats. I reached for his old Carhartt insulated hunting jacket, faded amber with green corduroy cuffs and collar. It had lots of pockets and the sleeves would be easy to roll up to accommodate my shorter arms. Plus, there was a hidden inside pocket for a handgun. I intended to fill it.

I rummaged through Dad's drawers, found his thermal underwear, and chose a fitted insulated pullover. I took off my bra for comfort and pulled the shirt on, making my breasts feel cozy and protected. His pants and socks were too big, but I had my own. I found one of his winter sweaters, a dorky blue and white wool job with elk and snowflakes. I knew I'd keep that one for myself, oversized and comfortable.

After I found the knit hat that matched the sweater, I was ready to seal off the bedroom for the time being. But an impulse sent me to the bedside table where I opened the top drawer, knowing what was there. My father was a consummate self-defense nut. Set out like an artist's tableau was a lovely Glock 36 along with its hand-tooled holster, belt, and two boxes of ammunition. I hefted and aimed the gun, noticing it was a little imbalanced for me but not unusable. Before snapping it into the holster, I checked to make sure the magazine was loaded. It was. I shoved the rest of the weighty ammo into a jacket pocket.

In the front hallway, I assembled and packed everything. I made sure I wore layers of clothes so that I could face the unpredictable northern Montana temperatures.

I kept the Glock and bullets in the jacket. I decided I would keep Grandma's little Ruger with me on the Murano console. Using the hallway phone, I called Billy, knowing he was working his tables and not answering his personal cell. I wanted to leave a message and not talk to him.

"Hey, it's me," I said after his outgoing message. "Listen, I want you to do me a favor. I'm going on an errand and won't be back until tomorrow afternoon. If I'm not around by supper, I'm probably in a little trouble. In that case, call the sheriff and tell her that I disobeyed her orders and need help. I know what you're thinking, but really, she can be trusted. That whole bed thing, it was her trying to protect me. Just call her, okay? I'm going to explore some property. Don't worry." Fat chance of that, I figured as I ended the call.

The hallway clock sounded midnight. "Time to head out," I said to the stuffed pheasant mounted next to the office door. He didn't blink.

CHAPTER THIRTY-TWO

The wind was wicked. Gusting to forty miles per hour, it belted the SUV every few miles, compelling me to grip the steering wheel to keep from lurching into the ditch. Typical Hi-Line weather, all the glorious stars carpeting the sky, but it's impossible to stand outside and gaze at them.

Jerusalem Rocks lay a few rugged miles outside the minuscule border-crossing town of Sweetgrass, thirty miles due north of Prairie View. There was no way I could drive the Murano to the Rocks because there were no trees or cover for the car. So I had to chance leaving the car in Sweetgrass and hike to the Rocks without being discovered by the Border Patrol or any of the Martin minions.

There was a notorious bar/hotel called the Glocca Morra Inn nestled at the edge of Sweetgrass. Its reputation rose and fell with each change in ownership. The Glocca Morra was used by folks stuck at the border for legal reasons. It was also frequented by drug and arms dealers who imagined they were unnoticed by the authorities. In actuality, there weren't enough authorities to police the border, so they let the less threatening offenders go about their offensive business. I was sure my old boyfriend Mike had conducted plenty of drug business while swigging Budweisers at the smoke-hazed bar.

There were a dozen vehicles in the bar parking lot, most of them pickups or fat American cars. I knew my Murano would be out of place, but hoped the Border Patrol would think I was one of the few guests at the inn upstairs. I parked in a central location, figuring it would look less shifty to curious eyes. Then I put on the Glock-heavy jacket and slipped the little loaded Ruger into the other front pocket with its box of bullets. I felt like a bandito. I snugged the knit hat onto my head and over my ears, climbed out of the car, and opened the rear end to retrieve my backpack. The *thump-thump* of the bar's jukebox was faint over the wind racket.

With the sleeping bag, the backpack weighed a little over twenty pounds and I thanked my yoga instructor for harping about weight-bearing exercise. I pulled the folded hunting knife from the pack and zipped it into an inside jacket pocket.

I hefted the pack onto my back, adjusted the straps and waist belt, checked my left coat pocket for the flashlight, slid on some outsized wool gloves, and faced southwest, considering Jerusalem Rocks. Already wind tears were jerked out of the corners of my eyes, their icy track angling into my hair. Soon I'd need the ski goggles, but I wanted to wait. I found any kind of eye protection disturbing because of what it did to my peripheral vision.

I had two choices, bushwhack cross country to avoid being seen or travel the faster level road but risk being seen. I chose the latter, assuming I could spot approaching headlights in time to duck into the roadside gullies. Besides, after leaving the main road, I remembered the road to the Rocks was basically washed out ruts that would have no middle-of-the-night travelers…I hoped.

I stepped onto the paved Loop Road, bending against the vicious wind and cursed the Hi-Line gods for their merciless treatment of the land's dwellers. I figured it was some gods of the Blackfeet Tribe, whose reservation lay to the west, taking out their just due on the foolish white people who thought they could capture this place.

Only once, while slogging down Loop Road, did I have to dive into the ditch. A military type of cargo truck went by and, by the red glints from cigarettes in the covered back, I could tell it was carrying people. Interesting. And, as far as I could tell, I wasn't spotted.

The going got far rougher when I moved onto the ruts leading to Jerusalem Rocks. The stars gave enough light that I knew where I was and could discern the course of the road, but it was impossible to see all the potholes. More than once, I stumbled into an oversized hole and was grateful I'd bought those hiking boots in Great Falls. With every stumble, the wind attempted to knock me on my butt, and I finally strapped on the goggles and then cussed myself for not having done it sooner. Now I could look around without squinting out the wind. I thought about using the flashlight to ferret out potholes but reckoned it was too risky if there were any lookouts at the Rocks.

Two grueling hours after leaving the Glocca Morra, I could make out tips of the bizarre shapes of Jerusalem Rocks eerily outlined in the faint moonlight. Time to be on alert. I found a large lichen-encrusted rock and crouched behind it to give me time to think this through and reflect on the terrain I was about to enter.

The Rocks were the artwork of northern Montana's wind. Eons of the wind's fingers carving and molding, had created her secret garden in an area no one cared about. A Dr. Seuss land consisting of hundreds of giant café table shapes, some straight and tall, others leaning drunken and squat. In between them were little alleyways, byways, and dead ends. It was a fascinating wonderland for both kids and adults. My grandfather bought the property to keep it from being developed. Not that there was ever a developer within a hundred miles of this site, but Hi-Liners viewed their land as desirable real estate. Bless their naïve hearts.

The formation wound along a ridge in an east-to-west strip, a few miles long and about fifty yards wide. The northern side, the side I was on, was flat, rocky table land. The southern edge of the formation dropped into cliffs, in some places seventy feet, less in others. That was the side my father would warn us about when I was a kid. It would be easy to tumble over given the loose stone and dirt. I remembered standing over those drop-offs, gazing over the alkali flats far below and doing the kid thing, thinking I could fly off that edge.

Once inside the Rocks, it was almost impossible to be detected unless you climbed on top of a sandstone café table, for lack of a better description, and waved your arms. Not likely in my case. So all I needed was to get into the Rocks and move west, sliding around and under formations. I knew the area of the rocks probably used by the Martins was at the far west end of the formations, where caves had formed from a million years of gouging wind and blizzards.

I was leaving the sanctuary of my rock when headlights appeared, moving toward my position. I crouched low, praying nothing would glint off my pack and call attention to me. When it was about forty feet away, the pickup slowed almost to a stop. I inched off my glove and reached into my outside pocket. Curling my fingers around the grip of the little Ruger, I felt remorse for earlier discounting its protective value.

For thirty seconds my heart didn't beat. The wind was nothing but backdrop against the sound of that engine. Then crunch, grind, and the driver put the truck in four-wheel drive and moved on.

"Shit!" I whispered to the sagebrush next to me.

When I peeked out to watch the truck head toward the Rocks, I could tell there were three people in the cab. I could also tell it was the same truck Josh Martin was driving when he left the Corral a few nights earlier.

I watched to see where they went into the formation and, as I predicted, they went to the west end of the Rocks before the truck dipped somewhere out of view. Now was the time to go.

The ground between the Rocks and me had few barriers, meaning no cover, so I crouched and scampered as best I could considering the wind and unwieldy backpack. A few times I tripped and skinned my knees on the flinty ground. Once, when I stood up, my pant leg stuck to my knee, telling me I was cut. Every step rubbed my pant leg on the knee scrape. Nothing I could do about it then, so I continued until I crossed into the boundaries of the formation. There, the wind torture subsided a little because of the protection from the Rocks.

The Rocks were full of rounded cubbies, protection from the wind, places to squeeze into and play house, or hide from bad guys. I pulled off my pack and scrambled into one such cubby, making sure I was facing away from the west end. I inspected my ripped jeans and pulled apart the tear to look at my knee using the flashlight. No open cut, just a bleeding scrape. Lucky. Using gauze from the first aid kit, I cleaned the blood away and taped the largest pad over the wound. I didn't think the bandage would last very long, but it would suffice to stop the bleeding.

I piled through the pack again and pulled out the folded maps and the drawing of a formation. I took a few minutes to study the drawing, cupping the flashlight beam with my hand. The drawing included two of the sandstone café tables, but one on the left had a smaller one sticking out of the top of it. Unusual. The formation of the right looked like lots of other café tables, but then I saw it. A faded penciled arrow on the far right, parallel to the right café table. It pointed down, into nowhere.

I wasn't going to move any farther until dawn, not wanting to call attention to myself with a roving flashlight. I released the sleeping bag from the frame of the pack, unfurled it, removed my shoes, and crawled in. Hiding the Glock inside the sleeping bag and placing the Ruger on the rock within reach, I felt safe. I also prayed for truth to the legend of no rattlers at Jerusalem Rocks. With my arm pillowing my head, I closed my eyes and waited for daybreak. The wind cried around the café tabletops while starlight spilled between them. I was lulled into sleep.

Chapter Thirty-three

A screeched grind of metal on metal woke me. Before I moved, I reminded myself of where I was and why the hell my upper arm was in roiling pain. I forced myself to keep from yelping as I inched it from under my head. An equally agonizing lump was under my lower rib. Feeling for it, I realized the Glock had drifted underneath me during the night.

"Ah jeez, sometimes I'm such a loser," I said to myself, then realized I'd better keep my noise level down. But sleeping on top of a loaded gun was not a brilliant career move.

Something odd was happening, so I quit the self-recriminations to pay attention and listen. No wind. But there were meadowlarks and truck engines. I sat up and concentrated on the trucks. More than one, that was for sure. And some of them had to gear down. So that explained the sounds that woke me.

I was certain nobody could see me because once inside the complicated Rocks, you could only be discovered if someone walked right up on you. I heard no footsteps. The trucks sounded like they were traveling the same route as the pickup from the night before. I'd wait until the sounds stopped before exploring.

I felt safe enough to down half a bottle of water, eat a granola bar and a blackened banana. By this point, I had to pee in the extreme. I wanted to move several feet away to do so and figured it would be a good time to do some initial reconnaissance.

Keeping to a crouch, I inched around some of the sandstone café tables, dropped my drawers, and took relief.

Just as I was finishing up, voices and footsteps thumped toward me. I had never been so compromised. Squatting with my pants around my knees, I prayed to every deity that I wouldn't be discovered and I wouldn't have a heart attack.

It came to me that they were walking along the outside edge of the formation and if I didn't move, including pulling up my pants, they probably wouldn't see me.

They were arguing. At first it was incomprehensible, then…

"Your guys don't get it. My people only take orders from me. They don't trust you foreigners, and they think you work for me. We gotta keep them thinking that or this whole thing will fall to shit." I was almost sure it was Josh Martin.

"You people get all money from our people. We can't help it you not understand that. We go with plan. You follow us or we go without you." The accent was not European or Hispanic.

Then a third voice spoke, not in English. I'd heard that language before. It was odd, singular but familiar at the same time.

"What's he saying?" demanded the Josh-sounding voice.

"We go as planned. Running out of time. No more stalls. Our leader…" The voices angled off to the west and became indistinct under the twinkle of meadowlark calls.

Still in the embarrassing squatting position, I waited several minutes until my calves and thighs begged for a change. With ginger, tottering movements, I arranged my pants and crept toward the edge of the Rocks. I could see nothing and made the decision to climb atop one of the stumpier stone café tables, at the same time realizing I had left my binoculars in the glove compartment of the Murano.

I edged around several formations before I found one that had climbing access. Being aware of my bandaged knee, I crawled and climbed atop the rock just in time to see another military-style cargo truck move from east to west across the path I had taken into the rocks during the night.

"What the hell? Do they have an entire army out here?" I said under my breath.

Then I remembered something that pissed me off. They were on my property! The whole thing, the Martin "township" and this, this…whatever it was, was all taking place on my land. My Montana landowner gene kicked in. I had to talk myself out of just tromping over there and firing a gun over their heads, screaming, "Git the hell off my land!" Thankful my reporter's instincts to get a story kept me planted on that rock, I pondered what I had heard in the earlier conversation.

It probably didn't matter in the moment, but I was baffled by the accent of the English-speaking foreigner and the language of the non-English speaker. I've traveled in more countries than I can count in one sitting. Language interpreters were some of my most valued assistants. I'd heard that language before, a unique kind of Arabic, tinged with something else. What was it?

I turned on my back and let the morning sun warm my face as I relaxed into memories of my Arabic interpreters. I could hear one voice, a woman's, moaning and whispering in my ear. We were alone in a bathhouse and I was taking her under the cover of water. I could feel my fingers sliding in her as she murmured in Arabic and…French. Morocco. That was it. The foreign men with the Martins were Moroccan. I was disappointed with myself that I didn't figure it out sooner. But I did get to relive an enticing little memory of that public bathhouse in Morocco. Who said quickies never pay off?

I shinnied down the rock and crouched back to my small "camp." As I gathered my stuff and rearranged my pack, I reviewed what I knew about Moroccans and terrorism. I was pretty sure that one 9/11 hijacker was Moroccan. I also knew there was rampant extremist recruitment occurring in several Moroccan cities juxtaposed with a Moroccan monarchy that was friendly to the United States. So these guys, as far as I knew, were operating without the sanction of their government. Therefore, the "leader" I heard mentioned might or might not have been Moroccan. Probably an international terrorist group but, considering their interest in the ballistic missiles of Montana, well funded and highly organized. Way over the Martins' heads.

I was cooked if they caught me. Beheaded on videotape. They loved icing reporters.

CHAPTER THIRTY-FOUR

After almost an hour of creeping west within the formation, I came upon a cliff dropping at least forty feet. Beneath the cliff, secreted by yet more formations, were a half dozen vehicles, mostly pickups and jeeps, but one cargo truck was there, too. I hunched behind a stone and waited several minutes to see if I had been spotted. No response to my presence. Lucky again. I slid off the pack and resigned myself to spying on the enemy without any backup plan except the call I'd made to Billy the night before. I started to worry he would barrel out here to get me and end up in deep trouble with the folks below me.

I looked around and found what felt like a safe observation point. Holding the Glock in one hand, I braced myself on my belly and elbows to watch the proceedings below.

Everyone was armed with assault weapons slung over their backs and holsters stuffed with high-caliber pistols. There was lots of activity. Several sweating men were moving various sized boxes into the pickups. Most of the boxes looked to contain weapons and their accoutrements. Some of the men were taking orders in Arabic. Others took orders in English. There was tense strain on all the players' faces and their movements were delivered with calculated speed. It appeared that the armaments were coming from a cave located below me to the right. I couldn't see its entrance, but gauging from the number of people moving in and out and what they were carrying, the entrance had to be fairly large.

To the right of the activity, I saw a primitive road that was the access for all those vehicles. From my vantage point, it appeared to loop around the western end of the formation, probably making a hair-raising ride for anyone determined to drive down there.

When all the trucks were full of the weapons crates, most of the men piled into the back of the cargo truck. Others took up driver positions in other vehicles. Then they waited. Ten minutes. Fifteen minutes. No movement. No talking. Just ironic meadowlark cheerfulness and a pungent aroma of sage, dirt, and gasoline.

Perspiration trickled down the faces of the men I could still see. They were scared and I was in no better shape. The sun was burning the back of my neck and sweat crawled through the roots of my hair. As I was reaching back to touch my scalding neck, three figures emerged from the cave entrance beneath me. A fatigue-attired, dark-haired man—Josh Martin. And Sheriff Rae Terabian.

"Jesus!" I gasped. And I dropped the goddamn Glock.

For a few seconds in slow motion, then picking up speed to tip over the edge, the Glock skittered and hopped down the cliff. Little puffs of dust punctuated each bounce just before it landed ten feet from Rae's feet. They were all looking at me.

Rae's face was a mask of fury. With one shout, the dark man lifted a finger and the cargo truck emptied. They were coming after me.

I scurried out of there heading east, back through to the formations. The rocks would give me cover, but I had little hope of escaping twelve determined men. It would take them four or five minutes, using that rough road, to get to where they saw me. My guess was some would circle round on the level ground and head me off, others following me. All the rock cubbies were wide-mouthed, useless for hiding.

While gripping the little Ruger still in my pocket, I kept moving, considering all options. None of them was promising. I was getting winded and realized I was still carrying the weighty Glock ammo. I needed to dump it without leaving a trail. For several minutes, I continued winding east, listening for footsteps, searching in vain for a place to hide. At one point, I heard a whistle but it sounded as if it came from where I left my pack. The bastards had my chocolate. With that thought, I let out a soft sob. Not about the chocolate, about Rae. The rage on her face.

I had to rest for a moment, so I plopped onto my knees like a petulant child. Tears spilled down my cheeks. I wiped them away with my sleeve and I looked up. There it was. The formation from the picture, exactly as it was drawn. The little table-shaped rock was still there on the left, sitting on top of a bigger one. To the far right, where the arrow in the old drawing was…air. It was a cliff. "Something's down there," I whispered.

I heard cloth scraping rock and boots scuffing across dirt. They were on me. I scrambled up and moved toward the same place where the arrow was in the picture. There was only one option. Without looking over the cliff or looking behind my back, I stepped over the ledge.

❖

My feet immediately struck loose rock and dirt and tore from under me. I cracked hard on my tailbone, then slid on my rear and lower back toward a giant sagebrush. I grappled for stability, but my left palm tore open on a jagged rock. I choked back a wail as my feet struck the base of the sage. I pushed myself underneath the huge bush and curled into a motionless fetal position. Squeezing my eyes closed and emitting soft grunts of pain and panic, I waited for bullets to come zinging at me. Nothing.

Agonizing pain in my clenched left hand brought me to my senses. I realized I was unconsciously holding it with my right hand. Blood was oozing between my fingers. I opened them to see a vicious two-inch gash through the pad at my thumb base. In one of my many jacket pockets was a red bandana, and I had to focus through the pain to remember which pocket. Too much movement could call attention to me. So would a red bandana.

"Fuck," I whimpered.

After several seconds of black despair and pain, I pulled myself together by pacing my breath. I checked my surroundings and hoped the heavy sage was adequate cover for the moment. There were tiny animal bones littering the ground around me, meaning this was a place coyotes dined on their prey. My blood dripping into the ground would have their interest for a few days. I was relieved to remember they're nocturnal beasts.

The blood was probably cleaning the wound for me since I didn't have any water. I brushed away any other debris from around the cut and dug in pockets until I found the bandana. To stop the blood flow, I had to risk using it. I wrapped the bandana around the base of my thumb several times, using my right hand and teeth to tie it off. I held the hand aloft by wrapping it around my neck behind my head, away from view. It was time to chew over my options.

Whoever was after me didn't see me go off the cliff. A few times I'd catch the glint of a gun as one of my hunters stepped to the edge of the Rocks to scan the ground below, but none came out directly above me. They were still looking. I also knew that I was holding up their operation. However, they couldn't just forget about me. I was a dangerous wild card in their carefully organized strategy. They would probably leave a few to hunt me and the rest would go on with their plan. I also reckoned one of them would walk the base of the cliff, to see if I'd found a way down. I was lying right in that path.

"Okay then, what was that arrow for?" I said.

The drawing was still in my jacket pocket, so I pulled it out again. It rendered no new information. I studied the base of the cliff I'd hurled myself from. I was dazed that I'd done something so crazy. A glint to my right and up about twenty feet caught my attention. A light greenish bottle lay at the base of the cliff I'd jumped. Next to the bottle rested a giant boulder, probably as tall as a large man. From my angle, the shape mimicked a rough arrowhead. Behind the boulder tangled several sizable sage plants pushing themselves against the base of the cliff.

My researcher's instincts fitted the arrow in the drawing, the bottle on the ground, and the giant rock together into a near-completed puzzle. A cave was behind that rock, maybe an old bootlegger's stash. It was no time to dither. I got the hunting knife out of the zipped pocket of my jacket and sawed off a branch of the sage. After I swept over the blood-drenched dirt under where I'd wrapped my hand, I checked the cliffs for any activity from my hunters. All quiet. I needed about twenty seconds to cover my tracks using the sage branch and scurry behind the arrowhead rock.

"Okay, Jilly-girl, stay focused. Don't screw this up," I said. "One…two…three…go."

I scrambled from under the bush, held my injured hand to my chest, and crept backward toward the arrowhead rock. As I moved, I whisked away my tracks with the sage branch, praying I wasn't missing anything. The rock slammed against my back, and I edged around it and pushed into the stiff, scratchy sage. Parting the resistant sage with my shoes and good hand, I spied my goal. A hole, hidden by the sage, the size of small refrigerator, in the cliff side. I took the Ruger in my right hand and the flashlight in my throbbing left. The sage grabbed at my legs as if trying to hold me back. Whispering another prayer that the no-rattlers myth held true, I entered the cave.

Damn, it was dark. Because my eyes had just been in the sun, even with the flashlight, the cave was blinding black. So I waited and listened. No rattles. No hissing. But there was a moist gurgling growl. It was coming from my left. My flashlight caught two lit dots several feet from me. Varmint eyes. An animal with a stripe from its nose down its back. No skunk because there was no smell, except something acrid and sweet.

"Oh hell, a badger," I muttered to the beast.

It was baring its nasty little teeth at me while scrabbling its two-inch claws in the dirt. That explained why there were no snakes in the cave. Badgers were the meanest little animals on the Hi-Line, maybe anywhere. And they were unpredictable, attacking only if they felt like sparing the time. This particular badger was about twenty pounds, implying he could back off a coyote, wolf, or small bear. Snakes were a source of sporting entertainment for him, appetizers. There was a bit of fur, blood, and bone near his claws, telling me he'd just lunched. At least he wasn't hungry.

I couldn't shoot it for fear of calling attention to myself. So I did the only thing I could do. I turned off the flashlight. I inched my injured hand inside my coat, unsure how well the badger could smell my blood. Then I waited, not moving. The light in the cave, filtered by the sagebrush, was finally sufficient for me to see. The badger was making indignant puffs out its nostrils but wasn't baring its teeth anymore. We each waited to see what the other would do.

While standing motionless, I heard the *clump clump* of boots passing by the arrowhead rock. The badger's head jerked at the noise. Sweat trickled down my neck and my legs.

The badger lunged. Brushed against me, and zipped out the cave entrance. A man's yelp mingled with growls and the tearing of fabric. I heard panicked Arabic and scuffling outside. Then a gunshot, silence, footsteps running, with uneven cadence, to the west. I hoped the badger made it with some ankle flesh as a dessert.

I dropped the pistol and flashlight and sank to my knees. I cradled my bloody excruciating hand and rocked back and forth in agony, relief, and gratitude. Nobody was going to look for me in an area where badgers prowled. For a while, I was safe. I waited for the fear and pain to diminish a few notches and took a few conscious breaths to dispel dizziness.

I needed to take stock of the cave, but I was reluctant to leave the entrance area. So I flipped on the flashlight and scanned the cavern. The back of my neck tingled when I ran the beam over dozens of grimy wooden crates. Piled four high and far into the cave, the crates were deteriorating. Some were disintegrating, causing their contents—bottles—to lean out the sides. I knew exactly what I'd found. This was one of my great-grandfather's bootlegging stashes, and it was a big one.

To the right was a dusty table, and an old fountain pen rested in tidy parallel with the top. The simple wooden desk chair had the remains of what appeared to be a blanket draped over its back. I was reluctant to step deeper into the cave because I was shuddering, not from cold, but from pain and finding myself in my family's notorious past. A past that was legend for me, never a reality.

"Jilly-girl, your grandpa and great-grandpa did what they had to. It wasn't always this side of the law, but their hard work set up our family today." My father stressed this several times while I was growing up, but I never understood what it meant. I just believed that the comfort I enjoyed was a product of caring ancestors.

It took Billy's gossiping to shed light on my family, bootlegging, and border running. The whole town knew except me. I suppose Daddy was going to tell me the whole thing one day, but never got around to it. And here, in front of me, stood the evidence of our past. The O'Hara family archaeology site.

And all I wanted to think about was the sheriff. She was keeping company with appalling people. Hell, she let them come after me. She would have let them shoot at me. The scream in my heart, when I realized she had sacrificed me, sliced something vital inside. I began hiccupping tears. Bending over my damaged hand, I fell apart. I had allowed myself to feel something, hope maybe, or love even.

"You stupid sucker." I gasped several times through the tears running over my lips. I've never cried like that before, not over my father's death or my grandma's. It was a different kind of crying, despair and loneliness so shattering I wanted to die in that cave, leaving a pathetic carcass for the critters to gnaw. "You were falling for her."

I noticed all my bodily fluids were soaking the dirt in front of me, so I pulled out the tail of the thermal shirt and wiped my face, blew my snot into the shirt, and wiped again. I figured I was going to live, and that depressed me even more. Since I was not a big supporter of outward self-pity, however, I worked to pull myself together.

"Fuck it. Just fuck it. I'm so sick of crying," I said to the booze boxes. Resolving to distract myself from the Rae situation, I ran the flashlight beam over the boxes and saw how far into the cave they stretched, at least fifty feet. When I pulled a bottle out of a dilapidated case, the label crumbled off it, landing in a wispy pile at my feet. I returned the bottle to its ancient coffin, edged around the cases, and worked myself to the back of the cave, ducking ever lower the farther back I got.

Odors of wet earth, mildewed wood, and something musky assailed me. My foot kicked something hollow and stiff. Pointing the beam to the area near my left foot, I found a withered work boot. The laces were long gone and the cracked leather of the tongue curled over the instep. It was a wretched lonely thing, but then I spotted another boot peeking from behind the last row of crates. An itching sensation of discovery crawled up my back when, crouching, I shone the beam behind the crates to spotlight a human pelvic bone.

There were other bones spread around the little space. The skull, lying on its side and facing away from me, was pushed up against a crate. I was grateful I didn't have to see its black hollow sockets. Clearly, the skeleton was old. No clothes survived, or maybe it didn't have any clothes when it was left there. It must have fed some animals because I could see teeth gouges on the few leg bones I forced myself to study without touching.

This was far from the first dead body I'd seen, but hidden here, on my land, with the remains of my family all around, I was sickened.

Before I backed away, I said, "Sorry, fella. I hope you didn't suffer."

My father's obsession with his maps and Rae's information started to make sense. I suspected that, somehow, Daddy knew about this. It also might account for the undelivered crates of booze left in the cave.

He wasn't some hero hoping to save the missile silos from terrorists. He was worried that body would be discovered by the sheriff. Then why didn't he just come out and move the body? More importantly, whose body was it and how did it get there?

I grabbed a bottle of the booze on my way to the mouth of the cave. Just inside the entrance where the light was best, I sat, dug out the hunting knife, and proceeded to chip away at the antique cork still plugging the whiskey bottle. Pretty soon I had most of the cork gouged out and it took little effort to push the rest of it inside the bottle, leaving it to float in the aged swill within. The pungent smell made my eyes water.

My aching hand needed tending, so I unraveled the blood-soaked bandana to study the wound. It was ugly, a jagged tear leaving the pad beneath the thumb hanging like a flap. I needed stitches and I needed to clean the wound. Since I had no water, I opted for the booze.

I was shivering in anticipation of the horrific sting. I blew all air out of my lungs and drizzled the whiskey on the cut. The jab of pain was worse than I had expected, causing my teeth to chatter and eyes to ooze tears. Somehow I kept from screaming. I used my knife to cut off the left sleeve of my thermal shirt and wrapped the stretchy material around the cut. The smell of whiskey mixed with blood filled my nose, and I spent several more minutes crouching and crying like a little kid.

I'd traveled to dozens of backwaters worldwide, but there, twenty miles from my childhood home, in a cave on my property, I had never felt so desperate and alone. The fleshless corpse behind the whiskey crates was not a cozy companion.

When I could finally string two thoughts together, I decided it was time to plan my escape from the cave. I was a dangerous loose end for Rae and her cronies. They would be back, badger or not. Every time I thought about Rae, my heart cracked again. It was dismaying to feel so devastated by someone I barely knew. She had struck a spark of hope in me and the spark had fizzled into despair. I may have been an unabashed opportunist, but opportunists deserved love too.

The sun had taken a yellowish glow, signaling the oncoming evening. I'd have to move in the dark along the base of the cliff. Jerusalem Rocks's eastern end was about one hundred yards from Interstate 15. But it was one hundred yards of rocky, uneven terrain and a barbed wire fence separating the elevated banked highway from the beginning of the formation. In Montana, you assumed all fences were barbed wire.

I didn't have much to collect and prepare for my cave escape. There was my flashlight, knife, and the little .22 Ruger Bearcat and its box of bullets. I emptied the Glock ammo from my jacket pocket and placed it on the old table. "Maybe you can find a use for these," I said to the dead guy. I forced thoughts of food and water out of my brain since there was nothing I could do about those needs. For a few moments, I fantasized about climbing back into the Rocks to see if my backpack was still around but knew it would remain just that, a fantasy.

After a lengthy inner debate, I grabbed two of the whiskey bottles and shoved one into each of the main pockets in my jacket. "Ya never know," I said loud enough for Dead Guy to hear. The thick green glass would weigh me down, but I could ditch them at any time. Somehow, they gave me a sense of having more resources than I really did.

I sat at the cave entrance, my throbbing torn hand in my lap, and waited for nightfall. The wind started clobbering the cliff face, making it impossible to listen for footsteps or someone scrabbling down the cliff. All I could hear was the wind blowing bleak whistles through the sagebrush at the entrance. Dead Guy had been listening to the macabre melody for decades. I was hell-bent not to join him, but I couldn't resist making up a mental cartoon of Dead Guy and his dead gal dancing in the cave to xylophone music. "Yup, I'm losing it," I decided after wiping laugh/cry tears from my eyes.

Dark didn't come fast enough, but when it finally arrived, a huge part of me wanted to stay in the cave's timeless safety. I checked my pockets for the fiftieth time to see if my flashlight still worked and if the Ruger was loaded. I had to say farewell to Dead Guy. "I have no idea if I'll be back, buddy, but if I live through this, I'll figure out what to do with you. I promise. Peaceful dreams." I crouched and moved out of the cave.

I decided that I'd need to keep close to the cliff and move between boulders and sage to stay out of sight. I had to assume someone was hunting me, but I was puzzled that I hadn't seen anybody since my badger buddy had chased the one pursuer. Either they had someone waiting for me to make a move, or they felt I wasn't important enough to bother with. I was pretty sure the second option was incorrect. These guys were up to something serious. Weapons, paramilitary troops, trucks, bunkers on the Martin farm, law enforcement collusion, and the damn missile silos. No, they couldn't afford to have big-mouthed me wandering around the countryside. The wind was blowing fear sweat into my eyes. "I'm too old and stupid for this," I said.

CHAPTER THIRTY-FIVE

From bush to boulder, I moved with all the deliberation of prey eluding its predator. At least the wind covered any noise I made, but it also tore at my eyes, making me squint so that I was half blind. My goggles were in the lost backpack, but I didn't miss them as much as the bottled water and granola bars. Sometimes the whiskey bottles clanked against rocks, but they never broke. They still made me feel safer.

Every few minutes I stopped and looked up the cliff face to see any evidence of my pursuers, and then I'd continue delicately moving around giant rocks and brush. After thirty anguished minutes, I could see an occasional set of headlights from vehicles moving north on I-95. Another quarter hour and I'd reached the barbed wire marking the separation of my father's property from the government land cradling the interstate.

"Well, what do I do now?" I asked the wind. Despite all my time in the cave, I hadn't really worked out what I would do when I reached the highway. I could either follow it into Sweetgrass and roust some help or try to hitch a ride south into Prairie View and find Billy. Since the lanes nearer me were southbound, I decided I'd try to make it to Prairie View, but first I needed to find a place where I could crawl through the barbed wire.

Keeping to a crouch, I moved north along the fence line, looking for a spot where fence meeting a boulder would create an opening to shinny under. About twenty feet along the line, I found a spot where the fencing crew must have been miffed about having to string barbed wire over and around boulders. The second strand from the bottom wrapped up and over a large rock, making a hole big enough for me to squeeze through. I almost made it unscathed, but my left knee rammed directly onto a barb, slicing the skinned knee I had forgotten about. I hissed but didn't scream as I pulled my leg through the fence. I could feel a dribble of blood running down the front of my leg and soaking into my sock.

For the first time in that unending day, I wanted to die, pack it in and let them shoot me. The damn barbed wire wound was the final indignity. I let despair and surrender course through me for several minutes while I held my pants against the puncture wound. When I caught myself calculating the years since my last tetanus booster, I knew my death wish had passed.

It was time to scrabble up the highway embankment and leave Jerusalem Rocks behind. Christ, that knee hurt. Along with my mangled hand, parched mouth, and empty belly, I felt like a real battle survivor. In my amused delirium, I silently whistled "Yankee Doodle" as encouragement to climb to the roadside.

In Montana, people drove at extreme speeds on the interstates. I had forgotten that. Every time I stepped out to flag a car, it sped by too fast for a driver to see me, except maybe as an antelope that had wandered roadside. This went on for twenty minutes or so while I trudged south. Finally, a semi-truck was barreling toward me at around eighty miles per hour while the wind was pushing close to forty miles per hour. The back draft from the truck, coupled with the wind, spun me flat onto the gravel bordering the asphalt. I lay there for a full minute and stared at the stars that were unfazed by my predicament. The not-quite-full moon reminded me of an eye looking at a specimen through a microscope. I was a sorry specimen.

I had just sat up when a long black car pulled up next to my prone body. The passenger door edged open and I saw an arm reaching from the driver's side working the door farther open. The driver's head was leaning toward me and a woman's voice said, "Get in!"

"Sylvia? Oh thank God!" It was Sylvia McCutcheon, my faithful attorney.

"Just get in…now!" She sounded strained so I knew better than to dawdle around. Stiff and hurting, I half crawled onto the ample passenger seat of her Mercedes. She was not looking at me but straight ahead to the south.

"You have impeccable timing, Counselor," I said and leaned back onto the headrest. Something pushed into my temple.

"Doesn't she though?" A man's giggle and a sharp jab into my temple warned me that we were not alone. The smell of putrid beer and tobacco breath was revolting.

Sylvia glanced at me, then continued looking south. "Eric Martin, you know…Josh's younger brother?" The hand with the gun bashed the side of Sylvia's skull. She was hit so hard, her head bounced off the side window.

"Never, ever call me Josh's younger brother," Eric screamed at her.

Slowly, Sylvia touched where she had been hit and I saw tears in her eyes.

"We're going to be okay, Sylvia," I said, but she looked at me with such intense bleakness that I doubted my own words.

"Oh, don't be so sure about that, dyke lady," said Eric in a nasally voice. "I'm doing my brother and his friends a big favor tonight. When they see what I've got here, I'll come out ahead on this deal, but you two, well, let's just say you'll come out behind." A snicker and another jab of the gunpoint into my temple. It was getting annoying.

It was common knowledge that Eric Martin was as sharp as a basketball, but he had the gun to my head. On the other hand, he didn't suspect that ladies could protect themselves. He didn't have the sense to search my jacket pockets, but as long as the gun was at my head, my pockets held little help, only hope. I decided to wait. From what he had said, he wasn't going to kill us, at least not right away. Maybe he was taking us to Josh and the others. To Rae.

"Drive, cunt. Turn when I say. Stop when I say. Nothing happens unless I say, or I'll blow someone's brains into the windshield. Don't really care who it is, either. Understand?"

Sylvia nodded and put her car into drive. I glanced at her and saw rivulets of sweat on her forehead, tears on her face, and the start of a nasty bruise on her cheekbone.

"I found your fuckin' friend hanging around the Glocca Morra parking lot." Eric sounded like he was having a friendly conversation with me. "She respects this gun, I can tell you, because she told me you were around, probably at roadside trying to hitch a ride outta here. Well, you got your wish, dyke lady. We're outta here."

He turned the gun into Sylvia's head. "When ya get to Prairie View, get onto Highway 2 going east. And if you try anything stupid, just remember, brains on the windshield. Got it?" Sylvia nodded.

The gun returned to my head. "Yeah, just do everything he says. We'll be okay. I guess Billy called you, huh?" She nodded. I saw the white knuckles of Sylvia's hand on the steering wheel. I knew I wasn't really helping her, but I wanted her to know that I was sorry for getting her into this shitty situation. If we got through it, I'd probably be out an attorney.

Pain smeared the side of my face. It was my turn to crack my skull on the side window. "Shut up, bitch! Don't talk to her." Eric pushed the gun barrel deeply into my temple and I fought throwing up. He backed off slightly when he saw the reflex action my belly was making. "Don't puke in the car! I hate puke in the car! Hear me?" he screamed in my ear.

My whole focus was to keep my stomach contents inside my belly. His rancid breath wasn't helping. I fought to calm my muscles and settle the contractions of my stomach. Hell, even if I had puked, there was very little to come out, but I wasn't going to chance it. After several minutes of breathing, shivering, and praying to whatever entity was in charge, I felt my stomach settle. I looked up and saw the lights of Prairie View and knew we'd soon be on Highway 2 headed east.

"Lock all the doors, bitch," Eric said. Sylvia felt for the door lock button on the left armrest, and I heard the click of all four locks engaging. "Just in case the dyke lady decides to exit our lovely joy ride." He was breathing in my ear, and I had to work with my nausea again.

Expecting another smack, I had to ask anyway. "Where are we going?"

Another unhinged giggle, but no smack. "Ah, to my secret place to hide sorry losers like you two, just a few miles east of Prairie View. A place so obvious, nobody'll find you…least not 'til after I've had some fun with you." Giggle. "Then I'll pass you to my bro and his woman. They'll take care of whatever's left. They just want you alive. Don't care about the condition as long as you can sign certain documents."

Rae again. She'd used me, knowing I was vulnerable because of

Daddy's death. Or was I missing something? Did she tell me all that classified information about the ICBMs because she knew I wasn't going to live long enough to tell anyone? She knew, with me, getting a good story comes before having good sense. Were there other reasons she confided in me? Personal ones? Calculated ones?

After passing through town, Sylvia accelerated on Highway 2 east. I noticed she was going a conservative fifty miles per hour, unheard of on Montana highways. She was probably buying time, time I was using to gradually move my hands into my pockets. I'd made a tactical error when packing the whiskey bottles; the one in my right pocket sat on top of the little Ruger. I'd have to move the bottle to get to the gun, a pistol that was only slightly better than a powerful bb gun.

For the moment, all I had were the whiskey bottles and desperation. I couldn't hit him in the car, not when he had his gun pressed to either Sylvia's or my head. Whiffs of various escape plans ran through my head, each discarded as impotent. Then I remembered that Eric viewed us as impractical girls. I might be able use his misguidance to get us free.

"Listen, dyke lady, fear turns me on. Get it?" Then Eric pushed the gun into Sylvia's bruised cheek. "At the Corral, turn left instead of right. Go to the back of the grain elevator. And don't fuckin' turn off the car until I tell you." He was repeatedly poking the gun into Sylvia's purple cheekbone. She made no sound but tears rolled in a steady dribble down her face. Her misery was my fault and I resolved to get her out of there alive.

Ahead I could see the flickering red and green neon of the Corral sign. The parking lot had only a few pickups in it. There wasn't a soul outside the building. To the left loomed the forsaken grain elevator. There was enough moonlight to make out the faded Montana Elevator Company logo. I could discern the access door eighty feet above, broken and feeble, with its rusted ladders extending to the weed-strewn ground below. I knew there were probably a few outbuildings around the elevator, but they were difficult to see in the gloom.

"Pull around to the back of the elevator and park between the sheds." Eric's breath was getting more revolting, and I pushed back another wave of nausea. "Leave the lights shining on the elevator but turn off the car."

Sylvia parked the car facing the deteriorating elevator, its rippled aluminum siding hung crookedly in several places. The two aluminum-covered outbuildings were on either side of us. Sylvia's right hand trembled when she put the car into Park. The gun barrel was punched into my temple again.

"Okay, you first, dyke. Get out…slowly, mind you, and move into the headlights. Pretend you're onstage and I'm your audience. If you run, I'll shoot your friend and then come after you. This is going to be fun. I promise."

I knew I had maybe three seconds of invisibility to Eric when I left the dome lighting in the car and walked into the headlights. As I eased out of the car and stood, I gripped the pocketed whiskey bottle in my right hand. Keeping my left side toward the car, I took two steps past the door. I pulled the bottle from my pocket in my three safe seconds and hook shot it hard over the top of the car. It banged and clattered against the outbuilding thirty feet away. It was louder than I expected it to be because we were protected from the wind.

"Fucking hell!" Eric was alarmed by the banging. "Get outta the car, bitch!" He poked Sylvia again while I wrapped my hand around the grip of the delicate Ruger and thumbed back its hammer. I needed a clean, close shot. Real close. The .22 bullets could be ineffective from a distance.

Eric kept his gun on Sylvia while he left the car and scanned the shed, looking for the noise source. I threw the second bottle over the car, behind Eric's back, and prayed. Prayers answered. The bottle made a lusty shattering sound off a rock. Eric turned toward it. I ran around the car, pushing Sylvia behind me. "Run! Now!" She was off. I was a few feet from Eric. With no thought, I pointed the Ruger at his torso and fired. The gun made a pop, like a firecracker in the deadly night.

"Hey!" Eric looked at his chest, at me, at his chest. I pulled the hammer and fired again, hitting him in the neck. His gun went off, making a deafening retort and concurrent metallic splat into the aluminum building. His knees buckled. His hand loosed the gun, and I kicked the weapon into the weeds.

Somewhere above, the wind banged a flap of aluminum against the elevator. It whistled through cracks and fissures in the giant structure. Forlorn music accompanying a sorry scene.

I squatted a few feet away to see if he was alive. In the dim light it was hard to tell. I hoped Sylvia was making her way to safety at the Corral. Garish lights flashed the scene and I looked into blinding pickup headlights. The pickup skidded to a stop behind Sylvia's car, spewing dust all around. The doors flew open. Annie and Josh Martin emerged.

The fear I suffered with Eric was nothing to what engulfed me when I saw the blind rage on Josh's face. His backlit white hair shone around his head, making him look like Satan's avenging angel.

"What'd you do to my brother?" Spit flew from his snarling lips. He clutched a gun. I looked at Annie. She pointed a gun at me, too.

"I didn't...he was crazy...he...Annie? Why are you here?"

"This is where I belong. With my man." She looked more determined than I'd ever seen her.

"Your man? Him? Josh? But you're taller than him!" Josh didn't find me funny. I saw his arm move the gun into aim position. I dove around the front of Syvia's car just as the gun blast hit the elevator. I scurried into the deep shadows between the outbuilding and the elevator. I prayed that Sylvia was calling for help. Then I remembered the "help" might be in cahoots with the Martins. I was on my own.

Chapter Thirty-six

Without the weight of the whiskey bottles I was more mobile, but I also felt more vulnerable. I still had my Ruger; its smooth, worn wooden grip was cradled in my right hand. I found my flashlight and knife in a chest pocket. Groping my way along the elevator siding, I found a padlocked door. I jimmied the padlock and found it was not squeezed into locked position. Someone had left the engine room of the elevator accessible. Probably Eric. I opened the door only wide enough to get in, betting the wind would drown out any squeaks the reluctant door made. Once inside I closed the door behind me and flipped on the flashlight. Josh would be on me any second, but he knew I was armed. He'd be careful. I shot his brother, after all.

The enormity of shooting someone tried to bully itself into my thoughts, but I resisted, promising myself I could self-flagellate later if I survived. I moved the flashlight around the room, looking for a spot for a standoff. Most of the dust-piled room was empty with some indefinable steel machinery pieces lying around. In the far corner was the service counter, a color-faded curled calendar still hanging on the wall behind. I strode over there intending to use the counter as a barricade. Bad idea. A distinctive rattle. I shone my flashlight at the floor. A rattlesnake had decided to spend the night there and wasn't sharing his accommodations. There was another rattler slithering into a knothole in the floorboard.

Nearly panicked, I backed off to the rotting staircase opposite the counter and started to climb. When I had reached the top of the first landing, I heard the engine room door open and the sound of feet inching across the gritty floor, trying to find their way in the inky dark.

I pocketed my flashlight. The Ruger was glued to my right hand. Sweat ran down my legs, my torso, even into the stinging cut on my palm. The interior of the elevator smelled of forty years' accumulation of mouse piss and dirt. The door opened again and I heard Annie and Josh have a whispered argument. I took that moment to move up some more steps to the second landing. My foot bonked a piece of pipe. I pushed it a little with my toe to see how big it was. I could move it easily, so I reached down and wrapped my injured hand around it and found it to be about an inch wide and maybe a foot long.

To distract them away from my whereabouts, I flung the pipe over the edge in the direction of the counter and my reptilian buddy. The pipe made an unseemly racket in the dark. Then silence, heavy and stultifying. It lasted for at least a minute, then someone was creeping toward the sound. The floorboards were creaking with each step.

"Ahhh! I've been shot!" Annie shouted. I heard Josh walk toward her voice.

"I didn't hear a gun. Are you sure you didn't—Jesus! It's a rattler! It struck my boot. Move back, move back!" From the thumping, shuffling sounds, they must have bumped into a wall.

"Josh, outta here. I got snake bites, maybe two." Annie whimpered a few times.

"Shut the fuck up. You find your own way outta here, 'cuz I need to kill me one bitch." Then he shouted up, "Ya hear that, bitch? I know you're upstairs and I'm going to kill you there. You've fucked up my life in too many ways. It's over."

"We should go help your brother." Annie's voice bordered on hysteria. There was the shuffling sound of another footstep, then a deafening crack, and several more. The floorboards were giving away beneath them. Annie screamed.

"Help. Oh God…biting me. Get me out. Help me…Josh, please. Josh…" There were the sounds of cloth tearing, grunts, and fingers scrabbling on wood.

"Jesus…Annie. Fuck…oh fuck." Josh took a few footsteps toward Annie.

Her pleading and gasping went on endlessly, and I had to grip the railing to keep from screaming myself. The horror of what was happening to Annie didn't crack my instinct for self-preservation.

Floorboards were creaking again, then the sound of something heavy dragged across the floor. No more cries or pleas came from Annie, just Josh's labored breathing. Tears were running into my collar.

"You bitch, O'Hara. My woman's hurt 'cuz of you. I'm gonna kill you and fuck you at the same time." His feet were grinding and sweeping around the floor, groping for the staircase. Above me, the loose aluminum siding continued to bang on the building.

I took several hurried steps to what felt like another landing, and I groped to my left, looking for the next step. I found it and climbed up. The rotten third step gave way under my foot. I was stuck to the knee in the decayed wood and gasping in fear as Josh inched up the groaning staircases.

"Are ya hurt, dyke?"

I put one hand on the wall and the other on what I hoped was a sturdy wood railing. It wasn't stable but it was enough for leverage. With a careful hoist up, I pulled my leg out of the broken step, causing pieces of wood to clatter on the stairway below. Keeping my feet from the middle of the steps while holding the railing and wall, I shimmied to the top of the stairs and onto the sagging catwalk that encircled the upper inside of the vast empty elevator. Then I grasped my little gun in my right hand, the flashlight in my left, turned back toward the stairs, and listened.

Josh's breath was coming in puffs and grunts as he labored his way up in the dark. When I was sure he was on the flight of steps below me, I pointed the gun and flashlight down the stairs. I flipped on the flashlight. Josh's face, eyes wide and angry, twenty feet below. I fired the gun, snapped off the light, crouched, and rolled to my right. I knew I hit him, but where?

"Cunt!" He fired his gun where he'd seen my flashlight. Its deafening retort stunned me and I lost hold of the flashlight. Feeling around for it, I knocked it off the catwalk with the side of my hand. My ears still ringing from the gunshot, I missed hearing it hit the decayed wheat far below.

I moved along the catwalk, hoping I'd hurt him enough to stop his assault. But his footsteps only moved faster. From the wheezing strain in his breath, though, I could tell he was wounded. A loud creak and snap echoed through the elevator, and I knew he'd gone through a rotten step. But his grunting and scrabbling noises told me he was still on the chase.

I felt my way along the wall on my right. I had to avoid the treacherous railing on the left. A fall from there would hurl me into the grain remnants seventy feet below. The thought of all the mice crawling around in the moldy wheat made me shudder.

Moving forward and feeling around, my left hand found what I was looking for, the metal handle to the upper grain access door. I pocketed my gun and grabbed the handle, giving it a hard shake. It was locked or jammed. I heard Josh moving along the catwalk, but it sounded as if he was staggering. Outside, behind the wind and flapping aluminum, sirens wailed.

"You're dead, bitch." He was close. I found the heavy hook and eye latch. A few jimmies of the door and I popped the ancient latch out. The wind grabbed the door and banged it flat against the outside of the elevator. Without a glance downward, I turned my back toward the vicious wind, knelt on all fours, and groped with my foot out the door to the top step of the outside access ladder.

My sweaty hair slapped into my eyes, but I eased myself down a few rungs of the ladder. The ladder wasn't sturdy but there was no time to care. I forced myself to forget I was at least eight stories above the ground, hanging on a dubious rusty ladder in forty-mile-per-hour wind.

I was a fish in a barrel for Josh and his gun, but I'd run out of options. I heard a gunshot and felt a burning sting on my right biceps, but I kept moving down. Nausea ballooned in my stomach, and I had to stop for a moment to fight vertigo. Taking the risk, I looked up at a bloody, grinning Josh Martin, standing at the access door pointing a large gun at my face.

Just before I looked away, his shoulder exploded, covering him and the side of the door with blood and gore. It took several seconds for me to understand he'd been shot. He staggered back, out of my sight, leaving a bloody smear on the door frame. Above the wind clamor, I heard him scream. There was a faint sound of wood snapping as he fell through the catwalk railing and to the vile wheat and mice below.

Unable to move, I wrapped my shaking arms around the ladder and looked behind me. On the highway, standing by a flashing police cruiser, was Sheriff Terabian. A large hunting rifle was at her shoulder and she peered along its sights, watching the access door, waiting to see if Josh would reappear. Several county vehicles lined the drive into the elevator, lights flashing, casting ethereal colors across the face of the elevator. Officers ran around the building looking like crazed ants.

Across the highway, standing at the door of the Corral, was Sylvia, hands on hips, surrounded by several enthralled bar customers. She must have called in the troops. Another attorney to my rescue.

Rae waited a few more moments, then skidded down the road embankment while yelling into her collar microphone. She disappeared around the elevator. They had Eric. Soon I'd know if I was a killer or not. I was in a piss-poor place to finally hit the wall with exhaustion and shock, but I could feel it overwhelming me. The makeshift bandage on my hand was soaked with blood. I wrapped my arms around the ladder and pressed my forehead into the rung in front of me. With every move I made, the ladder made little moans. From the west came cavalry sounds of ambulance sirens.

"Get it together, Jilly. It's almost over. Breathe. Focus. Don't look down." I was talking to myself loud enough to hear my voice over the wind that still tore at my hair and clothes. Every muscle in my body was shaking from fear and chill. A few dots of Josh's blood were on my jacket sleeves. Or maybe it was my blood. I knew I had received a glancing wound from Josh's gun; it stung but felt minimal.

"Jill. Jill. Look at me, sweetheart. Look up here." Rae's voice was gentle but carried command. I bent my neck back and gazed up at her. She was lying on her belly on the catwalk inside the door I had come out.

"Who's dead?"

Rae shook her head, sympathy in her eyes. "I don't know, honey. They're working on all three now."

"Then tell me something to make me trust you, goddamn it." Now I was crying again, sobbing really. The wind was drying the tears as fast as I could shed them. I hugged the ladder even harder and barely noticed how it creaked and reeled with each sob.

Rae looked as sincere as I'd ever seen anybody. "I didn't want anything to happen to you. I knew you'd rush out to the Rocks and nose around. It was too dangerous, so I cuffed you to the bed. I thought I'd be back in time to set you free and explain why I left you. Things got out of control because they sped up their attack plans, which included me, and I couldn't risk my cover."

"You let them hunt me like an animal. Why the hell didn't you help me?"

"Believe me, I was terrified for you, but I had to trust you knew the Rocks better than they did. There was no choice. They thought I was a bought cop on their side. Had I broken cover, more people would have died, including you. As it is, the operation was only partially successful. If you come up here, I can get you some help. Then we can talk about it later."

I shook my head. "I don't know if I can move. Tell me something that will make me want to climb up there."

She gave a tender grin. "We can play with my handcuffs again. This time you get to be in charge of them." She reached down, offering me her hand. I saw her glance at the spot where the ladder was bolted to the building.

"More, I want more," I said.

"I issued the speeding ticket because I wanted to check you out." She looked again at the ladder bolts. "It's only a few rungs, please try."

"You have a real touch with the ladies, Sheriff." I loosened my hug on the ladder and edged my hands on to the sides. The ladder crunched backward and down a few inches. My breath jumped into panicked gulps.

"C'mon sweetheart, take just one step. Then you can rest. Okay?"

I hoisted myself up one rung and squeezed the ladder again. "I don't know if I can do this. I'm so tired." The ladder shrieked and wobbled. My whipping hair was stinging my eyes.

"You have enough to get up here. I promise. And when you're here, I'll hold you and take care of you." I found the shaky strength to take another rung and then another.

Rae was still on her belly, hand outstretched to me, the other trying to pull the ladder in. I could see a deputy behind her, holding her legs. The screeching ladder swayed away from the building. I glanced at the moving ground. My stomach lurched. My whole body trembled as I reached for her hand.

She missed my pass…once…twice…three times. The fourth pass, she jerked the ladder in with her left hand and grabbed me with her right. When she pulled me onto the catwalk, I saw the top bolts that used to hold the ladder to the building were out of their moorings. The bolts farther down were nearly out, too. My foot pushed off the top rung and the ladder toppled away from the building.

Quaking and gasping, I lay atop Rae's body.

"It's okay. You're safe now. I'm here." Her soothing whispers brought back my slipping sanity.

From the ground floor the deputies were shining their powerful flashlights up to the catwalk. It was too rickety for them to ascend as a group. The deputy who had held Rae's legs was shining his flashlight down through the shattered railing to where Josh had fallen. Both jittery, Rae and I stood. Without hesitating, Rae put her arms around me and held me as if I were her most precious possession. She led me to the top of the stairs.

I stopped her a moment so I could look down the into the cavernous grain bin. A few deputies were aiming their flashlights through a lower access door. In the shadowed light, I could make out a leg and arm, all the rest was covered in rotten wheat and frantic, scurrying mice. Then we made our careful descent.

CHAPTER THIRTY-SEVEN

I wasn't happy in hospitals, but this one time I was grateful for the comfort of a clean bed and attentive nurses. The I.V. filled me with antibiotics, painkillers, and much-needed hydration. My knees were disinfected, but no stitches were necessary, just a few bulky bandages. My left hand was extensively stitched and wrapped, along with the bullet gash in my arm. Rae had watched, with rapt interest, the stitching process and discussed the technique with the bemused doctor. She never left me for more than the few minutes she needed to make calls and give orders. I spent the first night in the hospital in a drug-induced stupor with Rae in a chair next to the bed speaking into her phone, doing paperwork, or dozing.

The following morning, I was finally stable and irritable enough for nurses to leave me alone. I gave a complete statement to some federal officer who finally left when I started growling my answers.

Rae entered the room and ordered everyone to not disturb us. She closed the door, lay down next to me, and gingerly held my battered, exhausted body close. The comfort in that simple gesture delighted me, and my heart opened for her.

"Should we talk about it now?" I said.

"Some of it we can discuss, some of it we can't. Despite what's happening between us, I'm still an officer of the law and you're a reporter."

Lifting my head to look into her irresistible but weary eyes, I said, "But a reporter with a vested interest, wouldn't you say? After all, everything happened on my property, in my town, and—"

"Oh, suddenly you claim this town again?" She was laughing but she had a serious point.

I plopped my head back onto the pillow. "Let's just say I'm revising my opinion about Prairie View for the better."

"How so? Best funeral casseroles in Montana? No, I know, the best-managed sheriff's department in the United States. Now there's something you can put into one of your articles."

"Well, that part is true and I won't fail to mention it. But I was really speaking about the people here. I'm finally proud to count myself part of them. My obnoxious arrogance kept me from seeing clearly. But, darling, we are sliding off topic and you know it. You have some things to explain." I felt her sigh into my shoulder. "Tell me about the missiles. What happened? They're a big part of the story." I could have choked myself for saying that.

"See, there's how you see it, 'the story.' It isn't just a story; it was a real threat to all of us and our way of life." Her body tensed.

For a moment I was panicked she would shut herself off. "Sweetheart, I want you to understand this. Please listen and don't automatically flip into law enforcement slash politician mode. Please." When I felt her relax, I looked again into her eyes. "I love this country and the law every bit as much as you do. I have to protect it with the skills I have. Maybe I don't carry a badge or run for election, but I can write pretty. And sometimes I piss off people who have the same values I do but defend those values differently. I would never, never, knowingly compromise the security of this country. I live here, too, as do my friends. And my lover."

She looked at me pensively for a few moments, then put her head on my chest and was quiet for several minutes. As I awaited her reply, I felt my body finally give way to marrow-deep fatigue and I started drifting to sleep.

"Here's what I can tell you for now, and it's probably not enough for a story yet. One of these days I may be able to tell you the whole thing." Her voiced pulled me from my dreamy state. She was lightly rubbing my belly.

"Fine," I said, "but remember I'm trained to ask questions, and it happens without thinking."

"Well, you remember I'm trained to ignore and evade questions that shouldn't be answered. Deal?"

"Okay, deal." I placed my hand over hers and stopped the distracting rubbing.

Her speech was deliberate. "Since nine eleven, I've held 'special' law enforcement jobs—"

"In the interest of full disclosure, you should know that I know about your brother and nine eleven. And you need to know that it breaks my heart that you've had to suffer that."

She swallowed a few times before continuing. "He was my rock." She paused for a bit. "And I knew you were researching me. If I had your skills and drive, I'd do the same. Actually, I did do the same."

"You researched me? And found out what?"

"That you're a helluva great journalist and notoriously randy." She started laughing at my indignant yelp.

"Damn you, Sheriff, didn't you have anything better to do?"

"I did, but when a reporter, even a gorgeous lesbian reporter, starts digging around in a classified operation, I have to cover all vulnerable posteriors, even your delicious one. Now where was I?"

"'Special law enforcement jobs,' which I assume means undercover."

"Well, yes and no. This job became more undercover than we previously estimated. My original mission was to monitor the border and northern survivalist groups. But then we discovered the developments on the Martin farm, and my role changed."

"Who's 'we'?"

"My 'agency,' let's call it. If you ask me to be specific, I'll evade the questions with scintillating and clever parries. You'll end up angry and frustrated, and I'll regrettably have to leave. You choose."

I snuggled closer to her. "I choose ignorance, for now. Besides, I have plans for you when my body doesn't feel like it went through a trash compactor. Maybe I can weasel the information from you in a more pleasant way."

"I'm looking forward to seeing you try."

"So tell me what happened to the shitheads at the Martin farm."

"It's complicated, and there are aspects I can't tell you because I don't want to compromise anything, but I can give you a sketch."

I was disappointed but knew pushing her would drive a wedge between us, and I profoundly did not want that to happen. "Okay, I can work with a sketch."

"When you saw me at Jerusalem Rocks, we were moving a cache of weapons to the Martin farm. The weapons had been smuggled across the border and hidden there for months in preparation for the ICBM operation. The foreign terrorists convinced the Martins they were all working for the same thing: the destruction of the United States. That was true, but the terrorists couldn't have cared less about the Martins' dream of a right-wing utopia township. They just wanted a staging area for their operation."

"So the Martins were just pawns in a bigger game?" I hoisted myself up a little to face Rae. "Did the Martins know that?"

"I'm not sure. I do know that the Martins were so deluded by their righteousness and isolation that they really did believe that I was one of them. They touted me to the terrorists as if my defection proved their anti-U.S. credentials. The terrorists treated me like a necessary but distasteful ally. I was to keep all law enforcement away from them."

"So when you left me cuffed to the bed, what happened?" I was still a little emotionally bruised about that.

"The terrorist leader could see the Martins, especially Eric, were spinning out of control and endangering their operation. So they decided to deploy immediately, and I wasn't able to come back and release you. Besides, I believed you were safe anyway. You can't imagine how horrible I felt when I saw you on the Rocks."

"We can thank Billy and my pigheaded persistence for my freedom from the cuffs."

"Anyhow, while you spent the day hiding at Jerusalem Rocks, I spent the day helping federal agents round up and arrest as many people involved as we could find. Your appearance spooked the terrorists into aborting the ICBM operation. Several melted across the border, but we did get a few key players. The Martins and Annie were nowhere to be found."

"Annie," I said, "is she all right?" I could tell by Rae's silence that Annie was anything but all right.

"She didn't have a chance, sweetheart. By the time the paramedics got to her, the venom had infiltrated her entire system. No amount of antidote would have saved her. I'm sorry. I know she was a friend of sorts." Rae was smoothing my hair.

"I'll tell you the entire story some other time. She was someone I didn't know very well anymore. No matter what she tried to do to me, she didn't deserve to die, not like that. But I feel most sorry for Wayne."

Rae went on to tell me that I hadn't killed Eric Martin. He was locked up in the county jail with a big bandage where I had winged his neck. With Sylvia's and my complaints against him, plus his prior record, he would be making license plates for a long time.

We held each other for a long time after we quit talking, both of us lost in our thoughts. Finally, Rae stirred and said, "As lovely as this is, my dear, I have to be sheriff now. Billy is going to take you home in a few hours, but I'll be over tonight to play nurse."

"Will you wear a nurse uniform and kiss me where it hurts?"

"Let's give your stitches a day or two before we play doctor games, okay?"

The kiss she gave me before she left was so blistering hot that I considered ripping out my I.V. and following her.

When I settled back down, I started thinking about Dead Guy and his long entombment in that cave. I had every intention of eventually discovering his identity and giving him a proper burial, but I was in no hurry. "He's been there so long, a while longer won't hurt," I reasoned. I didn't have the energy to deal with another problem on O'Hara land. Truthfully, I thought there was a story to be had, but it could involve my family. And I wasn't ready for a murder investigation on my property. Not yet.

CHAPTER THIRTY-EIGHT

A few mornings later, I was finally up and moving stiffly around my father's house. Connie was hovering just enough to start annoying me when the doorbell rang the *Bonanza* theme. I assumed it was Billy since I wouldn't be seeing Rae until that evening.

Instead, it was Wayne Robison. He didn't shake my hand when I offered.

"I didn't come over to make friends with you, just to ask you a favor."

"Please, Wayne, know that I'd do anything in my power for none of this to have happened. And for Annie—"

"Annie was lost a long time ago. I want to ask you to not write about her. Not put her name in some newspaper for the world to judge. For the boys' sake."

"I'm not sure—"

"Just leave her out, dammit. She's what they'd call collateral damage. Look, she never loved me. I know that. I also know about you and her, what you did together in high school. She wasn't proud of that, maybe even hated herself for it."

"Hey, I don't need to listen—"

"No, you do. You do so you'll understand. I know I sound screwy, prejudiced even, but...listen, Annie's dad, you know what a prick he was?" It was no secret that Annie's dad was a womanizer, barfly, and lazy bastard. Annie and had I rarely discussed him. "He used Annie, you know. From the time she was maybe twelve or so. You get what I'm talking about here? He'd even make comments to me about it when he was drunk."

I buried my face in my hands, smelling the hospital bandage and underlying disinfectant that coated my stitched palm. I looked up at Wayne. "You mean her father was committing incest with her?"

"She blamed herself, even admitted she sometimes welcomed it. Until you came along. I think you showed her something different, but in the end, you were just another shameful secret to her. She wanted out of her father's home and her friendship with you. Did she ever tell you how often I asked her out and how often she turned me down?"

I shook my head. "Frankly, the only time I ever thought of you was when you two got married. As far as I knew, she only dated me."

Wayne's tanned hands hung limp off his knees as he stared at the floor. "She came clean before I married her, said her dad got her pregnant. I wanted to shoot the fucking pig, but I'm not made of that kind of stuff." Wayne stopped for a moment and took a sip of coffee. "We settled in over the years, had the second boy, and things were okay. Well, they were okay 'til we started hanging out at the Martins. Them and their patriot religion. Josh thought he was God out there, and some of those folks believed him, including Annie. Then those ragheads moved in with all their money, guns, and plans."

"What plans?" I was wondering what the rank-and-file Martin folks knew about their terrorist buddies.

"Ah, they kept that away from me. Annie quit telling me anything a few years ago. I was just useful but worn-out furniture to her. Well, actually, a while back, she told me one thing." Wayne sat up and looked at me.

"She told me that summer of our senior year, when we got married and I committed to raising her dad's kid, it was another one of her manipulations. Apparently, during that spring, she was dating another guy while giving you and me the brush-off. When he got her pregnant, he told her to get lost. So she convinced me to marry her, using Daddy's incest as her pity hook. I was such a dumb kid, in love, I believed everything she said. But she always loved the other guy, the one who dumped her when she needed him. The upshot is the father of our first boy is Josh Martin."

CHAPTER THIRTY-NINE

Wayne's revelations were all I could take for one day. I had a date with Rae that night and vowed to avoid discussing anything that would be upsetting. I wanted her to take me away from the images polluting my brain: Eric Martin hitting Sylvia's head, Josh's body half buried in moldy wheat, and Annie having sex with her dad.

Rae must have had similar plans for forgetting the trauma of the past few days because she showed up on her bike, wearing those jaw-dropping leather chaps. She stood in the doorway of the house, hair braided back from her temples and helmet under her arm. My knees almost buckled while my eyes took her in. She was carrying a clothes hanger, her dry-cleaned uniform protected by plastic.

"I hope you're off duty, Sheriff, because I have some private contracting I want you to do."

"I have more than twenty-four hours to do your bidding, ma'am." She reached to my face and cupped my cheek.

"Well, it's bedroom security, and I'm happy to see you've come dressed for the job."

"A woman with your injuries needs all the proper protection the law can afford."

"Oh please, Sheriff, it's not your protection I need, just the long arm of the law. Let's go upstairs." I hung her dry-cleaning in the hall closet.

The whole scene was set. Candles, a bottle of Leonetti, one half set of handcuffs still attached to the headboard. She had enough class to give a sheepish grin when she saw the cuff. "Guess I owe you, huh?"

"And it's time to pay up."

"How much?"

I looked her over for a moment and pondered. "I'm going to leave the room for two minutes. When I get back, I want you dressed in nothing but your jacket, boots, and chaps. Do you understand?"

She smiled, warming to the game. "I understand perfectly."

"Did you bring a fresh set of cuffs?"

"They're in my back pocket."

"I want them unlocked and ready on the dresser, and you standing in the middle of the room when I get back." Fitch would have been proud. I shut the door behind me and went into the bathroom to change into my robe. I was so turned on that I took a few swipes between my legs to help relieve the tension without wrecking the urge. When I reentered the bedroom, I concluded the sight of her bare ass in those chaps would follow me through my days and make my last few in the nursing home a little brighter.

Rae and I spent thirty-six hours in bed. We fueled our romp with reheated casseroles and a few bottles of 2000 Leonetti Cabernet. When she described the wine as "jammy, juicy with spicy undertones," my heart crawled onto her shoulder and wrapped its arms and tail around her like a baby monkey.

She finally had to leave, though. She was the sheriff, after all, and duty won out.

When she left me at the front door, I looked like a debauched tart, my bathrobe askew. She, on the other hand, was all pressed and starched, having retrieved her uniform from the hall closet. The juxtaposition of our attire made me want her again, and I know she felt the same way. We were shameless fantasy tramps.

After showering the luscious aroma of sex from my shaky, flaccid body, I went to my father's office to focus on his filing cabinet, particularly the drawer labeled "Personal."

The file with my name on it made me nervous, so I avoided it and went to the "Medical" file. Nothing in there surprised me except that his heart condition, coronary artery disease, had been diagnosed four years earlier.

From the little I could glean from the medical records, my father probably could have lived longer had he reduced his stress, eaten less fat, and exercised. He wasn't wired for any of those action plans, but it still pissed me off. "Shit, Daddy, you could never take a suggestion, could you." I thought about that giant slab of buttery salmon he'd consumed when he visited me in Seattle several months earlier.

Sadly chagrined, I went for the weighty, enigmatic file entitled "Meeker and Meeker." My journalist's tingle started when I realized Meeker and Meeker was a private investigation firm out of Denver. I lowered myself into the leather office chair and started one of the most astonishing reads of my life.

The reports from Alvin Meeker, P.I. started in 1981. They were centered around a woman, Eva Stark. My mother. The first report was a bio revealing what she'd done for fourteen years after I was born in 1967. A stint in Vegas as a hotel maid, then San Francisco as a dessert shop waitress, and finally to Portland, Oregon, to go to college. Earned a master's in library science.

"My mother isn't a dolly," I whispered. Hardly. She was currently head reference librarian for the Portland city library system. The yearly P.I. reports chronicled my mother's career and moves to and from several apartments and, finally, into a house. No mention of a husband or boyfriend.

One passage in a 1985 report stated that my mother agreed never to contact me or my father. "Subject accepted payment." A dispassionate description of my abandonment.

My father had paid her off. And, according to the reports, she was continuing to receive payments up to the present. And there they were: her address and phone number.

My mother lived one hundred and fifty miles from my Seattle condo.

I got up and made myself a Bombay gin and tonic. It was 10:35 a.m.

I sat swirling the icy drink, staring out the window at the cavorting gophers. I wasn't thinking, just waiting for the gin to numb my anger. Some of my life's mysteries had been solved the last few days, but I'd had no time to digest them. On top of all that, I was falling in love for the second time in my life. My mind couldn't conjure the discipline to file all that information into neat folders. I wanted to do something foul to the elk head balefully watching me from the wall. "Well, shoot me and stuff me," I muttered.

I looked at the open filing cabinet drawer, aware of the last folder with my name on it. With deliberate care, I stood, fought off the gin-induced dizziness, and retrieved the folder. I went to the kitchen and made an even stronger drink. Then I went to the living room, drink and folder in hand, and lay on the couch. Placing the drink on the floor, I opened the folder and found a handwritten letter from my father. His schoolboy writing made me smile a little.

5/10/06

My Dear Daughter,

Well, if you're reading this, then I've gone to the neon casino in the clouds. I'm sorry to leave you alone, sweetheart. Was it my ticker that gave out, or did I get a little whiskeyed-up and ran the car into the ditch? Guess it doesn't really matter. I'm gone and you're stuck with all my dealings. I hope you approve of my handing the day-to-day workings to Billy. He's a smart boy and I know you can trust him.

I suppose you've found the Meeker files and you are probably angry with me. You should be. I want to tell you that I couldn't share you, not even with your mother. For a few years, after she left you in your grandma's arms, she tried to see you. I was mad at her for leaving me with a kid and then I loved you too much to let you be gone from me for even a day. Your mom gave up finally, and I peppered her income to keep her from coming to get you. Not even your grandma knew this.

You get to decide what you want to do about your mother, except ending her payments. I've established those until she dies, which will be a long time from now. She's still fairly young, you see. I suggest you go meet her because I'm sure she's proud of such an accomplished daughter. In intellect and temperament, you two are much alike. I never met another one like her.

I have a few other things to ask of you, sweetheart. Please make sure Connie is taken care of. She is the closest thing to a sister I've ever had and deserves payment for putting up with me all these years. I know you'll be generous.

Another thing. Don't let Melvin Martin's boys have that

farm. If you don't know why by now, you will eventually. As for Melvin, make sure his bills are paid, will you? He's my friend and doesn't deserve what's happened to him.

This house belongs to you, my Jillian. I suggest you keep it for when you're in town. I know you'll remove the taxidermy; just make sure they all get good homes.

It appears I've left you a little bit rich. Making lots of money and raising a perfect daughter were the two things I did right with my life. I guess that ain't too bad.

I love you, my dear little girl, always have and always will.

Your Father

I rolled onto my side and cried myself to sleep.

CHAPTER FORTY

As I headed south, sun scrubbed the tarmac road and the vast buckled carpet of green wheat. The Rockies to the west were crisp, distinct. A few vibrant farm homes dotted the landscape, separated from each other by verdant miles and rustic abandoned structures. The cord connecting me to my roots stretched thinner but, despite my efforts, would never break. I flipped on the radio and searched for an oldies station. On the seat next to me lay the P.I. report with my mother's address and phone number.

Rae was leaning against the Rattlesnake Warning sign, the cinder-block restrooms for a backdrop. We had decided to meet there on my way out of Montana and back to Seattle.

As she folded me into her arms, I could smell her uniform starch and spicy perfume. The sun heated our shoulders and heads.

"I'm not sure I can leave you yet," I moaned into her chest.

"Even if we aren't physically together, we haven't left each other. It's only for a while," she said.

"I've never dreaded waking alone before."

"Text me as soon as you wake up. I'll text back what time I can call you."

"I'll find some geek at the airport who can show me speed texting."

"Just make sure it's a homely boy geek, then I won't worry about you fielding untoward advances."

"Maybe you should just take me into protective custody."

"Hmm, not a bad idea. But I'm not sure it's legal, and I have a reputation to uphold."

"To hell with your reputation," I said.

"No problem, it's already gone there." She hesitated for a moment. "In a few weeks, I'll have wrapped up lots of reports. Shall I make a quick trip to the Pacific Northwest?"

"If you do, I'll make you fall in love with it."

"Probably won't be too hard since I'm falling in love with one of its residents."

She gave me a double-barreled kiss. Another memory filed in my mental data bank for my days as an old lady in the nursing home. Old age was looking sweeter and sweeter.

I climbed into the now battered and filthy Murano while my meadowlarks serenaded each other. After a reassuring kiss through the window, Rae waved me onto the interstate. I felt her eyes following my car for miles.

About the Author

Kristin Marra spent the first thirty-five years of her life in Montana, where she never learned to love snow. Conceding defeat, she moved to the Pacific Northwest and freely admits she adores the clouds and gloom. Overcast days encourage delightfully obscene hours of reading and more hours for writing. Besides books, cooking, and movies, Kristin enjoys sharing adventures with her partner Judith, daughter Rachel, and varmint canine Spud. Kristin is employed in the public sector.

Books Available From Bold Strokes Books

Wind and Bones by Kristin Marra. Jill O'Hara, award-winning journalist, just wants to settle her deceased father's affairs and leave Prairie View, Montana, far, far behind—but an old girlfriend, a sexy sheriff, and a dangerous secret keep her down on the ranch. (978-1-60282-150-7)

Nightshade by Shea Godfrey. The story of a princess, betrothed as a political pawn, who falls for her intended husband's soldier sister, is a modern-day fairy tale to capture the heart. (978-1-60282-151-4)

Vieux Carré Voodoo by Greg Herren. Popular New Orleans detective Scotty Bradley just can't stay out of trouble—especially when an old flame turns up asking for help. (978-1-60282-152-1)

The Pleasure Set by Lisa Girolami. Laney DeGraff, a successful president of a family-owned bank on Rodeo Drive, finds her comfortable life taking a turn toward danger when Theresa Aguilar, a sleek, sexy lawyer, invites her to join an exclusive, secret group of powerful, alluring women. (978-1-60282-144-6)

A Perfect Match by Erin Dutton. The exciting world of pro golf forms the backdrop for a fast-paced, sexy romance. (978-1-60282-145-3)

Truths by Rebecca S. Buck. Two women separated by two hundred years are connected by fate and love. (978-1-60282-146-0)

Father Knows Best by Lynda Sandoval. High school juniors and best friends Lila Moreno, Meryl Morganstern, and Caressa Thibodoux plan to make the most of the summer before senior year. What they discover that amazing summer about girl power, growing up, and trusting friends and family more than prepares them to tackle that all-important senior year! (978-1-60282-147-7)

The Midnight Hunt by L.L. Raand. Medic Drake McKennan takes a chance and loses, and her life will never be the same—because when she wakes up after surviving a life-threatening illness, she is no longer human. (978-1-60282-140-8)